PLAGUE

FOR

PROFIT

BY

MIKE DUDEK

Heather! Enjoy! Mike Dudek

Publisher's note

This is a work of fiction. Names, characters, places, and incidents either are the product of the author's imagination or are used fictitiously, and any resemblance to actual persons, living or dead, business establishments, events, or locales is entirely coincidental.

ISBN NUMBER 0-9740380-0-8

First published by author October 2003.
Printed and bound in Canada.

For additional copies:

Mike Dudek
448 Strayer St
Johnstown, PA 15906-1649

I wish to thank the following:

My wife Dottie for putting up with me.
Jan Sawyer for proofreading it first.
Jane Dudek, my mother, for correcting my grammer.
Henry Dudek, my dad, for being an inspiration.
David Dudek, my brother, for being the only guy who could outshoot even DOC.
Carol Fris for final proofreading.
Bruce Betz for reading the novel.

Warning

Keep in mind that my villians are very bad to the point of being evil. The women are all beautiful, sexy, and devious. There is killing and sex in this book. The heroes are true to their own code of justice. I hope you enjoy this book.

Mike Dudek

Special note

Plague for Profit is a work of fiction. The Vaught Pharmaceutical Company, the special branch attached to the Supreme Court, and the individuals are all products of the author's imagination. Any resemblance of these entities in the novel to existing entities is purely coincidental. All of the characters and events portrayed herein are fictitious. Nothing should be interpreted as expressing the policies or depicting the procedures of any corporation, institution, university, or governmental department or agency.

The main thrust of this book is that good triumphs over evil. As terror strikes hit the United States, I hope that this book gives us an uplifting sense that we will survive stronger as a nation. In this book one man makes a big difference. I hope that all of us realize that each of us has that gift and can make the world a better place. I have used many technical gadgets, but you will notice that common sense is the final key solution, not the gadgets.

Enjoy,
Mike Dudek

Chapter 1

David Strathmore read the names engraved on the black Vietnam Memorial Wall and remembered the faces of his dead comrades. He ran his index finger over one name in particular. His name. Not his real name, but the identity he had used in the old days when he lived in the hell of deception and espionage. He was visiting his own grave. David turned away from the wall walking to a nearby bench. He couldn't shake the feeling that someone had just stepped on his grave. Perhaps it was his sixth sense kicking in. It was warning him that the decision he came to in the next few hours might cost him his life.

Two weeks earlier he had received a cryptic message from one of the three individuals who knew his true idenity. The message asked for his special help. Ten years earlier these persons had helped him leave the covert life of a deep cover espionage agent. He was morally obligated to help them.

The only way he was able to live a normal life was to die. His death had been faked, and he was now living the life of a normal businessman. He would to listen to the problem before he committed to return to his old life as an agent, code name Doc.

It was 11:17 in the morning. The black Lincoln pulled into the parking space and the driver waited. David's back straightened and his step quickened as he approached the waiting car. He saw the special briefcase on the seat. Five seconds after entering the car the cell phone in the briefcase rang. He opened the case and picked up the hand set of the scrambler then held it to his ear. "Yes."

A mechanical computer scrambled voice at the other end of the phone said, "Mr. Washington is ill Doctor. Please come in the car we sent. Perhaps you can diagnose the illness." The code was simply that something was endangering "Mr. Washington," the nation's security. "Illness," referred to something or someone internal to the security force as being the source of the problem. "Diagnose the illness," indicated that they had some information but no clue of who or what was behind it. Referring to him as "Doctor," indicated that his license to kill was reactivated.

David calmly replied, "Driver, take me to the patient."

At Camp David, the rural White House, security was monitoring the approaching vehicle. Meanwhile inside the main building at the long walnut conference table three men talked about their coming guest.

The Undersecretary of State voiced, "Why do we need this guy? We can use the CIA and find out who blew up the plane."

The Supreme Court Justice answered, "This *guy* goes and does things a battalion of men couldn't do, does it quietly, so the world community doesn't become upset. We are going to be operating on foreign soil. We don't need the extra involvement of foreign governments. We all know or at least suspect someone very high has committed treason. How far our security is damaged is still speculation. I for one don't want to take a chance. This operative is named Doc. Even I don't know his real name. Originally Doc's assignment was to find and eliminate moles within the CIA. The best agents off U.S. soil trained him. Not even his trainers know his identity."

The Undersecretary objected again, "How can we trust him, if we don't even know him? Do we have a hook into him? Is he expendable?"

Smiling, the judge answered, "He knows he is expendable. I don't have, nor do I suspect anyone else to have a hook on him. Finally, not only would I trust him with my life, I trust him with the future of the United States. Lord only knows what will happen if he fails. The hell of this bargain is that he knows we'll deny any and all knowledge of him and his operation. We did deny him before -- twice."

The Admiral broke his silence; "Do you remember the smart bombs in the Gulf war going down the stacks? Doc placed an infrared beacon at the inside base of those stacks so the bombs couldn't miss. A pick up chopper was to lift him out, but someone called it off and hoped Doc would die. Doc had been peeking and poking in all sorts of places and found some interesting facsimiles. One of the generals, stateside, had been selling critical information and spare parts to Sadam's friends. When he found out about Doc, and realized there was a distinct possibility Doc had found documentation that he was a traitor, he made sure the pickup was canceled in flight. The bastard then gave Sadam's people Doc's pickup point, and requested a shoot on site order. Doc always was resourceful. When he found the welcoming party, he realized he was no longer appreciated. He literally walked out of the country, went north, and ended up in Greece where he had a cache of funds. From there he made it to Rome, then England. He came to North America on a fake passport through Canada and then drove to Washington D.C. He went to a Staples store and made transparency copies of the faxes. Posing as a roach exterminator, he somehow gained access to the Pentagon. He walked in on a briefing the general was giving and put the faxes on the overhead display. Showing the faxes to everyone in the room proved our little general loved the God Almighty Dollar more than country. Our general pulled a handgun out of his attaché case and shot himself in the head. Doc suggested that the official record read that the general died of a sudden cerebral hemorrhage. Considering all of the blood and brains on the wall, I'm not sure whether Doc has a sadistic sense of humor or compassion for the man's family. The general's widow never knew the truth and he was buried with full military honor. It was better to have the man die than put his family and the government through the humiliation of explaining the general's traitorous activity. I approved that cover-up myself."

Meanwhile, the black Lincoln pulled up to the guard gate. The guard motioned for the driver to lower the windows and open the trunk as a security precaution. While a second guard checked the rear of the vehicle, the first guard checked the driver's identification. The driver explained that Doc, sitting in the back seat, was a guest. The guard bent forward to look at Doc, then stood erect and gave the vehicle a salute. Doc acknowledged the salute with a short quick nod of his head and a crinkle of a smile at the left side of his mouth.

Following the driver, Doc headed to the main building. Both men were patted down by the Secret Service before being admitted into the building. The driver waited outside the meeting room.

Alone, Doc entered the room and the judge stood. "Gentlemen, may I introduce Doc. Doc, you know the admiral, and myself. For purpose of this meeting our companion will be Mr. Jones, representing the executive branch."

"Pleased to meet you Mr. Undersecretary *Jones,*" Doc said grinning.

"So much for secrecy," said the Undersecretary, livid. "Now who the hell are you Mister?"

"I'm a concerned citizen. Now gentlemen, What's the problem?"

The judge took control as he usually did at critical meetings. "Last week an aircraft was destroyed by a bomb. This was a unique bomb, placed onboard the plane in Germany. According to Scotland Yard, the trigger mechanism was armed when the plane reached a certain altitude. The plane landed at Heathrow. After refueling, it hit a critical attitude and the timer for the bomb started. Most probably the plane was to be far out in the Atlantic when it was to disappear, making recovery relatively impossible. As luck… if you can call it that, had it, the plane developed trouble and had to return to Heathrow. It was only two kilometers off the coast when the explosion disintegrated the plane."

"Sir," Doc responded, "I don't usually deal with acts of terrorism. That type of activity is better left to the standard government agencies. The Yard has excellent people and the FBI labs can cooperate for any technical help."

"That bombing isn't the real problem. Yes, the appropriate agencies are working on the bomb. Our problem, and the reason why you're here, deals with who and what was onboard the plane and who almost was onboard. If it's as we suspect, we need to take action to protect the sovereignty of the United States. In particular we need you to investigate in cooperation with the other governments. There is a possibility this may have been a preliminary act of war. Other possibilities include a terrorist bomb, or a contract hit on someone on the plane."

"Before you go further sir," Doc interrupted. "I'm no longer in your employ. In fact I now have a private life and I'm content. While I'm flattered that you consider me a working spy, I'm retired. As a matter of fact, Admiral, I can't get a pension, military benefits or even any Social Security for the time I served. I realize the cost of my private life is the elimination of my existence in government service. That stint in Desert Storm as a special investigator for the Supreme Court wasn't worth it. Of the $50,000 I was paid, I had to shell out over $40,000 in bribes and costs just to get back to the states."

Therefore gentleman, if you need me it will cost you one million dollars ... per month ... plus expenses. And..."

Silence in the room was inordinate. Undersecretary Jones's neck veins were straining as his blood pressure increased. The audacity.

In a managed voice the judge responded, "And what?"

"And a voucher showing the taxes were paid so that the million is clear"

Jones was ready to respond in a flurry of obscenities. The judge, reaching with his left hand to hold Jones's right hand onto the table, said, "Done. However, the salvage and or recovery of funds or valuables are naturally the property of the United States. In the event recovery is on foreign soil, it shall be split equally between the two governments involved."

Nodding in agreement Doc muttered, "Fine."

The judge was smiling and Doc knew something else was going to hit the proverbial fan. The judge said, "You normally work alone, but in this instance you'll have an officer assigned to you for support, communication, and accounting."

"You can't stick me with a damned bureaucrat and expect me to carry off a mission."

"You already met your liaison officer. He is a Brit., trained by the SAS, and possibly the best procurement officer in Europe. He is your driver."Pressing a call button on the phone the judge commanded, "Send in officer Smythe."

Chapter 2

Joseph Smythe entered the room carrying a gray three-inch Samsonite hard shell brief case. Pulling out a chair adjacent to Doc, he apologized, “Sorry Sir. I was under orders not to engage in conversation in order to conceal my accent.”

Addressing the room in general the judge began. “Doc has agreed to cooperate. He is outside all normal loops. It’s an extreme possibility we either have a leak or a traitor in a position of high influence. For this, and other reasons we’ll be using the United Kingdom as the point of all communications. The specifics of what we know already make the U.K. a critical player. With that in mind I defer to Mr. Smythe to go over the unique problems."

Smythe opened the Samsonite case and handed folders to everyone seated.

“Point One -- The detonation device itself has been identified as a German prototype, but the machining and alloy most probably came from the United States. The explosive had trace chemicals consistent with explosives used by the old Soviet Union. A substantial amount of these explosives have been sold all over the world to the highest bidder as a source of funds. Essentially there are too many variables to determine a source or origin. The proper services are trying to find the terrorists with the expertise to build such a device.”

“Point two -- The reconstruction to determine the initial point of the explosion puts it in the passenger compartment just forward of the wing fuel tanks. Probably it was among the carryon luggage of a female passenger going by the name of Marie Valasko. Although Marie had proper identification, that identification was faked. When we realized this, we were able to recover the security tapes. They show Marie was possibly a Pearl Lewis. Pearl is, I mean was, the love interest of a low level German thug. Why he would blow up his lover is beyond reasoning.”

"Point three -- A biological weapon was found in Iraq in a stainless steel container the size of a workman's thermos bottle. British site administrators found it. The hazardous material was put in a bio-transport container and then placed in a bio-transport vault. This was being sent to the United States for identification and destruction. All three containers had monitors on them and we did find them intact in the wreckage. Monitors show all three containers have the seals intact. The United States Navy will be doing the recovery on it tomorrow. They will then take it back to the States."

"Point four -- The British Prime Minister was to be onboard that flight. Fortunately one hour before takeoff the P.M. sprained an ankle. That was a lucky sprain in that it saved the P.M.'s life. MI-5 and MI-6 are looking into any possible assassination attempt, but that isn't probable at present."

"Point five – This could have been an act of terrorism or an act totally unrelated to our primary four concerns."

"Pardon me," interrupted Doc. "What makes a hit on the P.M. a low possibility?"

Before he answered the question, Smythe reached into the briefcase and spread a map of Great Britain on the tabletop. "Whatever the reason for destroying the plane, it was successful. We received information there is supposed to be a payoff. It's supposed to happen here." He poked his index finger at a point on the map north west of London.

Taking over the conversation the admiral said, "A chopper will be here in 20 minutes to take you both to Quantico. From there you'll fly to England. We need to know who ordered this plane destroyed and why they did such a heinous thing. Observe what goes on and work that thread back to the source of our problem. Thanks to officer Smythe MI-6 will be supplying some observational *tools* for the mission."

Cupping his hand to his ear the judge said, "The chopper is early. Communications will be through my secretary, Shelly Coyne." The judge pulled two pens from an inside pocket of his suit coat and handed one to Doc and the other to Smythe. "These are Motorola pen phones. They have only three numbers programmed into them. One is the required 911 and the other is a secured number to Shelly Coyne, the last is the opposite pen. Naturally there is an encrypter chip that scrambles the communications to Shelly. Essentially these are cell phones that work off a satellite bounce rather than the conventional repeater system." He reached out and shook doc's hand, "Good hunting."

The blade wash of the chopper thumped overhead. "We should go now," said Smythe. They left, crossing the grassy lawn, they headed to where the chopper had just landed.

After they had gone the Undersecretary was shaking his head from side to side. "I just don't understand why you place so much faith in these two men."

The Judge replied, "Simply put, those are probably the two most dangerous men in the world. Not because of their killing skills, but because they think and reason. They take whatever action is necessary to complete a mission. They never give up."

Upon arrival at Quantico base, both men were escorted to a nondescript building adjacent the FBI complex. Smythe took a deep breath, "Now we can finally talk. This is a sound proof area. "What name do you want to use for a passport, Sir?"

"I prefer David as a first name and the middle should be just the letter 'O' and the last can vary so long as it begins with a 'C.' That way the name will match the code. And, please call me David, not Sir."

"Photos are this way, "Smythe said as he started down a long hall. Entering a room complete with camera, laminating and other machines, Smythe took a seat and had the technician make three passports showing he was a U. S. Citizen. David Strathmore also had three passports made, each with a different name using the mnemonic of DOC.

"David, are you ready to fly?"

"Lets go."

Both men headed toward a hangar where a Harrier aircraft was being pulled out for flight. They changed to flight suits, in the locker room, placing their street clothes and passports in flight cases. Smythe took the pilot seat and David took the back seat in the Harrier. "Do you know how to fly this?" quipped David.

"I damn well better. This is the craft I flew over here in," answered Smythe. "I've to return it."

"You were referred to as a procurement officer at the meeting. Don't tell me you stole this aircraft?"

"I don't steal things, sometimes I borrow them for a while. This machine was assigned to me for this mission. We may need to go places without airfields."

"Out of curiosity, What's the biggest thing you've ever borrowed?"

Grinning, Smythe replied, "The QE II, but only for three hours."

Doc tightened his oxygen mask, then activated the plane's onboard secured communications. "Where are we going? I hope we are not going to fly the whole way to England."

"Not quite, we are going to New York and to catch a transatlantic flight on the Concord. I don't know about you, but I want to see a movie and catch some sleep. We have to be ready for a long night of surveillance tomorrow."

"Sounds good to me. This seat could get to me after several hours."

Smythe and Doc continued through the pre-flight checklist. When they hit the ordnance sections Doc asked, "Is this a full complement of ordnance?"

"Of course we are fully loaded. We are not carrying any nuclear devices or bombs, only conventional guns and rockets. You'll learn never to expect less of me."

Rotating the jet turbines for a vertical takeoff, Smythe imitated Captain Picard from Star Trek as he quipped, "Engage thrusters." They were airborne.

Over the Atlantic, they were soon beyond the 3-mile territorial limit. Smythe opened the throttle and they broke the sound barrier over the open water. Doc looked in a cockpit mirror and he could see a trail as the sonic cone left a concussion impression on the water for just an instant before being washed into oblivion by the waves. When they first reached Mach 1, the ambient noise of the aircraft diminished substantially. David had forgotten this phenomenon. It had been a few years since he traveled at a speed over Mach 1. When they approached the air corridor for New York, Smythe reduced the airspeed to .82 mach to match more conventional aircraft. Thc trip was surprisingly quick. Smythe entered a flight pattern for a landing at Kennedy. To be less conspicuous, he left the jet turbines in the horizontal position. An incidental observer would just note that a military plane had landed and not think twice about the type of aircraft. They taxied to a private hangar near the perimeter of the airfield. The doors opened and a little tow motor was driven out to guide the plane to its berth in the secured hangar.

"This way gentlemen," said the guard as they climbed out of the cockpit. They were ushered to a locker room where Smythe and Doc showered and changed to business suits. They double-checked their identifications were in order. Then drove to the main terminal building in a utility vehicle.

Posing as two businessmen, Smythe and Doc showed their boarding passes to the steward as they boarded the Concorde for the transatlantic flight. Both men cat napped as the plane sped toward England.

Two other things were happening at that same moment that would have critical implications for the next few days. First, a single female form guided a 10-foot aluminum fishing boat with a 15-hp electric motor onto the shore on the Welsh coast. After beaching the craft with the little trawling motor, she left a simple note on the seat of the boat. "Finders' keepers -- I've given up fishing. Enjoy the boat. May your luck be better than mine."

The second incident was occurring on the other side of England. In a bus terminal near Dover, a Frenchman in a checked sports coat unlocked a locker and removed a briefcase. Heading for his rental car, he looked for anyone paying particular attention to him. Seeing nothing abnormal, he gently opened the case and looked at many little packets of white powder. The street value of the case was far in excess of Three million US dollars. All the Frenchman needed to do to earn his $50,000 US dollars was to deliver this case to a deserted farmer's field in a moor in northern England. He was already spending his fee in his mind. Tomorrow he would have earned his money.

Chapter 3

The Frenchman steered the Volvo away from the parking space and drove to a nearby restaurant. In a rear lot he waited and watched to see if anyone was following him. He always was careful when he did payoffs, but in this case he was exceptionally careful. Normally payments were made in large sums of cash. Once he even made payment in gold coins. This was the first time he paid someone in dope. He disliked the concept. Musing, he thought about the way the world was going to hell.

The briefcase contained only 50 kilograms of white powder. It had a wholesale value of one million US dollars. The street value was slightly over three million US dollars. If he were caught with the case, the value would translate to life in prison. More probably his failure would result in a death sentence carried out by an inmate and made to look like an accident. Secure in the knowledge that he had never been caught, he started the engine and pulled out. Still watchful of the other vehicles, he drove north on the main highway until he came to a shopping plaza.

Parked in the back lot, he slouched in the seat to avoid being seen. He kept up the security vigil. After he was sure no one noticed him, he pulled out of the lot, drove south to the next village, and waited again. Satisfied that he didn't have anyone watching him, he headed north to his exchange location. It was only 10:00 in the morning and the meeting would not happen until 2:00 the next morning. He needed to scout the area in full daylight to avoid any surprises at night. He would get a good meal and some rest before his late night jaunt. It was about one in the afternoon when he drove by the field where the transfer was to take place. He observed a few sheep grazing and wondered if he might accidentally step in anything in the dark. It would be very embarrassing if he slipped in some droppings. He would be very careful tonight.

He found a bed and breakfast, checked in. After checking in, he went up to his room and stretched out on the comfortable bed.

He was thinking about the coming night rendezvous. One question still nagged at his mind. Why did his boss order the payoff in dope?

The man with the American accent explained that the payoff could no longer be in U.S. currency because most of the currency now had magnetic strips imbedded in the bills. The pretense for the magnetic strip was to stop counterfeiting, but an additional benefit was found. Metal detectors in airports could be modified to read and count the value of the currency passing through the sensing area. They were sensitive enough to count the money in a man's wallet or a woman's purse. Money couldn't be hidden from the device by putting it in socks or garters.

Thousands of dollars in a sealed envelope inside a closed brief case could be counted in less than a second. Amounts of $2,000 set off warning sensors for the airport security. Amounts of $10,000 or more alerted both airport security and Federal officials. Automatic cameras photographed individuals for later identification. Granted although these arrangements were meant to deter drug payments, it also put a crimp in payoffs and bribes.

British and European currencies were not suitable because both were changing. The new issue of the standard European currency would cause suspicion if one individual of modest means were to try to convert large sums to the new currency. Gold couldn't be used because of the enormous weight of such high values.

The Frenchman guessed they knew what they were doing. After all they were up front with him on disclosing the contents of the payoff case. They had even figured a way to give him a legitimate payoff of funds. A unique arrangement was made so he would be named as beneficiary of a life insurance policy. The policy would pay off a benefit from a dear departed loved one directly into his bank. He did question this, as he didn't have any relatives in the United States. The United.States was where the funds would come from. It was explained that only at the time a policy is issued, the beneficiary must have an insurable interest, such as a blood relationship. Later, after issue, the beneficiary on the policy could be legally changed to anyone. He was assured no one would be killed just to get him a payoff. After all, murder for money would be close to a sin in his skewed version of religion.

He subconsciously felt this would be his last job. He was getting too old for the stress. He focused his thoughts on a clean $50,000 for a day's work. He left the cool breeze from the open window blow over his body, lulling him to sleep.

Meanwhile, the Concord delivered David Strathmore and Smythe to Heathrow without incident. The plane taxied to the terminal building. Soon an umbilical like walkway was attached to the exit hatch of the plane. Passengers with passports in hand filed out to the waiting customs officials. An elderly woman was trying to engage David in polite conversation. "When I come to England I must stop at Harrods and get woolen socks for my feet. They are always so warm and soft. I really think they must feed the sheep something special to make the wool so nice."

Attentively answering her David said, "Yes I always get my woolen sweaters at Harrods. I really like the sales. Do you like shopping at the sales?"

Nudging him, Smythe muttering, "Have you lost your mind?"

"Just being social."

Just then an airport security guard approached the men. "Gentlemen, could you please come this way. We believe you left a piece of carryon luggage onboard the plane. Could you come with me to identify it?"

Pretending to just realize that he was missing something, David thanked the officer. "I'll be lost without my laptop computer. Thank you for finding it. Sometimes I think I would forget my head if it were not fastened on."

Leaving the line and following the guard Smythe commented, "Damn, you almost made me think that you actually had a laptop with you."

They entered a small alcove. The guard sat behind a large desk and opened the drawer. He pulled out the passport stamp. "Smythe, how many do you need stamped today?"

"Only three each Geoffrey."

Geoffrey stamped the six passports with entry stamps. "Sure beats the Hell out of standing in that long line. By the way, your vehicle is the Land Rover parked outside the emergency exit." He flipped a set of keys to Smythe. "They want you at HQ to pick up your play toys. You're to be there in 45 minutes."

"Thanks again Geoffrey," Smythe said as he headed out the side door to the Land Rover.

David asked smiling, "Do you've connections everywhere?"

"Not quite, but I'm working on it."

, Smythe got behind the wheel of the Land Rover. David took the passenger seat.

"H.Q.?" David questioned.

"H.Q." Smythe confirmed without explanation, as he started the motor. The drive was just over 30 minutes. At the perimeter guardhouse, Smythe identified himself and his passenger. Satisfied by the identifications, the guard pushed down the weighted end of the pole barricade. Smythe slipped the Rover under the still rising pole.

The third building on the left had grassy fields behind it. The fields were unnaturally flat. They ended in a raised embankment at 100 meters and had another slope at 300 meters. These were ranges to test weapons. The landscaping was situated to catch the deadly bullets so they could bury themselves in the tons of clay that comprised the earthen walls.

Smythe pulled the Rover into a space behind a furniture van. Both men walked toward the main door of the building. A little camera mounted high on the side of the building hummed as it tracked their approach. While they were still three feet away from the door there was an audible click as the electric lock snapped open

A man in his 50's sat on a stool working on a rifle. The walnut stock was held firmly by the large carpeted jaws of two wood vises. Without looking up, he said, "You must be Smythe." After he tightened the protective caps on the alignment screws of the telescopic site, he got off the stool and turned to David. "Good to see you again Doc," he said clapping David on the back.

Under his breath Smythe barely muttered to David, "And you thought ***I*** had connections."

Responding to the comment, David explained, "He taught me sniper techniques years ago."

Turning to the armorer he asked, "What's the latest intelligence on our problem?"

The armorer pulled out a topographical map from beneath the table. "Nothing new at the crash site. We did locate the bagman. He came in from France using the new channel train. He rented a Volvo and went to a bus station at Dover."

Smythe interrupted, "Did you keep him under surveillance?"

"Yes and no. Actually we didn't identify him at the station. One of the technicians ran a tape of disembarkation through an image comparison computer and the damn machine found him. We didn't realize he was in the country until three hours after he left the train station. We traced him to a rental car agency at the station where he rented a sky blue Volvo. We did luck out because the rental car agency had been having a problem with stolen and non-returned cars. As a result they changed company policy and installed transponders in all rental units. The rental company can trigger the transponder and it will give the exact satellite navigation coordinates. One of our men sat in the rental car office drinking coffee and eating doughnuts while our bird was laying down false trails and doubling back on himself. When he was satisfied he wasn't being followed; he went to the bus station. We figure he picked up the money for the payoff at a station locker. He played cat and mouse looking for a tail for another hour. Finally he must have been satisfied that he was safe and headed north to the general area of where our snitch said the payoff would be located."

Smythe interrupted again. "Do we know the payoff site?"

The armorer continued his story. "Originally we knew it would probably be one of two fields. Because of the intersecting roads one was very probable. When he drove by one of the fields and stopped for over fifteen minutes surveying the countryside, I knew we had him. I figure he was checking out the location.

With the deference of a student approaching an instructor, David asked, "Sir, several people mentioned ***toys***. What are they alluding to?"

Smiling a broad smile that filled his whole face with satisfaction, the armorer said, " Let me show you."

Chapter 4

The armorer led David and Smythe to a loading dock at the rear of the building. In the middle of the dock was a huge boulder with moss and lichens forming splotches on the irregular creases of the stone. "We leased three of these from Pine Wood Studio."

"Why would you lease rocks?" Smythe puzzled.

"Pine Wood Studio shoots a lot of action films. When you've actors running all over the scene you often lose sound. They developed these listening stations to capture the sound for motion pictures." Pushing on a clump of moss caused a latch to release. Hydraulic struts similar to those on a hatch back car lifted the entrance hatch to the boulder.

"These are directional microphones," the armorer said as he motioned to one wall. "An operator can use a combination of directional and parabolic microphones to follow the action. We already have a listening post in place at the two suspected fields and this third is a spare to cover any contingency plans." Gesturing to Smythe to enter the fiberglass boulder he said, "Be my guest."

Pointing to the bottom of the console he continued, "Three 12 volt batteries power the microphones and recorders. The panel has ten switches. Eight of these are numbered to correspond to the eight microphones. Each microphone has a pistol grip on the back to point it in the proper direction and the associated number is on the grip. Basically the operator flips a button with a number and then points the corresponding microphone in a particular direction. The sound is routed into the headset. The yellow button on the far left lets you listen to a combination of sounds from all eight microphones. The red button on the far right turns on all eight recorders. Each microphone has its own recorder. If you're in doubt, flip on the red button and let the sound experts analyze the tapes later."

Smythe smiled. "Sounds easy enough. Where's the light?"

The armorer pointed to a green pressure switch along the side of the control panel. “Illumination will be a green light similar to what the photo labs use when working on color film. It only gives off a green glow. It will take at least five minutes to get your eyes accustomed to the dim light. Remember, you don’t want to be a target with a light leak.” Motioning for Smythe to get in he said, “Try it.”

Smythe sat in the operator's seat and put on the headphones. Flipping switch number one he grabbed the associated pistol grip and moved the parabolic microphone so that it pointed out onto the shooting range. His eyes glinted as he aimed at a bird, “Got you,” he said as he hit the red button on the pistol grip.

“Smythe, you’re lucky. It may rain in the night and this fiber-glass shell will keep you dry. Your listening station is already in position about ten meters off the roadway. We are going to drop you off a hay wagon. If no one is around you can slip out of the hay unnoticed, and into the listening post. Be careful with the electronic equipment. It’s on loan for two weeks and then I’ll have to return them or pay for the ones that are damaged.”

“Anything for me sir?" asked David.

“Two things actually. First is a pop-up survival tent similar to the type used by mountain climbers. Yours is camouflaged to look like a fieldstone. The real security is woven into the Gortex shell. We have a mesh of fine thermal transfer wires woven into the entire mesh of the tent. They will pick up the ground temperature from the wires under the tent and dissipate the lower temperature over the upper surface of the tent. This will mask any thermal image of the person inside the tent. Similar webbing of thermal transfer wires covers the listening post that Smythe will be inside. Both of you’ll be shielded from any optic or thermal scan of the area.”

"Where do you want to position me?” questioned David.

Going to the topographical map, the armorer pointed, “Here, this ridge should give you the best location for visual surveillance. Natural rock in the area is about the size of the surveillance tent so you should be able to blend with the surroundings. Unfortunately, you'll have to walk into the area."

"Do you want me to photograph the exchange?"

"Yes, with the camera you saw me working on when you came into the workshop."

"You were working on a rifle."

"Exactly. Wait here and I'll bring it out." With that comment the armorer left the dock and went back into the workshop. Two minutes later he brought out the rifle.

"There are only six of these in existence," the armorer stated with pride. "Parts were made to my specifications and I assembled them myself."

"What's so special about a rifle with a scope?" chided Smythe.

"This rifle has a hollow graphic composite stock that is reinforced by fluted titanium rods for strength. The hollow of the stock holds batteries and computer chips that connect to the telescopic site. The shooter has the selection of normal view with natural light, infrared viewing to detect heat, and starlight mode to amplify nighttime ambient light to daylight intensity. The controls for the scope are located on the stack adjacent to where the shooter's thumb rests. The button above the trigger guard controls the most interesting feature. It enables the shooter to capture an image of what he sees through the riflescope onto computer chips as a digital image that can be uploaded later into a computer. If the rifle is fired, the scope and computer chips atomically save the image. Naturally the crosshairs have optional red viewing for low light situations."

"How big a bore is it?" commented David. "The barrel and action look a bit heavy."

"I'm glad that your recognized the difference. The barrel is 20% thicker than normal and has radius rifling to take the extra pressures of high-speed rounds. The bolt has three locking lugs to secure the chamber."

"What type of round causes such high pressures," questioned Smythe?

"Desegregating bullets, naturally. Do you remember the heat shields on the United States Mercury space capsules?"

"Yes," Smythe confirmed.

"I've adapted the bullets so that air friction heats the lead to a molten sludge held together by a thin copper jacket acting like the heat shield. At impact the copper collapses, spattering the lead. The effect on the target is like an exploding bullet. The effect for the shooter is the bullet can't be traced by rifling marks."

"What prevents someone from hand loading a similar shell?" questioned Smythe.

"Nothing from loading a casing, but if they were to fire it from most commercially made rifles, the pressure would break the action causing the bolt to fly back, and kill the shooter."

Addressing David, Smythe quipped, "I'm glad you've the rifle, not me."

Disapprovingly the armorer reprimanded Smythe, "Don't be an ass. Anything I do is safe and I test every device myself."

"Sorry." Smythe apologized.

"Care to try it Doc? I've it set for point of aim, point of impact at 300 meters"

The armorer pulled three packets of ear protectors out of his pocket. Handing a pack to David and one to Smythe, he commented, "Even with a sound suppresser it's loud."

David inserted three cartridges into the rifle. The armorer went to the targeting panel. He triggered a device buried in the ground 300 meters away from the loading dock. An automated frame holding a cardboard target rose one and a half meters into the air in front of the backstop. David felt the balance of the rifle and nodded approvingly at his former instructor. He shouldered the rifle and looked through the scope.

The armorer interrupted David's concentration. "Doc, the starlight setting has a safety sensor that disables it in daylight so that you don't accidentally blind yourself."

At the fiberglass shell of the listening station David chambered the first round. Resting the fingers of his left hand on the hard surface he formed a support for the rifle in the webbing of his hand and palm.

"Be a sport and shoot offhand," quipped Smythe.

"When I shoot, it's never sport," replied Doc. "Watch you ears," he said as he flipped off the safety. The first shot echoed across the meadow. Chambering the second round, Doc took aim and fired. Working the bolt, he slid the third into the chamber, sited, and fired.

"Damn, you still got it," said the armorer. "All three holes on the target touched. Reset your site two clicks left and one down." He handed Doc three more shells. "This should be it." He then went to the targeting panel and brought up a fresh cardboard target. Doc fired three shots into a single hole in the center of the target.

"Excellent! Now try one more," the armorer said as he set the third target. He then opened a plastic case and withdrew a single cartridge. "Recoil will be an additional four kilograms and the impact will be four millimeters higher."

David chambered the round. Adjusting his aim to compensate, he held the crosshairs slightly below the target. He squeezed the trigger and the barrel of the rifle spewed a stream of fire toward the target. A ten-centimeter hole blew out from the center of the cardboard.

Amazed, Smythe commented," With that cartridge, close counts."

"Let's go inside and get ready to leave," said the armorer gesturing for them to follow him back to the workshop. "There are warm hiking clothes in your sizes in the locker room. While you change I'll clean the rifle."

Within ten minutes both Smythe and David changed into hiking clothes. The armorer had just finished cleaning the rifle and was putting it into a case fitted to a shoulder frame holding a rucksack and the mountaineer tent. "Each rucksack contains two small bottles of water and three energy bars to keep you alert. I'll drive you to the drop off points. My car is out back."

Chapter 5

The three men went out the back door of the workshop and headed toward an old sky blue Rover. Popping the rear hatch they stowed the two rucksacks and rifle case in the back of the vehicle. The armorer slid in behind the wheel and Doc took the front passenger seat. Smythe was left with the rear seat.

As he pulled out of the parking space the armorer commented, "I almost forgot. Doc, open the glove box. I've two low frequency transceivers so that you can communicate."

Doc opened the glove box door and found the two cigarette pack sized transceivers. He handed one to Smythe.

The armorer continued, "The unit has three settings, voice, vibrate, and diode. For God sakes don't use the voice mode until everything is over to signal me to come back. Only use the light emitting diode or vibrate to communicate with each other and only on the hour. The diode and vibrate modes use a special low power setting. The voice is set for full power transmission. Depress the SEND once for everything. If you've trouble press SEND once. Wait a full two seconds then press it a second time. This is critical if the receiving unit's in vibrating mode in order to differentiate the number of signals. To signal a 'heads-up' when our visitors come use only one pulse at a time other than on the hour."

Conversation was very limited for the rest of the trip. Doc opened the topographical map and studied the terrain where the surveillance would be set up. The location has a road on the west side of a shallow valley. Smythe would have the listening station located a short distance off that roadway. The area was primarily farmland. A roadway, little more than a cow path, came into the valley from the north, widened substantially at a pond situated near the center of the valley and exited to the east. Smythe supposed this road would probably be the way the midnight visitors would come to the meeting. His entrance would be from the south and end in the midst of a protrusion of rocks, giving him a good view of whatever would happen that night. His concentration was interrupted by a change in the motor noise. The armorer was slowing down and pulling onto the berm of the road near a grove of trees.

"Time to stretch your legs," commented the armorer. "The site is two miles north of here. Just follow the stream." Doc opened the door, went to the back of the vehicle, and strapped the rifle case to the rucksack frame. He swung the pack onto his back and tightened the chest straps.

"With luck I'll see you in the morning," he said, as he walked away from the car.

"I'll beep you on the hour," called Smythe to the retreating form.

The Rover pulled back onto the dirt roadway and picked up speed. "I was going to drop you off at a farm and have the farmer drop you from the hay wagon at the listening station. The hay wagon travels so slowly that you could run faster than it moves. So far I've not seen any cars on this road. If we don't run into any, I'll just pull off to the side of the road and you can jump out and get into the fiberglass shell."

"Fine by me"

"No vehicles that I see. Get ready." He pulled approximately three meters off the berm of the roadway and Smythe opened the door and ran to the listening station. He popped the hatch and was inside within a minute. As the hatch closed, the armorer checked to make sure no cars were on the roadway in either direction. Since everything was still clear, he pulled out onto the road. He drove north to wait out the night, ten miles away in a comfortable bed.

Doc was enjoying stretching his legs. It was a beautiful day. He moved slowly through a wooded section and stopped to listen to the wildlife. If someone else were in the area, the surest sign would be a change in the wildlife sounds. Hearing no change, he proceeded the last half mile toward the outcrop of rocks. He stopped in the shade of a large maple. He unbuckled the rucksack frame, sat on the ground, and wiggled out of the shoulder straps.

He opened the pack, searched for the binoculars and found them at the bottom. He stood and raised the binoculars to his eyes and scanned the area in front of him.

Doc wanted to select the perfect spot for the show tonight. He settled on a flat area in front at a big granite rock. He figured the granite could guard his back. His concentration would be focused on the events to unfold in front of him. Kneeling down at the rucksack he freed the camouflage tent. He held the tent in his right hand and the binoculars in his left, and he walked the last 50 meters to where he would set up shop for the night. He knelt on the ground in front of the large stone and studied the valley in front of him. This would suite just fine. Two sheep were drinking at the edge of a pond. He spotted the fiberglass shell presumably holding Smythe. It really did match the surroundings. Had he not seen the shape of it beforehand, he would not have realized it was anything other than a boulder.

He kicked at the ground knocking a few small stones to the side so he would be on smooth ground. Doc popped the catch on the tent. Spring metal stays opened the tent in an instant. He fastened four anchors in the ground so the tent wouldn't show any movement even if the wind picked up. Satisfied the tent was secure, he went back to the tree to retrieve the rucksack and rifle. He took the rifle from the case and held it to his shoulder. Looking through the telescopic sight, Doc again checked everything in the valley to be doubly sure no one would see him going into the tent. He picked up the rucksack and rifle, then walked quickly to the tent and slid inside.

The tent, unlike its mountain climbing archetype had slits along the sides so the rifle could slide and site through the side of the tent without exposing the shooter. There was also a shooting prop inside the case that the armorer had failed to mention. This allowed the shooter to rest the forearm of the stock in a padded U shaped rod stand for better support. He took the little transponder from his pocket and slid the switch to vibrate. The sunset would set shortly and he didn't need an accidental flash of a diode from the transponder to illuminate his position in the dark. He remembered the flashing lights on planes were originally only seven-watt bulbs. That little light could be seen at great distances in blackness, and he didn't want to be a target.

In spite of the pad under the tent he still felt the dampness penetrating as nightfall came. Carefully covering the illumination from his watch he checked the time. It was almost on the hour. Smythe should be checking in. Four minutes later the little transponder vibrated once. He waited for a count of ten then pressed the SEND button once to confirm he was OK. Since it was now dark he decided to try out the heat sensing capabilities of the scope. The pond showed fluoresced in the heat sensor showing it still retained some of the heat of the sun from earlier in the day. The sheep had long since returned to the farm. He focused on Smythe's listening station. The metal fibers really did mask any sign of heat from his body. Just then he spotted a car coming from the southwest along the road where Smythe was situated. With the heat sensor, he was able to discern two occupants in the front seat. The warm engine actually glowed in his scope. As the car continued out of sight, he tried the starlight feature. The starlight setting let him see the shrubs and contours of every detail of the land. He scanned the entire valley.

Shortly after the ten o'clock check-in, he was looking at the roadway behind Smythe when he noticed a flash of light from his right. Quickly resetting the scope he again checked out the area. Finding nothing he switched to the heat-sensing mode and re-swept the area. Nothing. Not even animals were visible.

The time was 11:45. In fifteen minutes he would get another confirmation from Smythe. He heard a rumble of a truck motor in the distance. It was growing louder. He focused the scope on the roadway southeast of Smythe's listening post. He could see headlights weaving in the distance. The truck was swaying all over the road. He focused attention on the truck. From the erratic driving, the driver must be either drunk or on drugs. Smythe's listening station was on a slight curve of the road. The truck was approaching it at a fairly high rate of speed. The truck hit the berm of the road and blew a cloud of dust, preventing Doc from seeing exactly what was happening. He heard a dull thud as the truck sideswiped the listening post. It was knocked on the side. Doc flipped off the safety of the rifle. The truck gained the roadway again and Doc focused on the license plate. Steadying the rifle he squeezed the digital image capture and record the license plate of the truck. He was seriously considering shooting out a tire, but he knew if he did, they would lose the capability of getting information from the coming meeting. He was still keeping the crosshairs on the tire when he saw the truck slow to a stop. The driver stumbled out, holding his stomach, and retched violently into the grass at the edge of the roadway. Either this man was drunk or sick thought Doc. The driver fell to his knees and continued to retch, for another five minutes, before staggering back to the truck He had to hold onto the fender and door just to keep himself upright. Behind the wheel, he engaged the gears and the truck continued up the road oblivious to the damage on the side caused by the impact with Smythe's *rock*.

Doc focused on the listening station. Nothing was moving, but then again nothing should be moving. It was now 11:56, four minutes until check-in. Switching to heat sensors he again looked at the listening station. The heat dispersing wires must still be intact because he couldn't see any heat signature from the rock. He noticed something on the ground. Zooming the scope to a spot on the ground to the left of the fiberglass shell, he saw something warm spreading on the ground. "Shit," he said to himself. Concerned that his partner may be bleeding to death inside the fiberglass shell or worse yet killed by a drunk driver. Anxiety made time pass in slow motion. He held the transceiver in his hand. He willed it to give a signal. Nothing. It was 12:00, and the transceiver didn't vibrate. He looked again through the scope and the warm patch of liquid wasn't growing any larger. The transceiver still didn't vibrate. At 12:05 the single vibration in his left hand startled him. Thank God. Doc returned the signal, then again scanned the horizon for anything, anything at all.

As one o'clock approached, he was anxious for the single vibration to confirm that Smythe was still in the world of the living. The vibration came at the precise moment that the second hand hit the 12 on the watch. Smiling to himself, Doc knew he still had a show to watch

Earlier that day a woman had left the aluminum fishing boat on the shore of Wales. She carried a long case and a piece of luggage as she left the area. She went into the little town at 4:00 the prior morning and found an old church. At the back of the Abbey there was an old Chevrolet in the parking space reserved for the Abbott. She opened the suitcase and put on latex gloves. Reaching into the suitcase she found a pre-typed note. It said simply, "Dear Abbott, please forgive me. I must borrow your vehicle without your permission. It's very early and I don't wish to wake you. It's a matter of life and death. I'll return your car tomorrow afternoon. Please don't notify the police. I've included 100 American dollars to help the parish. Please pray for me that I may save a life. Your devoted servant"

"I hope he buys it," she muttered to herself as she reached for the wires under the dash. She hot-wired the ignition and the car came to life. She drove northeast to Heathrow. At the airport she parked the Abbot's car in the long term parking area.

She took her luggage to the car rental area and obtained a small Audi by using false identification. She paid cash for the rental. While the rental agent ran a driver report on the false identification she went into a nearby restaurant. She called the Abbott and left a message on his answering machine. "Thank you so much. I was able to spend twenty minutes with my sister before she died. That time was invaluable. Just after she passed, the phone rang and my brother-in- law was in a very bad accident in France. I've caught a plane to go to his side. You car is in the long-term parking area of Heathrow airport section C row 14 about halfway down the aisle. I locked the door and left enough money in the glove box to reimburse you for the use of the car. May God be with you." The false identification had cleared as not having any driving violation and the rental agent had topped off the petrol tank.

She placed her luggage in the car and headed to where the meeting was scheduled to take place. It was about 4:00 in the afternoon when she drove the cow path of a road and up the east side of the valley. She found a grove of trees and parked the car where it couldn't be seen from the road. Next she opened the suitcase and took out a little screwdriver. She removed the courtesy lights from the door panels, as well as the overhead light, and placed the bulbs into the glove box. When she opened the box she realized that it too had a light, so she removed that bulb. She opened the door and checked that no light would be triggered. Double-checking, she turned over the ignition and looked at the instrumentation, adjusting the illumination control for the dashboard lights to absolute minimum. Next she went to the trunk and removed her long case. Inside was a disassembled rifle. She attached the barrel to the stock with an Allen wrench. The scope had been set to the barrel at the shooting range in Ireland and sealed with super glue on the screw threads to insure that they would not move. Next she loaded the weapon with five rounds, depressing the first round so the bolt of the rifle would slide over it and then slid an extra cartridge into the chamber, so the rifle had now been loaded with six rounds. After putting on the safety she placed the rifle on the floor of the back seat. Finally she changed into a dark blue jogging suit and put dark socks on her feet. She left the shoes on the floorboard for later, and curled up for a quick nap.

It was 10:15 at night when she woke. Reaching over the seat, she retrieved her shoes. She removed the rifle. Closing the door carefully, she left the vehicle and began to make her way to the rim of the valley. At the rim she found a ground swell. She set the rolled up dress on the ground to steady the rifle. Resting the forearm of the stock on the cushioning of the dress gave her a very good gun rest. Her body was hidden by the shallow indentation in the ground. Only the barrel, telescopic sight and her head showed above the rim of the valley. She could see the pond at the bottom. That was where the exchange was to take place. She had an excellent sighting position. She surveyed the rest of the valley but couldn't see anything of interest. She pulled the gun back beside her and lay on the ground waiting.

At about 11:00 she heard the approaching truck, but knew that this would not be of interest, as the meeting wasn't scheduled until two o'clock that morning. She heard the thud. She steadied the telescopic site on the retreating truck, saw it stop and saw the driver get out and retch. "Stupid bastard," she thought to herself. She then brought the rifle back beside her so that nothing would be exposed. Midnight came and went, as did one o'clock. Only the night birds occasionally flying overhead and the frogs in the pond kept her company. Then she heard the distinctive sound of a motor. Pressing the illuminate button on her watch she saw that it was 1:28 in the morning.

The motor stopped. She repositioned her rolled up dress as a gun rest and looked for the source of the offending noise. She couldn't see anything. Possibly the sound had carried. It was probably someone for the meeting who had arrived early and wanted to wait a safe distance. She continued her vigil but to no avail. Nothing could be seen. They must be too far away.

Across the valley Doc also heard the sound of the motor. He pressed the send button once. Smythe returned a single vibration. Both men were waiting.

Finally at 1:52 by Doc's watch the motor started again. The vehicle came carefully from the north. It stopped approximately 100 meters from the pond. The driver killed the headlights and left the motor running. Just when he had doused the lights a second vehicle came another road from southwest. It also stopped about 100 meters south of the pond. At exactly two o'clock both vehicles blinked their parking lights twice then continued to within 10 meters of each other. They left the parking lights on for visibility due to the overcast night. A man with a slight build emerged from the truck. He was carrying a large attaché case. He stood by the vehicle until two men exited the second truck. Both men were of normal height but both had massive upper bodies

As Doc watched, the men gestured to each other. Then one man knelt on the ground and opened the case. Another opened a knife and probed inside of the case. As the third reached into his pocket and pulled out a glass vial. The man with the knife used it to sample the powder from in the case, putting some of it into a glass vial. He shook it and the contents turned very dark. As he started to stand, a shot rang out and he fell backward. Doc pressed the camera button catching the scene. Another man started running for the vehicle when a second shot rang out and he also fell to the ground. The remaining man grabbed the case and started running for his truck. He was shot in the center of the back, causing him to lurch forward, and fall on his face. Another shot caught the struggling man in the head. His body lay twitching. Doc had captured the action in a series of ten images. He switched to the heat-sensing mode and was able to see the heat trails from the shots. He followed them to a ridge. The light breeze caused the red trace lines from the flight of the bullets to waver like loose strings caught in the wind. He scanned the ridge but no one was visible.

Doc continued to watch for the shooter, but to no avail. He figured that whoever did the shooting was watching. He could almost feel it. The shooter would want whatever was in the case, so doc waited he waited for someone to show themselves. No one did.

A full hour went by and Doc continued to monitor the ridge. Nothing was moving. Two hours went by and still nothing.

Shortly after 4:00 in the morning he was scanning the ridge with the starlight mode when he saw something. It was an unlit vehicle with a driver.. The driver was pulling off a ski mask and Doc saw long hair. Something was unusual. The hair looked dark purple. Evidently a red indicator light on the dash was emitting a low glow illuminating the driver. He snapped four more images of the driver.

The vehicle turned and was out of sight. This had to be the shooter, but why would the shooter leave a small fortune on the ground and drive away. Survival instinct told him to wait another half-hour before moving.

Chapter 6

"Smythe, I think it's over," called Doc on the transceiver. "Are you all right?"

"Bruised but functioning," replied Smythe over the communication link.

"Can you meet me at the bodies?"

"Not really. You're going to have to come and get me out"

"I'm coming," confirmed Doc. He crawled out of the camouflaged tent and took the rifle in his arm. He didn't want to be unarmed, just in case. Picking up the binoculars he looped the lanyard over his head, tucked the transceiver in his pocket and headed down the grade to Smythe.

The transceiver crackled with the voice of the armorer, "Ready for a pickup?"

Doc replied, "We need a clean-up crew. Also, do you've any dogs available for tracking?"

"How many did you eliminate?"

"Not me, sir. Three are dead and the merchandise is all over the ground."

Doc made his way across the kilometer from where he was watching to where Smythe was still trapped in the overturned fiberglass shell. Tapping the outside Doc whispered, "Damn, Smythe you had me worried." The shell had rolled onto the hatch so Smythe couldn't open it. Unfortunately it was the only way out of the device.

"I'm going to rock it forward. Try to help"

"Go ahead and rock my boat," mimicked Smythe.

Doc pushed and the shell rolled upright. Smythe opened the hatch and crawled out. Relieved, Doc said, "I thought you had bought the farm."

"What in the Hell happened? I feel like a truck hit me," mumbled Smythe.

"A truck did hit you. Are you bleeding? I saw warm liquid leaking out of the shell and thought that you were losing blood."

Embarrassed, Smythe began, "Well earlier in the evening I drank the water from the one flask. I had started on the second when I had a need to tap my kidney. The only place to go was to use the empty flask, so I refilled it. I didn't even have the cap on when my world was turned upside down. The urine went one way and my head went another. By the way, did you shoot everybody? "

"Only digital pictures." Doc smiled as he tapped the stock. "Let's take a walk and look at the dead."

Both men left the listening post and walked to where the three men were gunned down. The case was open and bags of white powder were all over the ground. Two of the bags had broken. "We are going to have to clean up the cocaine or the sheep will be flying high if it ever gets into the pond water," commented Smythe.

Looking across the field to his right Doc pointed, "The shooter was up on the rise to the east. It was almost like shooting fish in a barrel. For a secret meeting, they may just as well have sent out invitations. I don't believe in coincidence. The driver who hit your station looked as if he were drunk but I'm not so sure that he didn't know exactly what he was doing. Certainly the shooter knew about the meeting." Doc looked up and saw a white Isuzu panel van pulling up to the listening post. Behind it came the light blue rover driven by the armorer. "I guess the technicians have arrived."

The armorer approached with two men in white lab coats following closely. One of the lab men carried a collapsible stretcher in one hand and black body bags in the other. The second technician had a camera and film bag. First they photographed the area, and then photographed the bodies from different angles. They measured the distances between the bodies. Then using latex gloves, they carefully bagged each body and transported them back to the panel van using the stretcher. When the technicians had removed of the third body, they returned to bag the Samsonite case and white cocaine. In a separate bag they cleaned up the spilled powder. It was more for evidence verification than caring for the sheep as Smythe had joked.

"Where was the shooter?" questioned the armorer.

"On the rise over there," Doc pointed. "Perhaps a dog could help us to get evidence."

"What happened to you?" the armorer said, as he looked Smythe up and down for the first time since arriving. "You look like you've been hit by a truck."

"I was."

"Is there a scoop and extra bags in the truck?" Doc asked.

"Yes, why?"

"I would like to get something analyzed," he said as he started walking toward the panel van where the technicians were securing the evidence for transport.

Doc stuck his head into the back of the van. "When you're done, come with me. Bring the camera, scoop and evidence bag. You might as well keep the rifle in the van, you'll need to download the pictures." With that he started walking down the road.

Smythe followed. "Where are you going?"

"I want to know more about the truck that hit you. The driver was swaying all over the road, but you're the only thing he hit. About a half kilometer down this road he pulled off, got out of the truck, and threw up. It looked very real, but I want to check"

"You want to check vomit?" questioned Smythe.

"Yes. If it has alcohol in it, he may have been a normal drunk. If not, he knew about the listening post and needed you out of commission before the meeting."

Doc found the area where the truck had stopped just as the technicians caught up. Doc didn't need to look very hard for the vomit. It was pea green in a culvert. "Here," he said pointing at the disgusting mess. "I'll need a toxicology looking for alcohol or other substance."

One technician asked, "Do you want any plaster casts of the tire tracks where it went into the mud?"

"Yes, we may need them later."

The armorer was a practical man. He got in his Rover and drove down the road to catch up to Doc, Smythe and the technicians. "I've been on the radio. We'll have a bloodhound here in another hour. The technicians can work with the handler to try to find out whatever they can. I want you two to come with me and get some sleep until I can put this together. I've liberated the rifle from the van and will download the pictures while you're getting rest." Without any hesitation Doc and Smythe got into the car and headed back to the workshop to get some much-needed sleep.

Four hours later the armorer woke Doc and Smythe. "I've some news. The technicians have a preliminary report and I downloaded the digital pictures. Here's a copy of the report for each of you."

Initial Findings

Vehicle plate identified from digital photos. Plate belongs to a furniture delivery division of a local department store. The vehicle was supposedly garaged at the time of the accident. It wasn't reported stolen until 10:00 this morning, after the incident. Plate and vehicle are properly matched.

Driver identified from digital photos as matching a corpse found in the van 30 kilometers north of the drop site. Driver ostensibly smelled of alcohol and an open bottle of whisky was found on the van floor. Bruise at back of neck wasn't compatible with collision trauma. Blood didn't flow from the glass cuts to the face and arms when they were cut by flying glass as the van crashed into a maple tree. Lack of blood splatter or even flow suggests that the heart was stopped prior to the collision. Blood was submitted for toxicology testing and blood alcohol testing. Fingerprints were taken from corpse for identification.

The corpse of André Bouche, also know as the 'The Frenchman,' shows that a 243 caliber soft nosed bullet killed him. The shot was to the base of the skull. Death was instantaneous. From the digital photos, he was the first shot. Initial conclusion is that the shooter placed the shot.

Corpse of Gerry Gerber indicates that he was the second victim. The individual was shot in the center of the back. The bullet impacted the spine. A shard of vertebrae ruptured the heart. A section of lead perforated the right lung. Due to the proximity of the body to that of André, it's concluded that he was shot second as he was running away. This corresponds with the digital photos. Gerry was known for his anti-British sentiment. He often worked with the German mobsters stealing whatever they could from the remains of the USSR and selling it to the highest bidder.

The third corpse was tentatively identified as Big George. George worked for the underworld as local muscle for hire. Sometimes he would be used for intimidation, other times it would be as a bodyguard. The body had two impacts from bullets. First was the shot in the back below the right shoulder blade. The bullet entered the chest cavity rupturing much of the lung tissue. This is evidence by the blood found in the mouth and nose as he was aspirating during his last breaths. The second shot was into his head. From the angle of entry he was lying on the ground. The bullet hit at the base of the skull and blew out the top of the skull. This was a placed shot similar to the first corpse. The shooter was an excellent shot as evidenced by the consistent type of impact location.

Samples of the white powder confirm cocaine of extremely high concentration. Initial testing suggests Turkey as the country of origin.

Vomit recovered is almost all split pea soup. No alcohol was noticeable. Toxicology screen showed the presence of Ipecac. Ipecac is used to induce vomiting as a basic form of first aid for children who have ingested toxic substances.

Bloodhound was able to locate the position of the shooter. From marks on the ground the shooter was there for some time. Fibers recovered show dark clothing made of cotton. The bloodhound traced the scent back to where a vehicle was parked among some trees. Tire prints from the cast suggest a common Michelin tire with an all-season tread.

Digital photos of the vehicle with the shooter are too magnified on the shooter to determine the type of vehicle other than to make it a sedan.

Computer at a 93% probability tentatively identifies the shooter as Pearl Lewis. We know that this must be wrong. We were able to confirm thru dental records that Pearl Lewis was killed in the plane crash. Lighting of the subject is unique. Evidently a red indicator light was on in the dashboard. Image of the mask being removed doesn't show any shoulder strap. Probably the light was the seat belt indicator. The color of the hair from illumination of a red indicator light combined with the pale green of the drive indicator make it 92% probable that the subject has natural red hair. Spectrum analysis shows that this wasn't a synthetic wig or dye. Lack of protrusion of the larynx from the profile picture suggests that the subject is female.

Photos attached:

Smythe started, "I think that fake drunk knew that we were onto the meeting and he tried to kill me."

Doc had a somber look of concentration on his face. "Close, I don't think he knew about me. I do believe that he knew only about the listening post and wanted to kill whoever was inside." Turning to the armorer he asked, "Who knew about the listening post but not about me?"

Concerned, the armorer nodded in agreement. "I think that you may be onto something. I'll find out. Only 10 people knew about the meeting." As he looked at Doc, he mumbled to himself, "We need someone who didn't know about you but did know about the listening post. They may not have even known about Smythe being in the shell."

Doc continued, "The shooter concerns me. Either Pearl is dead, or she was the shooter. I can't conceive how she could get off the plane in mid-air and survive to kill those men. Let's get a complete personnel file on her. I want to know everything we can find out."

The armorer walked to a computer terminal and started typing. "I've a T-1 line to Whitehall. They should be able to give us the information shortly." He finished the query and nodded. "Let's get something to eat, I'm hungry. He led the way to a small kitchen located to the side of the lab. In the freezer he found several frozen dinners. "I've turkey, or spaghetti dinners."

Smythe chimed in first, "Turkey."

Doc said, "Same."

The armorer smiled, "May as well make it three." He then pulled the three microwave dinners out of the freezer and put them into three separate microwaves in the kitchen. He grabbed a roll of paper towels and he tore off three sheets, "Today we are not going to be fancy. Do you want coffee or tea? "

"Coffee," said Doc.

"Same," said Smythe.

The armorer put a large Erlymer flask of water into a fourth microwave and heated the water. "I've instant."

All three ate the quickly improvised lunch. As they finished eating, the computer in the outer office chimed. The laser printer switched from standby mode and the pages started printing. "It looks like perfect timing for our answer," commented the armorer.

They went back into the workshop. Doc took the papers from the laser printer.

"This may be worth a trip to Germany," he said as he flipped one sheet for Smythe to read. As he continued to read, he looked up and queried the armorer, "Do you've access to United States military personnel records?"

"I've access to the computers but not to any personnel records. They are very touchy about that," replied the armorer.

Doc reached into his pocket and pulled the pen phone from his pocket. "Lets see how good these are" He pressed the call button.

"Yes," said Shelly Coyne at the other end of the connection.

"Hello Shelly, this is Doc. I need a guest code for the military personnel files. One that will last for three hours would be good."

"That will take a little time. Call back in 20 minutes. I'll see if I can get you one," she answered.

"In twenty," Doc replied and clicked off the connection. "

"Why do you need military records?" questioned Smythe.

"Pearl's father was probably in the military. She was born on a United States military base in Germany. A Captain Mitchell not Doctor Mitchell signed her birth certificate. I want to find out if she has any relatives still living and if so where they are located."

Twenty minutes passed. Doc called Shelly back and got a guest password good for six hours. He had the armorer access the United States military personnel records using the computer in the workshop. It only took a half-hour to find what he wanted.

"Pearl's father was a sergeant Philip Lewis. He was in the motor pool on base. He became involved with a German girl named Gretchen. They married on base. He stayed in Germany for an additional six years after the marriage. Upon discharge he moved back to Illinois and opened a repair garage. He was killed five years later in a car accident. Records show wife Gretchen, and three children, Pearl, Ruby, and Jade survived him. Gretchen Lewis remained in Illinois with the girls. It looks like she is still alive and living at the same location. The girls all graduated in Illinois. Pearl moved to Germany. Ruby went to law school and became a lawyer for an insurance company. Jade is a fashion model and works all over the world. "

Smythe commented, "I'm willing to bet that when Pearl went back to Germany, she got mixed up with that German gangster. He was probably the one behind the bombing."

"Could be," said the armorer. "Part of the bomb came from a German design. One of the dead men at the meeting worked occasionally for the German mob. Finally Pearl was the person with the bomb."

"Let's talk to the mobster. What's his name?" said Doc.

"Mueller, Frederick Mueller," said Smythe as he read the report.

Doc got onto the Internet and downloaded some insurance death claim forms. He customized them with the name of the victim of the plane crash naming her as seat 12A a.k.a. Marie Valasko, a.k.a. Pearl Lewis. He then inserted the address of Frederick Mueller into the form. "Can you arrange transportation to Muller's?" he said as he turned to Smythe.

"Yes," smiled Smythe. "Do you've a plan to get in to Mueller's house?"

"I was thinking of knocking on the front door," grinned Doc.

Chapter 7

Smythe was grinning, "The chopper will pick us up in 45 minutes and take us to the airfield. I've a Gulf Stream waiting there to take us directly to Germany."

"You never fail to amaze me," said Doc. "How did you get the jet so fast?"

"We need parts from the Benz factory. I just increased the urgency of the need and I hitched a ride for both of us. Finagling is easy in a large bureaucracy. While the left hand is trying to figure out what the right hand is doing, we slip through the cracks in the system."

The armorer asked, "Can you get me a trip to Bermuda?"

Smythe replied, "Sorry. Politicians are wise to that location and have used up all the trips."

The helicopter came and picked up Doc and Smythe, flying them to the airfield where the jet was waiting. The Gulf Stream pilot was already going through the pre-flight checklist when they arrived. The flight to the Benz factory went without a hitch. When they disembarked, they showed the passports to security, and then caught a taxi into the city. When they were passing a massive gray building that was an old bank, Doc asked the driver to stop. As they left the cab he said, "We need to do some shopping."

"We only have $200.00 each in U.S. currency. That will not go to far if you go shopping."

Doc pointed down the street. "If I remember correctly there is a nice little restaurant about a half a block further down the street on the left side. Wait for me there. Order a dinner for each of us. What I need to do will take about 15 to 20 minutes." Without further discussion he turned and went into the bank.

The bank was old, built in the 20's and survived WW II intact. It had been remodeled several times since, but kept much of the massive demeanor of an Old World financial institution. Doc found the vice president in charge of new accounts and was ushered into the private office.

"I would like to transfer $250,000 U.S. currency into this bank for purchases while I'm on vacation. Could you arrange the wire transfer so that it will go directly into an account and have it converted at the correct exchange? Naturally I would like access to the funds, so I don't need any interest-bearing account." This made the banker smile.

The banker replied, "Yes we can set up such an account, but there will be fees for the wire transfer, and other setup fees for the bank."

"I'll also need a safety deposit box. As I hope to make this a yearly event, I would like to pay for it 10 years in advance. Do you've any large boxes available immediately?"

Doc gave the banker the name and phone number of a bank in Nassau. When the banker in Nassau recognized Doc's voice he became elated and offered to make sure the transfer was sent immediately to the German bank. Doc provided the numbers in a unique way. "The authorization for transfer is 21854687. Add your wife's birth date and divide by the code number we preset."

The German banker was curious about the security, but also pleased that it existed. "While we are waiting for the transfer can I show you the boxes we have available?"

"Certainly."

They headed to the box section and Doc picked out a large one. It was at waist level on the far wall of the box section. They returned to the banker's private office. The banker had his secretary bring in the necessary forms. Doc used the fake passport as identification and signed all the forms. Doc asked, "Can you prepare three envelopes with the equivalent of $5,000 U. S in each? I'll be needing some walking around money."

"Certainly, but would you not prefer checks? They would be much safer should you lose the currency."

"No, the currency would be better. I'm going to get something to eat, I trust everything will be complete when I return." He stood up, opened the door of the private office and left the bank.

The banker was surprised, as no one had ever acted so casually about transfers of larger funds of money. The secretary came in as he was still staring at the empty doorway. She said, "Sir, we are receiving a wire from Nassau."

He was surprised. Normally banks sent the wires at their convenience, and almost never immediately. He gathered the papers and went to a teller to prepare the accounts and transfer the money appropriately. He had his secretary locate the key to the safety deposit box. Finally he had the teller prepare the three packets of currency for his new customer. All of this took the better part of a half-hour. He got out a large manila envelope and put all of the forms into the parcel. Then he waited.

Doc left the bank and walked down the street to the restaurant where he found Smythe eating a fruit salad. "Sorry. It took a little longer than I expected."

Smythe swallowed quickly so he could talk. "Don't worry, I had them bring out the salad but hold the meal until you showed. Were you able to do whatever you needed done?"

"Almost. After we are done eating I've to pick up some money." Doc smiled as he started on his fruit salad. He was actually hungry. Smythe had ordered braised chicken for each of them. It tasted exceptionally good. They decided not to have dessert. They paid for the meals, and left the restaurant.

David said, "I'm going to introduce you as the head of security for my company, and a personal body guard. I'll need you to sign a form for a safety deposit box. Use one of the fake passports, but remember which one. Don't ask any questions, and avoid talking. When we get into the bank, wait in the private area by the banker's secretary."

"Why do we need a safety deposit box?"

"We may need a place to leave cash or weapons. Keep in mind that someone knew of the surveillance in England. We may be cut off and we need a back door. This will be the back door."

Smythe smiled, "I like your thinking, and I like the idea of an escape plan just in case."

The banker watched the two men approaching. He had not seen the second man before. David opened the swinging door of the little railing separating the banker's private area from the general public area. He and Smythe entered. David nodded to the seat adjacent the secretary. "I'm sure that my friend can wait here." The secretary acquiesced and the banker himself met David at the inter office door to his private office.

The banker greeted David warmly. "I've your forms ready for signature." They closed the office door for privacy.

David said, "I've an additional request. The gentleman with me is the head of security for my firm and I want him to have access to the safety deposit box. I realize that you'll need his signature, so I brought him along."

The banker and David completed the other forms. After David signed the safety deposit box form, he went to the door and motioned Smythe into the office. He pointed to the signature area of the form with the pen then handed it to Smythe. Smythe took the pen and signed the form without saying a word, then left the office, closing the door behind him. "He doesn't say much," commented the banker.

Keeping the meeting under his control David changed the direction of the conversation. "The three envelopes?" he stated.

The banker opened the top desk drawer and pulled out the three envelopes. "They have been converted to Deutsche Mark per you request."

David took the three envelopes and noted the amounts were marked on the top of each envelope. He took one and handed it to the banker. "In my country we give tips in order to cement relationships."

"Nothing is necessary sir, the bank has charged the appropriate fees as noted on the disclosure form."

David looked at the banker and saw in his eyes that he could be bought. The gaze of the banker drifted to the envelope on the desktop. David pushed the envelope back to the banker and said, "I may need special services, and I expect them to be done. For these services I'm paying in advance. If you feel these services are above and beyond the duty of a bank officer naturally the funds are yours. If you feel that the funds belong to the bank, you may pay the bank for these services. The banker looked at David and his eyes became wide with a mixture of concern and panic.

"I can't engage in anything illegal, it would cost me my job."

David laughed. "I would never have you do anything illegal. What I need is no delays. For example, was the transfer to your bank done immediately?"

"Yes."

"If I need funds transferred, I expect it to be done expediently. Naturally the bank does these things as a matter of routine and charges fees. I want you to make sure there are not any delays. I may be doing business with firms within your country. I need to be sure of their reliability. What I need to know would be available to a banker but not written in formal credit reports. "

The banker smiled, "I understand. Such information is available through discrete channels."

David continued, "Lastly, I may want referrals to vendors. Specifically I need the name of a good hotel, and a car service where we can get a car with driver for a week."

The banker consulted his private directory and found the name of a hotel. He wrote the name on the back of his business card. He looked up a car service facility, making note of it on the back of a second business card. He handed these to David. "I'm sure you'll be pleased with the service that these places provide."

"Could I impose one more favor? I would appreciate it if your secretary could show my friend the location of the box while you call for a taxi." The banker nodded and called Greta on the intercom.

She got up from behind her desk and asked Smythe, "Could you please follow me? I've been directed to show you the location of the safety deposit box."

"I'll follow you any time and anywhere," commented Smythe as he got out of his chair. Greta glared at him.

David asked the banker to reserve the private suite for a week and pay for it with a bank check drawn from David's account. He also directed the banker to arrange for the rental car and driver to be paid for a minimum of a week with a second bank check from David's account. David asked that the car and driver be available in two hours at the hotel.

"Make sure that the driver has an overnight bag as we may be touring the countryside." The banker had David sign two withdrawal forms in order to comply. David decided to ask one last question, "What can you tell me about a man named Frederick Mueller?"

"I understand that he was in the local underworld of criminals. He has now expanded the operation to include business arrangements with former Soviet officials to sell scraps of merchandise to other countries. Those smuggled bits of merchandise started out to be clothes and then optics. I understand that he is now reselling all types of small armament. It's said that he could get almost anything, legal or not. He lives in a guarded compound a little over an hour's travel north of the city. Be very careful with him, as you may not end up on the safe side of the law. Moreover, you may not end up in the realm of the living. It's rumored that he can be vicious."

David and Smythe left the bank to wait on the front steps for the taxi. When the car arrived, they both got into the back seat. "Driver, our luggage was lost. We have to get some suits for a business meeting. Can you recommend any good men's shops?"

"Certainly sirs, we have very fine shops here is Stuttgart."

Ten minutes later they pulled into a fine men's shop. David had the cab wait with the meter running. They purchased two hardshell traveling cases and a leather valise. They tried on clothing and bought suits, shirts, and shoes as well as personal toiletries. As small talk, David mentioned that he always had problems with buttons getting caught and coming loose. For this purpose he asked the salesman for a small spool of gray thread to sew the buttons should they become loose. The salesman gave him a spool of gray polyester thread at no charge. After removing the tags at the counter, they put the clothing into the traveling cases. All of this was put into the cab.

David gave the driver the name of the hotel and they were driven there in another 15 minutes. David tipped the driver and they entered the hotel. At the front desk the clerk had the room reservation from the banker. Once in their suite, David opened the valise and put in the life insurance claim forms he had made on the laser printer at the armorer's workshop. They showered and shaved, and then dressed in the new clothing for their ride in the country.

"How are we going to approach Frederick Mueller?" questioned Smythe.

"I'll approach him alone. As I said, walking up to the front door and knocking."

Chapter 8

The telephone rang. It was the front desk. "Sir, your car is here."

Doc picked up the leather valise containing the insurance forms he had made on the laser printer in England. He and Smythe took the elevator to the main lobby. Sitting in an overstuffed leather chair was a man wearing a blazer emblazoned with the insignia of a rental car service. They approached him and introduced themselves.

David asked, "Do you've the overnight bag for yourself if we stay overnight at some areas?"

"Yes sir. I stopped at home and prepared a suitcase for myself before I came here," replied the driver.

"Let's go," said David as he headed for the main entrance to the hotel lobby.

Smythe shrugged his shoulders and said, "He is like that."

David took off his sports coat and folded it neatly in the open trunk of the car. Smythe did the same with his coat.

David got into the front seat and Smythe in the back seat of the vehicle.

"Do you've any luggage?" asked the driver.

"Only the valise. I'll keep it with me." replied Doc.

"Where do you want to go?" asked the driver.

"Take E-1 north for about an hour. The man I've an appointment with lives in a little village. We'll stop and ask directions to find the house when we get closer," replied David.

An hour and fifteen minutes later they found the residence of Frederick Mueller. It was a private compound surrounded by a stone wall approximately ten feet tall. It was topped with broken glass embedded into the mortar at the top of the stone. Rods were mounted at about 4 meter intervals and had porcelain insulators shielding the barbed wire strung between them. Most probably the wire was electrified. A bypass wrought iron gate protected the main entrance. A small guardhouse was to the side of the vehicle entrance where a separate pedestrian gate afforded entrance to those on foot. They drove past the property and both Smythe and Doc took mental notes of the property defenses. They continued about two kilometers up the road then pulled off to the side of the road for discussion.

David directed the driver, “I want you to pull up opposite the main gate, and I’ll get out. What ever happens, stay in the car unless I specifically ask you to come.”

Smythe asked, “Are you sure you don’t want me to come with you?”

“Stay here. I’ll be about an hour or so. Leave the air-conditioning on.”

While they were stopped, Doc went to the trunk and retrieved his sport coat. He straightened his tie and picked up the valise. “Let’s go.”

They pulled beside the curb opposite the pedestrian wrought iron gate. The gate was mounted into massive concrete pillars that were the demarcation of the stonewall. Doc crossed the street and rang the buzzer at the gate entrance. A large watchman answered from a phone in the guardhouse. Doc asked to see Mr. Mueller regarding some business that required a signature. Doc was dressed like a businessman and held the valise at his right side. The guard left the enclosure and came to stand opposite the pedestrian entrance of the wrought iron gate. Doc knew that this wasn’t going to be easy as the guard had his arms folded across his massive chest. Doc estimated that the guard was 250 pounds of pure muscle. Probably the guard had been a professional athlete.The guard stood opposite the iron bars of the gate and insisted that Doc give him the papers for Herr Mueller to review. Doc refused and again requested to be let in for just a few minutes to obtain the signature. The guard moved in an instant and blocked the gate with his massive frame. He again asked the nature of the papers. Doc relented and said, “I’m an insurance man. These papers deal with the flight that went down off the coast of England, and the death of Marie Valasko."

The guard's face turned red. He pressed the lock release button and charged out of the gate, right fist clenched.. The guard was coming out the gate at a fast walk. Doc positioned himself so that his back was about ten inches in front of the cement pillar. Smythe was watching from the car and saw the guard coming at Doc like a runaway train. "Dumb shit. Move." Smythe said to himself.

Doc let the valise slip from his right hand. The guard pulled his right fist backward. Suddenly the massive fist started forward moving directly toward Doc's solar plexus. Doc reached forward catching the forearm as it came toward him then pulling the arm with all of his might. The guard was off balance. Doc could smell the garlic on the guard's breath. Doc twisted sideways in the 10-inch space between his back and the concrete wall. Still pulling the guard's forearm, he directed the increasing velocity and momentum of the giant's fist to impact with the concrete wall. Bones snapped and the guard's face contorted into a grimace of pain. He swore in German. Doc responded by snapping the guard's head against the concrete wall. "Don't talk about my mother like that."

The guard was unconscious on the sidewalk. Doc deftly removed the nine-millimeter Browning from the guard's shoulder holster. He released the clip and slid each bullet from the clip, and pulled back the slide emptying the cartridge from the firing chamber. Next he patted the guard, looking for additional weapons, and found a spare clip. He took the cartridges from it one at a time. He put the unspent bullets into the guard's left-hand pocket, and slid the Browning back into the shoulder holster.

Although the guard was unconscious, his face still held a grimace of pain. Doc reached into his own pants pocket and pulled out the little Spiderco knife he always carried. He cut off the guard's coat sleeve. Underneath the jacket the guard had on a short sleeve shirt. Doc felt the broken arm. The radius bone was broken. He felt the hand. Two fingers were also broken. He felt the guard's pulse at the neck. The pulse was stable. Doc placed his knee on the man's shoulder, and pulled the broken arm. He felt the click as the radius bone was put into position. Doc slit two strips off the severed coat sleeve and used these to secure the ammo clips to either side of the broken arm. He cut off another narrow strip of cloth, leaving a wide strip remaining. He rolled the wide strip into a wide oblong ball of cloth. He pulled the fingers into position setting the two remaining broken bones. Doc closed the unconscious guard's hand over the large ball of cloth. Finally he secured the hand by lashing it around the ball of cloth to prevent further damage to the broken fingers.

Doc was wondering why the guard went ballistic. He had intended to make a scene to get to see Mueller, but something else happened. He could see a flutter of the guard's eyelid as he was starting to come around. Doc leaned over so that his mouth was close to the guard's ear. His right hand reached to the guard's groin and he grabbed the guards' testicles. He whispered into the guard's ear, "Don't move. Just listen. You broke your arm and two fingers. I've set the bones, so that the swelling holds them into position. You should probably see a doctor to have the arm put into a cast. If you give me any problem I'll rip your testicles off." With that statement he squeezed slightly to make sure the guard realized that he wasn't kidding. "Why did you try to damage me?"

The guard answered, "You said you're the insurance man."

"So what, I've insurance papers for Mr. Mueller to sign, that is all."

"Insurance man is responsible for death of Herr Mueller's mistress. You killed her, I'll kill you." With that the guard started to move, so Doc squeezed.

"I didn't kill anyone associated with Herr Mueller. Do you want to be the first?"

The guard stopped struggling. "Now I'm going to help you to stand. Then we'll go to the main house."

The guard looked questioningly at his arm and hand, and then looked at Doc. "You didn't kill anyone? What's in the case, a gun to kill, or a bomb?"

Doc smiled, “You could have just asked.” He opened the case and removed the three papers leaving the open case on the sidewalk. “Will you escort me to the house with these papers?”

The guard was still suspicious, and finally said “Now?”

“Now.” Doc helped him to his feet.

Both men walked up to the main house and Doc knocked on the front door.

In the car, Smythe muttered to himself, “I’ll be a son of a bitch. He did it.”

A matronly woman in a maid’s uniform answered the door. She looked at Doc, then was horrified as she looked at the guard’s arm and hand. “I fell down," the guard explained. "Could you please let us into the den and ask Herr Mueller to meet us there.” The guard led the way to a room to the right of the entrance hall. “Could you please get the door? My arm isn’t working properly.”

Doc opened the door and helped the guard into the room. The drapes were drawn and the room was dimly lit. Doc noticed the glow of a red diode of a video monitor among some books as a light snapped on. “Lean against the wall while I check you for weapons,” said a blonde man holding a Mac-10.

Across the room the action of an automatic weapon snapped shut with a click. A young man with closely trimmed hair pointing another Mac-10 at Doc said, “Please.”

Doc placed the three sheets of paper onto the desktop and then moved to the wall. The blond guard put the Mac-10 onto a tabletop then patted Doc down looking for weapons. He found the wallet with the fake ID and the little knife. He placed these on the desk and asked Doc to have a seat. Doc took a seat opposite the desk so that he was in position to write on the desktop. While they were waiting, the injured guard asked, “Why did you set my bones?”

Doc answered, “My parents taught me that if I break something, I’ve to fix it. Besides, you had me confused with someone else, and I want to know who you’ve me confused with?”

Before the guard could answer, the door opened and heavyset man in his late 50’s entered the room. He looked very much at home in this office with the oak furniture, leather covered chairs, and armed men. He sat behind the desk. Placing his hands palm down on the blotter, he inhaled deeply. "Most people try to contact me by phone and make an appointment."

Doc answered, "I understand that most people who try to reach you by phone never succeed. I also understand that anyone making an appointment meets with your subordinates."

"True."

Doc continued, "I need to confirm a bit of information and witness your signature on some forms. A subordinate would not be legal representation for my paperwork."

"What's this paper about?"

Doc reached for the three papers on the desk and started explaining. "A plane was blown up. The 1929 Warsaw Convention as amended by the United Kingdom specifies that each passenger onboard the plane have a death benefit of 100,000 Special Drawing Rights. That amounts to approximately 100,600 ECU or 119,600 English Pounds. A treaty, rather than a policy that names a beneficiary controls the death benefit. The treaty suggests that the next of kin or household be used to control the settlement. Marie Valasko was in seat 15 A of the doomed aircraft. Later Marie Valasko was correctly identified as being Pearl Lewis. The ticket was purchased from a German travel agency and delivered to your post office box. I'm here to fill out the death claim in order to pay the required amount."

"I'm surprised that you found out so quickly about the false name. Pearl is, or rather was, my mistress. I wanted her to travel safely under an assumed name. My competitors may have wished harm to come to her as a means of getting at me. I still don't know if that is what happened." Frederick Mueller stared at the writing mat. "I've made inquiries, but I think that the bomb was meant for someone or something else. My Pearl was just aboard the wrong plane."

Doc reached for the pen held in an ornate holder at the edge of the desk. He picked it up and marked an x at the bottom of one of the forms. "I'll need you to sign this to confirm that she was a resident in your household in order to release the check."

Mueller's eyes flared. "I don't want any money, much less blood money of my lover. She has a mother in the United States. Give the money to her."

Doc was still playing at being an insurance man. "I'll need you to sign this other paper. It's a waiver of benefit so that we can pay her mother."

Mueller grabbed the paper and signed without reading it. Handing it back to Doc, he said, "What can you tell me about the crash?"

"I can tell you that it was a bomb. It exploded near the transfer pipes for the fuel. The igniting fuel intensified the explosion. The placement of the bomb was probably deliberate." Doc's eyes concentrated on Mueller's face. "The bomb was probably next to Pearl when it went off."

Mueller clenched his fists and his knuckles went white. "Some bastard did kill her."

Doc could see the grief in Mueller's face. The man in front of him lost his lover. Evidently he had been hoping that it was a random act that killed his beloved, but the realization that it was deliberate made Mueller angry. He glared at Doc. "You're more than an insurance man with a death claim. Anyone who can handle Otto is much more than a paper pusher. You came here to ask me if I had Pearl killed didn't you?"

"Yes."

"The answer is no. My wife left my bed 20 years ago. She uses my money from a generous monthly stipend provided the bitch never returns. Pearl was my recreation, as well as helping me keep an objective view of my business. Find me that man who ordered this catastrophe. I'll have him and all his family killed." Mueller stared at Doc for a full minute. Neither man said anything. Finally Mueller spoke. "Make him suffer when you find him. If you need help, call this number and ask for Otto. Whatever we can do, will be done." With that he wrote a private number on a paper.

"When I find the person responsible I'll be sure to send you regards. I do need information about Pearl. Why was she on that plane?"

"Mueller replied, "She received a call from the States. Essentially the caller was a woman who said Pearl's mother was ill with cancer, and was to go into the hospital the following Monday. Pearl contacted her sister in Canada. They were to meet in Toronto, then fly together to see her mother.

"I didn't know that she had a sister. Do you've a picture?"

Mueller reached into the top left hand desk drawer and pulled out a color photo of himself with a beautiful redhead. "This is Pearl. Her sister is identical. They even had similar hair styles."

Doc was astonished. "They were twins?"

"No, triplets. The third sister works for a law firm in Washington D.C."

"I've another question," said Doc. "Did any of the sisters know anything about guns?"

Mueller rocked back in his seat laughing. "Three years ago the sister in Washington was almost a victim of a mugger. She was very upset and told Pearl. Pearl in turn made it my problem. I've friends; one of them is a Russian who is very good with guns. I had all three women come to the compound. There is a shooting range in the back. They became familiar with all sorts of weapons and learned hand-to-hand defense. They didn't learn how to bow politely, but rather how to disable the assailant. All three were very excellent with rifles with scopes. Pearl liked to bounce cans across the range." Mueller's face sobered "Why do you ask?"

"I was watching a meeting of someone connected to the bombing. I thought I saw a redheaded woman also watching."

"It would not have been one of Pearls sisters. If it were, no one would have left the meeting."

"No one did."

Frederick Mueller nodded. "Ruby is an actress and model working in Canada. Jade is the lawyer's assistant in Washington." If I were a betting man, I'd say you probably saw Ruby. She has a temper. Don't stand in her way. When she has her mind made up;

she is like an avalanche tumbling down a mountain. There is just no stopping her."

"May I've picture of Pearl?"

Mueller opened his wallet and withdrew a small photo of Pearl. She was sitting in a rowboat smiling at the photographer. "Use this. It doesn't have my face in the picture. I would appreciate its return after this is over."

"Where can I find Ruby?" asked Doc.

"The last information I had on her, she was in a play in Toronto. She had an apartment in the city."

"Thank you." With that remark Doc got up from his seat. He stopped for a second then turned and asked, "One last question. When I was at the gate and identified myself as an insurance man, Otto became very hostile. Why?"

Mueller answered, "When we first were questioning our informants about the bomb, we got information that the man behind it was known as The Insurance Man."

"Would it be possible for me to talk to that informant?"

"Unfortunately, the informant died at the end of the interrogation"

Doc rose from his seat and then walked out of the room. He opened the front door just as the housekeeper was racing across the hall to reach the door. He turned to her and said, "Take care of Otto. He does have three broken bones."

She nodded with understanding.

Doc walked down the long driveway. As he approached the gate, the new watchman in the guardhouse pressed the release button. The gate buzzed until Doc released the catch. He picked up his valise, then walked across the street to the car. He still could feel the tension in every muscle of his being. Smythe and the driver just stared at him.

"Pull out. I need to get to the top of a hill, away from everyone."

The driver gave a questioning look. Smythe interjected. "He needs to use a radio and has to get away from this place to use it."

Nodding understanding, the driver engaged the engine and pulled away. He drove about 4 kilometers when they came to a rise overlooking a valley with grazing fields along the slopes. "This will do," said Doc.

The car pulled off to the side of the roadway and Doc got out with Smythe. They both walked away from the car. "May I've my pen back?" Doc asked.

Smythe reached in his breast pocket and pulled out the little transmitter. Doc took the instrument and pressed SEND. "Shelly, I feel Mueller is clean. We'll be going to Toronto. This is for your information only. We may be compromised by the incident in England."

Although he expected a recorded line, the instrument in his hand responded with Shelly's voice. "We agree on the English compromise."

"Please check on any reference to insurance or The Insurance Man. It may be the pseudonym of the bomber. Also check to see if there are any connections with insurance and the English incident. I'll be in touch"

"Be careful Doc," Shelly whispered into the transmitter as she switched the instrument to standby mode.

Smythe asked, "Where to now?"

"Back to England, then to Toronto."

Chapter 9

Smythe and Doc stood on the hillside. Smythe gave Doc a funny look, "What's with the communication from a hilltop? You and I know that the satellite communications connection goes straight up to the satellite and doesn't need to be high to carry the signal. Anyway, what went on in the house?"

Doc smiled. "You're partially right. The pen has an excellent connection from anywhere except underground or in buildings. I think that the bug they put into the valise probably needs to be high to carry the signal."

"A bug?"

"Should the circumstances be reversed, I would have bugged it myself."

"Damn."

"So far as the house, I guess you saw me going up to the main house with a guard named Otto."

"The guy you helped to punch out a concrete buttress?"

"Yes. The cameras caught the encounter and they were waiting for us by the time we made it to the house. We entered a den and two men were waiting for us with Mac-10 machine pistols. They were for show. The den was trimmed with lots of ornate wood and flocked wallpaper. The furniture was good hardwood and some of it was trimmed in leather. They couldn't afford a Mac-10 going off in that room. If I remember correctly that gun fires 30 rounds of 45-caliber ammo per second. It would have caused thousands of dollars in damage just to kill me. I'm positive the guns were for show only."

"Did you talk with Mueller?"

"Yes, but something wasn't right. I don't think he downed that flight, but something wasn't right with the meeting. I know he is holding back information. I think he is after blood from the person or persons who killed his lover. I would not be surprised if he personally wants to pull the trigger. Still, there's something else . . ."

"Where to now? You told Shelly that we were going to England. When do we leave?"

"Perhaps we'll leave tomorrow. Now we are going back to the hotel and let the bug listen to what we want to tell it. I think that we both need a good night's sleep."

They arraigned for the driver to have a room down the hall from the suite. Doc took the bedroom to the right of the central receiving room and Smythe took the smaller bedroom to the left. Each of the bedrooms had a bathroom attached and a separate doorway to the main hallway. Doc and Smythe went down to the bar and sat in a little booth at the rear of the room.

"I think that we may have visitors tonight. If we do I may be able to get the answers to the nagging feeling I've about the meeting at Mueller's home."

"Do you think Mueller lied to you?"

"No, but I think he didn't tell me the entire truth."

"I could go to the base and borrow two Browning automatics for safety," offered Smythe.

"I don't think that would help. I don't want to have to explain gunshots in this country. Certainly whomever you borrow the guns from would be upset if they were confiscated and the serial numbers tracked back to the owner."

"I'll take the first watch if you want," offered Smythe.

"Just come when I ring your room. I think there is probably a homing signal in that case in addition to the microphone. I want them to come to my room. When I question our intruders, don't question what I threaten. I mean to scare the Hell out of them, possibly quite literally."

"I take it you never read the Geneva Convention."

"Actually I did. You're right, but what I intend to do is more psychological than physical. They should be quite all right in the morning, but by then we'll have our answers."

On the way back to the room Doc stopped at the front desk and asked if the desk clerk was on for the rest of the night. He confirmed that he would be. He added that not much activity was expected this evening, as all of the guests had already checked in to the hotel. Doc smiled and headed down the hall with Smythe. Both men were exhausted and retired early to their separate rooms.

Doc draped his clothing over a wooden butler. Because the leather belt prevented the pants from folding properly he emptied the pockets onto the nightstand and removed the belt, curling it and placing it on the nightstand. He folded the pants over the crossbar of the polished wooden butler and draped his shirt over the curved wooden hangar that framed the top of the butler. Wearing only his shorts and T-shirt he crossed the room to the dresser, and opened the top drawer. He took out the spool of gray polyester thread he had gotten at the shop where he had purchased his suit. Next he went to the nightstand and found the complimentary writing paper and pens. He tied the thread to the one pen and put it into the desk drawer. He pulled the thread so that it crossed the room in front of the door. He looped the end around a table lamp at the far end of the room. Returning to the desk, he emptied the contents of the drawer onto the desktop. He removed the drawer and positioned it upside down on the floor at the foot of the desk. He balanced the pen with the thread tied around it at the edge of the desktop so that it would fall onto the upturned drawer causing a noise. The hollow veneer wood of the upturned drawer would amplify the concussion on its surface much as a drum does.

He cinched the thread tightly around the lamp so that anyone entering the room would hit the trigger line. The sound of the pen falling would be a distraction.

Years ago he had learned the art of combat naps; the deliberate relaxing of the muscles of the body as the mind slipped into a twilight state of conscious. He was in that semi-conscious state when he heard a noise. The hotel had equipped each room with the newest magnetic card locks to prevent theft of property. The magnetic lock does an excellent job, provided you're the one with the magnetic card key. Someone evidently had borrowed one of the master magnetic cards from a maintenance person and had slipped it into the lock. Doc was instantly alert and rolled carefully onto the carpeted floor. He grabbed the leather belt from the nightstand, and flicked his wrist while holding the end of the leather with the holes. The belt buckle arched in a tightening circle wrapping the leather around his right hand.

The intruder stepped into the room. It was totally dark and his vision had not adjusted sufficiently from the light of the hallway. He moved cautiously toward the bed with a knife gripped in his right hand, the blade held low.

Doc stood up beside the bed, startling the intruder. "Can I help you?" he said.

"Yes, by dying."

Doc watched the blade of the knife. The intruder held it with four fingers gripping the hilt of the knife and the thumb resting against the blade guard. The knife was held just above waist level and the intruder was positioned to thrust into Doc's heart. "What do you want?" asked Doc again as he moved slightly to the right.

" Only for you to die."

The intruder was approaching the thread. Doc deliberately glanced toward the nightstand with the pen to watch the intruder's response. Nothing happened. The intruder advanced another step, pushing against the unseen thread knocking the pen from the nightstand onto the upturned drawer. When it thumped, he glanced in that direction for an instant. Doc did the unexpected and grabbed the knife blade with his right hand, which was protected by the leather belt. The intruder had been holding the knife in a loose grip, expecting to be thrusting it. Doc ripped the knife from his grip and swung his hand back against the man's face. The weight of the belt, buckle and knife had the effect of brass knuckles, and the intruder's jaw snapped as it broke. The intruder lost two teeth in a spray of blood. Simultaneously Doc kneed the intruder and the man slumped to the floor, face down. Doc lifted the man, supporting his weight by grabbing the back of his belt to lift the body. He grabbed the back of the collar of the shirt to lift the man's head. Using the body as a battering ram he slammed the man's head into the cast iron bathtub causing a bong to sound like a bell from a gothic church. Instantly the intruder was unconscious.

Doc checked for identification and weapons. The man had no papers on him, but did have a Makarov 9mm automatic in the front of his waistband. The automatic was the Russian version of the Walter PK. Doc was familiar with the 6.3 inch weapon which weighed only 1.46 pounds without it's magazine. He checked and it had all full eight rounds in the magazine. Doc walked back across the carpet, sat on the edge of the bed, and dialed the extension for Smythe's room. He answered on the second ring. "What was that noise, are you all right?"

"I'm fine, but my guest fell in the bathtub and has a concussion."

"You ***did*** get a girl in."

"No. One of the guards from Mueller's house stopped by. I think we'll have some answers when he wakes up. You better get dressed and come over."

Doc slipped on a pair of slacks and threaded his leather belt through the loops. He noted that he would have to get another belt as this one had a couple of deep cuts in it from the knife. Smythe knocked on the still partially open door. " Is it OK to come in?"

"Yes, come on in. Our guest is lying on the bathroom floor. You keep a watch over him while I clean up in here."

Doc got two washcloths and scrubbed the blood off the carpet. He found the two teeth and put them in a paper cup from the bathroom. He put the drawer back in the nightstand and wound up the thread, depositing it in a trash container. He returned to the bathroom to rinse out the washcloths. His guest was still unconscious. "I'm going down the hall to the maintenance closet. I might find something there that we can use to restrain him when he wakes."

Doc took the magnetic pass card from the intruder's pocket and headed down the hall. When he opened the closet he found the unconscious body of the night maid slumped against a wash pail. He checked her pulse and it seemed stable. He found a roll of adhesive tape similar to the duct tape used in the United States. He left the girl in the closet and returned to the room. "Tape his mouth, arms and feet," he said to Smythe as he left again. He returned to the closet, picked up the unconscious maid and took her back to the room. He opened the door to the center living area and positioned her on the couch. Next he called down to the front desk and asked the night manager to come up to his room. The night manager came up immediately and Doc greeted him at the bedroom door. He explained that there was an attempted robbery and that the thief had injured the night maid. The night manager was alarmed more for his guests than the maid. Doc assured the manager that the thief had left and that he was all right. He then helped the manager walk the half-conscious girl to the manager's office downstairs. Doc took several bills from his wallet and gave them to the manager asking him to care for the girl as needed, but not make any report. He then returned to his room where Smythe was sitting on the edge of the bathtub looking at the unconscious man.

"I need to make a call," Doc said as he sat on the bed, dialing the number Mueller had given him. He was surprised that Otto answered the phone. "How is the arm, Otto?"

"You," responded Otto.

"I don't like knives, Otto. Tell Mueller that I've the package he sent me all wrapped up. He can pick it up in an hour at the loading dock at the back of the hotel."

"I don't know what you're talking about," replied Otto.

"One of the blonde guards that I saw in the house tried to kill me tonight."

"It wasn't Herr Mueller's doing. We'll both meet you. Is he dead?"

"No."

"We'll want to question him."

"Me first." With that Doc hung up the phone.

Doc and Smythe revived the blonde intruder but he was uncooperative. When they removed the tape from his mouth he winced with pain from the broken jaw, but just spat on the floor when they asked him questions. At one point they pushed his face into the commode water to try to make him talk. Doc was watching the clock and 40 minutes had passed since his call to Mueller. Doc re-taped the man's mouth and both he and Smythe took their prisoner down the freight elevator to the loading dock at the back of the hotel. Headlights from Mueller's car came around the corner just as they lead the intruder onto the loading platform.

Smythe held the blond in front of himself as a shield, staying further back next to a trash dumpster. He reasoned that if someone started shooting it would make a respectable shield. Doc pulled the Makarov out of his waistband and held it at his side as the car slowly pulled alongside the loading dock. The back door of the vehicle opened, and Mueller stepped out, holding his hands high. The interior light of the car showed that Otto was the only person visible in the vehicle.

"Where is this *package?*" said Mueller.

Doc motioned and Smythe stepped out of the shadows, pushing the blonde into the light cone thrown by a 40-watt bulb over the rear entrance to the hotel. Mueller nodded. "This may be an answer to one of my own questions. Did you get your answers from him?"

"No. I tried for about a half hour, but didn't find out anything," replied Doc.

"Is that Makarov from him?" asked Mueller.

"Yes"

"Are the last numbers of the serial number in the 500 series?"

Doc turned slightly so that as he raised the weapon to look at the serial number it would still be pointed at Mueller. Looking at the weapon he caught the reflection of the door light against the polished barrel and saw the serial number. He lowered the automatic to his side. "Yes. What's the significance of the serial number?"

"I had a shipment of 70 Makarov automatics sold to me by a Soviet officer in return for a nominal pension. I also had a thief break into the records department and all records of these serial numbers disappeared. They were manufactured to high tolerance for the NKVD and the manufacturer turned all records of the serial numbers over to the Soviet Secret Police. Only the NKVD knew the serial numbers until their records were given to me and I personally destroyed the only copy of the weapons inventory on that shipment. The problem is that I never received the shipment. Someone stole it from me while I was stealing it from the Russians. There were to be several explosive devices and special timers as well as the Makarov automatics in the inventory. I inadvertently arranged a car accident with the Russian whom I thought cheated me. Now that I see one of the weapons, I think that this man, who was in my own employ, stole from me. I don't tolerate that. What would be important to you is that the timer and explosive that blew up the plane was probably in that same shipment. I've been trying to find out what happened to it myself. Very few people knew that I had such merchandise. You had me puzzled when you showed up asking questions. But, now is the time for answers. Would you and your friend like to accompany us back to my chateau where we can talk to this gentleman discreetly?"

Doc nodded his consent and Otto came up the old steel steps to the loading dock and took the prisoner from Smythe. Otto escorted the man to the rear of the vehicle and opened the trunk. The prisoner resisted for a second. Otto hit him in the stomach so fiercely he literally picked the man off his feet. He slung the doubled up form into the open trunk. Doc looked puzzled at Otto. Otto smiled back. Holding up the hand so that the sleeve on this arm was pulled back slightly he said, " Steel rods in the fiberglass make a formable weapon."

Doc got into the rear seat with Mueller and Smythe got into the front seat with Otto. As soon as they closed the doors, Otto started the engine and pulled out of the alley, heading toward the chateau. The car sped through the early morning making the trip in just over a half-hour. As the car approached, the garage door opened. Once inside, Otto turned off the engine and the door closed completely. Otto motioned toward the garage door. "It's armor plated to protect against a possible sniper."

Mueller led the way into the basement of the chateau, followed by Doc and Smythe. Otto brought up the rear with the blond prisoner over his shoulder. They entered a room that resembled an operating room except that the operation table had a trough around the edge to collect blood with a tube that led downward to an empty container under the table. This would be an interrogation room from which few people would emerge alive.

Otto strapped the unconscious man onto the table using wide leather straps lined with sheep's wool. The wool would lessen the chances of marks on the body from the straps. When he was done, he proudly said, "The doctor put on my cast while I sat on the table."

Mueller went to a cabinet and withdrew a small vial with a dropper top. He opened the man's eyes and put a drop in each. Replacing the vial, he motioned for everyone to follow him to an adjacent room. He locked the door behind him. "I put a dilation solution in his eyes. It will intensify the illumination from the overhead operation light effectively nearly blinding him and also causing pain. I don't want to use a hypodermic medicine as it could be traced if we end up with a dead body. I'm going to use a wire brush to cause abrasions on the skin similar to what would happen in a car crash. This will enable me apply an oil over the brush burn that will give the indication of intense heat and pain. Actually, Mexican cooks use the oil as a flavoring spice. It's oil of the Habanero pepper plant. He will tell us what ever you need to know. What do you want me to ask him?"

Doc answered, " I need to know if the highjack explosives were what was used to blow up the plane. If they were, who ordered it? Who paid him? Who planted the bomb? What did they expect to accomplish with the explosion? Lastly I want to know if he knows anything about the payoff in England?"

"This you shall have if he knows it. Have a seat. There is a monitor to watch our thief. Some of the techniques that I'll employ are not nice and you should be shielded from the sounds and light."

Smythe questioned, " What do you mean lights and sound?"

"Watch and learn," Mueller said as he walked over to a console in the adjacent room. He switched on a power button and a deep base sound could be felt rather than heard. "This is a very low base sound set at 72 beats per minute. That is the normal heart rate. As time progresses over the next ten minutes it will increase to 85 beats per minute and within 30 minutes be at 120. Our subject's nervous system will attune itself to the beat and very shortly he will find his heart racing. As I already explained, I dilated his eyes. Now I'll increase the light in the room so that it increases slowly over the next half-hour to levels where we'll need sunglasses to see. Our subject will not be blind, but what he sees will be reflections of blood vessels in the back of his retina, causing distortions. Remember the old trick of cooking a frog? If you put a frog in hot water he will jump out. If you put a frog in room temperature water and slowly increase the temperature he will not even try to escape, and will be cooked alive."

"The principal is much the same, I want his body to respond to the subliminal sounds and light until his nervous system goes into overload. Then I'll get answers. If he dies, I don't want any trace of drugs in his system."

"You mentioned Habanero oil earlier," questioned Smythe?

"Oh yes, I'll cause abrasions on the skin with the wire brush and put on the oil. This causes a sensation much like the skin being on fire. I'll assure him it's an acid and his skin is being eaten away. I can stop the reaction with buttermilk, and of course I'll tell him that this is an antidote for the acid. I'm sure he will talk."

The next two hours were pure hell for the former guard of the Mueller estate. As Mueller had expected the guard did collapse mentally after only one hour. He told an interesting story. It began with a solicitation from Mueller's competitor offering the guard money and power.

In the meantime the driver slept peacefully at the hotel, unaware of any disturbance.

Chapter 10

Under devious and twisted torture at the hands of Mueller, Hans told the perverted tale of his part in the death of Pearl and the downing of the aircraft. His story also revealed that he was very much a pawn in the scenario. This is the story that Hans revealed.

A French gangster named Jacque offered money and power. The money wasn't real, nor was the power. He proposed an idea of how to destroy Mueller financially. The plot was simple. Jacque had been trying to bargain with the dissentient Russian at the same time Mueller was also engaged in negotiation with the Russian. As a result, he knew the specifics of what could be had. Jacque's motive for doing anything was profit, so he found a market for the explosives, and had actually sold them before he was in possession of the merchandise. When his buyer wanted delivery of the merchandise, Jacque recruited Hans, the blond point man for the operation run by Mueller. He told Hans of the bad blood between himself and Mueller and suggested that perhaps if Hans could take over Mueller's operation they could work together. He offered his buyer to Hans as a means of funding the takeover. He also failed to mention that he had been paid in advance and there would be no money for Hans. Jacque set up the meeting for the sale of the explosives and timers. The Makarov automatics were of no consequence. He suggested that they could be used as throwaway weapons since they were not registered.

Hans further revealed how he arranged to hijack the Russian armament and kept a Makarov for himself as a treasure. He delivered the explosives and timers to a prearranged site. At that meeting he was thanked, but didn't receive any money. They said that it would be transferred into his account. He checked his bank every day for a week but never saw any funds. He felt foolish. He contacted Jacque and demanded his money. Jacque told him that it would be at the main airport in Stuttgart. Hans was to meet a man at a particular time and get a key to a locker where the money would be in a bag. This was very convenient for him, as he had to drive Herr Mueller's mistress to the airport that same afternoon. Hans arrived at the airport drop off area, let Pearl out of the vehicle, and gave the luggage to a porter to mark and transfer to the baggage area. He parked the car in the short term parking area and walked the distance to the airport terminal. Hans found his contact man in the baggage claim area. He recognized the man as one of Jacque's men from the meeting where he was recruited. The man shook his hand and grabbed him by the shoulder as if he were a long lost friend. He transferred the key to Hans in the handshake, mumbling, "Your instructions are in the locker."

Hans said he could see the bank of lockers behind Jacque's man. He crossed over to the enameled green lockers, and found the locker with the same number as the one stamped on the brass key in his sweating hand. Hans inserted the key and opened the door, not knowing what to expect, but wishing for the money. Inside was a small gift-wrapped package with a bow. Underneath it was a sheet with instructions for him. The typing stated that the package was a radio to be given to Frau Pearl for her mother. "Tell her that this present is from Herr Mueller. You may tell her it's a radio, as the x-ray machine will identify it as a radio." He looked at the bottom of the sheet and even turned it over, only to find the back was blank. He was looking for a mention of the money still owed him.

Hans went to the boarding area and gave her the package, giving credit for the present to Herr Mueller. He stayed at the debarkation area until the plane was actually airborne, then walked back to the car. As Hans approached the vehicle, he spotted the man who had given him the key. His step quickened in anticipation of the still awaited money. "I've given her the gift, but I don't understand the significance of what it has to do with the money still owed to me?"

The man smiled and answered, "It's insurance. You'll be paid shortly; it will be over in about ten days. You'll get your payment then."

Mueller's interrogation of Hans intensified. He wanted answers to questions that Hans didn't know. Believing that Hans was keeping something back; he put pepper oil on Hans' eyes, blinding him. He continued questioning for any other information that could possibly be of use. Mueller realized a time line had developed. Effectively it was a countdown to some bigger event. He counted backward and knew that seven days had passed since the plane was blown out of the sky. The clock was ticking and the game was almost over. Unfortunately he still didn't know what the game was or what the rules of the game were.

David was thinking the same thoughts. He was pondering the possible scenarios for destruction of the plane. He now had a strong suspicion that Pearl's death was convenient to an additional situation.

Mueller continued his questioning on the details of every bit of conversation. David sensed Mueller was becoming stressed and that Hans didn't know any more. Mueller crossed over the line between interrogator with controlled direction of thought and avenging angel. Hans' bare chest was covered with perspiration as he stared up with blind eyes. Mueller insisted in a rage, "Tell me what he said" Hans could add nothing else. Mueller screamed, "Tell me what Jacque's man told you." Hans said nothing. A third time Mueller screamed, "Tell me."

Hans muttered "He said it was insurance so that I would be paid later."

Mueller lost control and dumped the Habanero oil over Hans' exposed chest. Hans' muscles contracted and his body went into spasms. His muscles twisted and jerked, straining against the leather straps and sending the body into a grotesque contorted shape. His pectoral muscles were outlined in complete detail from the extremes of the contraction. The pressure on his heart was too much. After about two minutes the body relaxed. His heart had stopped.

Walking out of the interrogation room Mueller ordered Otto to wash the body down with buttermilk then again with soap and water. The buttermilk would dissolve the residue from the

Habanero oil and the soap would get rid of the buttermilk. For all intents and purpose it would look like Hans had a heart attack, which he actually did have. There would be no trace of what actually caused the heart attack.

Smythe was upset that Mueller had murdered Hans. David grabbed him by the shoulder pushing him back into his seat. " Hans betrayed Mueller. These people deal with different values than those of a court of law. Hans violated those rules and the trust of Mueller. That by itself would be enough to give him a death sentence. The fact that he participated in the death of Pearl made him guilty of murdering her, as well as everyone onboard the plane. This court of justice just convicted him and sentenced him to death. It's our job to use that information and prevent the next deaths from happening."

"What makes you so sure that this isn't the end?"

"The man Hans met at the airport said that it would be over in 10 days. Something is going on other than the plane crash. I think the crash was a cover-up for something else. If killing all of those people onboard the plane is inconsequential to their plan, I hate to see what the plan is."

"Where do we go from here?"

"Outside"

Otto had just come back from getting two men to finish up with Hans' body. Doc asked him where he could be safe to transmit. Otto asked him to follow. The giant led the way to a courtyard inside the complex. Buildings surrounded it on all sides to give shelter from the prying eyes of a sniper. Doc asked to be alone with Smythe so Otto left. He pulled out the pen and extended the antenna for better reception.

"Shelly, do you've any information on what I asked for regarding the use of the word insurance? It came up again."

"The insurance on the plane was with Lloyds who had the risk parceled out among several carriers. The Toronto office will handle the checks for this incident. The passenger life policies were with a firm out of Chicago, Illinois in the United States. The special cargo they were transporting, you know what I mean, wasn't insured. The insurance on the surveillance rock was through Lloyds. Coincidentally it was also through the Toronto branch. The actual policy was for the Pinewood Studios but was endorsed for our special use."

Doc asked, "Check with the local Lloyds people and see if anything strange has been happening in their Toronto office. We found out that something is to happen ten days from the date of the plane crash. Ask all offices to watch for any activity scheduled at that date. Did the Navy recover and destroy the merchandise?"

"Recovery was fine. The seals were intact, but the vault was empty when it arrived in Georgia."

"Damn. It fits."

"Be careful David."

"I'll. Out."

Doc walked back through the house followed by Smythe. "We're going to Toronto."

"When?"

"Now." They walked into the observation room adjacent to where Hans died.

Mueller had recovered most of his composure and had just entered the room wearing a new shirt and slacks. The old ones were soaked through with perspiration from the heat of the interrogation room. "That bastard killed my Pearl," said Mueller.

Doc sighed, "He may have been part of a bigger plan to kill a lot more." With that opening statement he filled both Mueller and Smythe in on what he had just learned about the canisters of anthrax and VX gas that were now missing from Shelly.

"We'll need a ride back to the hotel immediately."

"Done", said Mueller. He nodded to Otto, who got up from the chair as he reached for the car keys in his pocket. Doc and Smythe followed on his heels with Mueller walking behind, lost in thought. "I'll check with my French friend and find out what I can. How can I reach you? "

I'll have someone contact you by way of the number you originally gave me. I'm going to Toronto and see if I can follow up on that angle. You may have to leave me messages with a woman named Shelly. She is to be trusted as though you were talking to me directly."

"Fine. I'll find out what the Frenchman knows even if it kills him."

Doc smiled, "I'm sure you'll." He then closed the door of the sedan as Otto turned over the engine.

As fast as he had driven to the Mueller compound, he drove even faster back to town. It was just after ten in the morning when they entered the city limits. Doc directed Otto to stop at the bank. Doc went into the safety deposit area while Smythe and Otto waited in the car.

He put the Markoff in the safety deposit box. Doc was careful to remove the ammo from the clip so that it would not weaken the spring tension if it were loaded for a long time. He wiped the individual cartridges free of any prints as well as the clip and weapon. He also put in an envelope with currency. He had just made another 'black' drop just in case he was ever trapped in this area of the world. This done, he locked the box and returned to the car where Smythe and Otto waited with the motor running.

The next stop was the hotel where Doc and Smythe checked out, leaving a substantial tip for the desk clerk. They gave a cash bonus to the sleepy rental car driver who they found watching an American soap opera dubbed into German on the television in the room. He was quite happy to have earned a considerable sum for very little work. Doc swore him to silence as to where they went. Doc called the airport from the pay phone in the lobby and made reservations for both he and Smythe for a flight to London with a connection to Toronto.

Otto was waiting alongside the curb as Smythe and Doc came out of the hotel. He drove them to the airport where they boarded the plane after only a 45-minute wait. Smythe was quiet and Doc thought of the possibilities of the looming disaster if nerve gas or Anthrax were let loose. He also wondered who was involved. The canisters were put into the bio-vault. Someone had to have stolen the full canisters and switched them, someone on the inside, someone trusted someone who intended to cause a massive amount of death.

In the back of his mind something else stirred. Pearl's flight was going to Toronto. Toronto was the servicing office for two of the insurance companies. Was there a connection? At Heathrow airport they transferred to the transatlantic flight to Toronto.

Chapter 11

The trip from Stuttgart to London was broken by only one brief stop. Both Doc and Smythe transferred to the connecting transatlantic flight to Toronto after only a 42-minute layover. Doc's mind drifted to some documents he had seen back in Iraq. One of the documents dealt with supplies during the Gulf Desert Storm War coming from a French source. Perhaps that source was the same man who tried to eliminate Mueller? It was possible but improbable. He had faith that Mueller would find the truth.

The gnawing feeling in the pit of Doc's stomach was from an idea that the Frenchman named Jacque was only a very small part of a very big plan. If the plane full of people being killed, a small fortune of dope splattered over the ground, and the hijacking of Russian military ordnance were small items, whatever the end-game goal was it had to be very big. He drifted off to a fitful sleep with these items spinning in his mind.

The chime of the seatbelt light coming on awakened him. Smythe was already alert and reading a magazine. They disembarked and went to the baggage pickup. They went through customs using the same fake passports used in Germany. As they exited the customs area , Doc spotted a shapely young woman holding a sign reading DR. SMYTHE AND ASSOCIATE. "I think that is for us," he said to Smythe. "Do you happen to know her?"

"Yes, Carrie is from the field office. Let's go, she probably has a car."

They went over to the 20 something year old blond and she blushed as Smythe said, "Good to see you Carrie."

"I've a car waiting in the loading zone. They only just let the office know that you were coming in an hour ago. We haven't had time to straighten things up. Please don't tell London."

"Stop. We're not even going to the office. This is an unofficial visit. Just slow down and relax." assured Smythe.

"Are you one of the spooks too?" questioned Carrie as she looked Doc up and down.

Doc answered, "I'm an auditor from accounting. Smythe and I lost a bet so we had to leave the office for a week while they re-do the computers and such. We figured it would be a vacation of sorts."

Carrie responded, "Bull. You're one of them. I can see it in your eyes. There is no way a man like you is going on vacation with the likes of Smythe. I saw the way you both were watching the women picking up the luggage. Besides I know Smythe in the biblical way," she said with a smile. "Get in the car, then we can talk."

Doc nodded to Smythe and whispered, "She's pretty sharp for being so young."

"Don't tell her I told you, but she is actually 32, and was a field operator until she decided to settle down a bit. Now she is the assistant to the administrator of the field office here in Toronto."

They found a black Saab in the baggage drop-off area. A porter approached and said, " Don't worry Missy, I was watching your car. No one bothered it."

"Thank you sir," she said as she slipped him a few dollars.

Smythe went to get into the driver's seat, but Carrie cut him off with a swing of her posterior. "I drive my own car."

Smythe walked around to the front of the car and sat in the passenger seat. Doc got into the back seat. As they pulled away from the curb, Carrie asked, "Where to?"

"Let's start by taking a look at the office of Amalgamated Insurance Technology, Inc., "Doc answered.

Carrie commented, "I never heard of that one. I keep a phone book under the seat. Look it up."

Doc found the address and Carrie located the tall gray building which housed Amalgamated Insurance Technology, Inc. "Park here," said Doc. "I want to look around on foot." He crossed the street and went into the first floor of a bank building, which had offices on the upper floors. Doc went to a teller, and using one of his credit cards, obtained some Canadian currency. He spoke briefly with the teller and took a good look around the lobby, noting on the marquis that the entire tenth floor was the domain of the insurance company. He straightened his tie in the reflection of the glass cover of the fire hose reel. In the shadow of the reel the glass refracted the light in such a way that he was able to discern that infrared beam emitters crisscrossed the lobby behind the security officer's desk. He went up to the tenth floor to see what was there. The elevator doors slid open, and he was facing a narrow vestibule with a padded bench. To his left the emergency stairway led down to the ground. The office complex in front of him was screened off by glass panels sitting on a three foot wainscoting wall about fourteen feet in front of the elevator. A simple Weiser lock with only a night catch. No deadbolt secured the door to the complex. Through the glass he saw several desks with secretaries working at computer terminals. He remained on the elevator, pretending he had gotten a wrong floor. After the doors closed he pressed the L for Lobby. He knew what he would have to do. He left the bank and returned to Carrie and Smythe in the car. "Is there an electronic store nearby?" he asked Carrie.

"In the mall by the Needle tower. That would be the closest. I think it's a Radio Shack store," answered Carrie. "What do you need?"

"I want to buy a radar detector with laser capability."

"Why do you want something like that? You're not borrowing this car and you sure as hell are not going speeding in my wheels," stated Carrie emphatically.

" I'm not even going to drive," explained Doc. "I want the detector so that I can monitor when the alarms are active in the bank lobby."

"I don't care if you're a spook, I'm not going to help you rob a bank. That sure as hell isn't in my job description," spouted Carrie.

Doc spoke is a clear calm voice, "We are not going to rob the bank, but we are going to have a look at the insurance company on the tenth floor. I've a bad feeling, and I hope it's unfounded. If

I'm right, all that I'm going to do is take photos. You do have a camera available?"

"I've a low light, high resolution pocket camera. It's a fixed focus lens. You hold it 15 inches above the paper and it makes a very clear copy," said Carrie very proudly.

"How am I to know when I'm exactly 15 inches above the paper?" asked Doc.

"Silly, I've a string wound around the camera. When the end touches the paper you've a good shot." As she was talking she reached in her purse and retrieved the small gray camera.

Doc took the camera. "I had one of these once. It used a thin metal wire that came out of the case to measure the distance."

With a sheepish grin she said, "I broke the wire, so I just use the string."

Changing the subject, Carrie said, "Let's get going," and started the engine. The trio drove to the mall and went in through the food court. "Now what all do you need?" she said.

Doc answered, "You and Smythe go to the electronic store and buy a battery powered radar detector that also senses laser. I'm going to the drug store and buy a few items." As he walked down the concourse he spotted a kiosk specializing in computer-generated business cards and stationary. The machine recognized both U.S. and Canadian currency. Doc put in three bills to activate the computer's keyboard. He made 10 business cards for himself. The phone number he typed was a special 800 number with a specific extension.

He headed to the side hall of the mall where the restrooms were located, and found a phone. He called the number imprinted on the business cards. The computer answered and asked for an extension. Pressing the extension he used on his business card he connected to an answering machine. He pressed the pound sign twice, and then entered his pass code. He recorded a message. "This is Daniel O'Connor with Her Majesty's Royal auditors. I'll be in Canada on assignment. For verification I'm about 5 foot 10 inches tall and weigh about 175 pounds. I've brown hair and green eyes. The code name for the week is Popsicle."

He hung up the phone and went into a children's toy store. He found a wind up, spring driven truck, and bought it. He left the toy store, turned right, and went into a Sears store. He located the hardware section at the rear of the store where he bought a tri-corner file, a Weiser lock, metal snips, and a small auto tool kit. Finally he went to the drug store and bought a spray can of under-arm deodorant. His shopping completed, he headed back to the car.

On the way to the car Doc spotted Smythe and Carrie heading to the car from another exit of the mall. He slowed his pace so that he would arrive at the vehicle at the same time.

"Got it," said Smythe holding plastic bag in the air. "Did you get whatever else you needed?"

"I got my stuff, but now I need a place to work quietly for about 20 minutes," Doc answered.

Carrie interjected, "My apartment is only 10 minutes away. Would that do?"

"Works for me!" Doc replied.

They all got into the little black Saab and Carrie drove across town and pulled up in front of a little white home. "This is all mine," she said proudly.

"May I use the kitchen?" Doc asked.

"Sure," she answered.

Carrie unlocked the front door and Doc and Smythe followed her. They entered the living room. Doc picked up two magazines from a coffee table and then followed Carrie to the kitchen. He pulled out two chairs. He sat on one and positioned the other so that he could put his packages on the seat to face him. Doc put the magazines onto the tabletop to protect its finish. Next he opened the small auto tool kit from Sears and took out a flat blade screwdriver and pliers. He got out the toy truck and removed the bottom plate. As Doc was doing this, Smythe pulled out a chair opposite him and rested his head in his hands to watch in silence. Carrie asked, "Anyone want some coffee?"

"Sure," Smythe said.

"Good," agreed Doc.

The bottom of the toy truck was now off, and Doc was removing the coiled flat wire spring. Twisting it opposite the coil, he straightened a section and cut it off. The flat wire was now about 3 inches long. Clamping the pliers about half way on the flat wire, he made a ninety-degree bend in the wire. "One done," said Doc.

Next Doc took out the metal snips and cut a strip of metal approximately three eighths of an inch wide by 3 inches long. He opened the Weiser lock box and held a key from the lock against the strip of metal. Using the tri-corner file he made a rake style lock pick. The angle of the rake matched the angle of the notches on the key. "Two done," he said.

Doc looked at his watch, "Now I'll have the coffee."

"I've a question." Smythe asked.

"What?"

"Exactly – What and when?" Smythe asked.

Holding up the 'L' shaped bent spring Doc stated, "This is the wrench. It's used to turn the pin system in a lock." Picking up the other piece, he said, "And this is a rake. It runs against the pins flipping them up. I've the angle cut to match the Weiser lock on the door of the insurance company. I hope to slip the lock without having to pick it, but I need a backup. Now be a good fellow and bring in the case from the car."

Smythe went to the vehicle and retrieved the valise. Setting it on the floor beside Doc, he quipped, "Do I get a tip?"

"Yes, don't cross the street in heavy traffic. Now I need a towel. Carrie, can I borrow a dishtowel?"

"Sure, no problem," she replied and went to the top left-hand drawer of the kitchen counter for a terry cloth towel. "Will this do?"

"Excellent," replied Doc. He opened the bag from the drug store and retrieved the aerosol can of deodorant.

"Are you expecting to work up a sweat on this job?" asked Smythe.

"Not really. This deodorant uses aluminum chordate as the drying agent. If the room has any laser or infrared detectors, the car alarm, which you were kind enough to purchase, will alert me. If I spray a burst of this dust it will create a prism effect and will refract the light, allowing me see the normally invisible beams without tripping the alarm. That way I can just step over or under the light beams."

"And what's the towel for?" asked Carrie.

" To keep the can from banging in my case."

"When do we go?" asked Smythe.

"Shift change is 3:00. Many of the offices including the bank close at 4:00. I want to introduce myself to the guards at about 3:30 and then wait until about 5:15 until I go up."

"OK. How did you find out about the shift changes?" inquired Smythe.

"I told a teller that I used to work with a man who was a guard here and that I didn't see him. I then simply asked when the shift changed so that I could come back and say hello. She told me the rest."

"You've to be out of your damn mind, introducing yourself to the guards. What in the hell are you going to do? Say, I'm the person who is going to pilfer the insurance company. Do you mind if I wait here until everyone is gone?" mimicked Smythe.

Smiling, Doc said, "Close, but look at this before you mouth off." He reached into his pocket and then flipped Smythe a business card.

" Where did you get these?"

"At the mall."

"What if the guard calls the number? What are you going to do then?"

"I'll ask him to call to confirm my identity. I've a blind voice mail drop that will answer and confirm my identity. I'm surprised that you don't use one yourself."

"I've a blind mailbox. That is the only thing I've ever used," replied Smythe meekly.

"You had better get up with technology or you'll be left behind my friend."

Carrie interjected, " What do you want us to do?"

"Drop me off and then come back after 7:00. Park about two blocks south of the bank building and wait until I find you. It may be later, but definitely before the shift change at 11:00."

Looking at her watch Carrie said, "It's 2:40"

"Let's get ready," Doc said. " May I use your bathroom?"

"Up the steps to the left." Carrie replied.

Chapter 12

The trip from Carrie's home took only 10 minutes. They drove around several blocks and found an area next to a park where Smythe and Carrie would wait that evening for Doc to return. Carrie pulled beside the curb about a block from the bank and Doc got out. Doc straightened his tie and smoothed his coat as he stood looking at the gray building in front of him. Nodding to Carrie, Doc picked up the valise and started walking toward the bank. Carrie pulled the car away from the curb and headed south with Smythe looking in the side mirror as they turned the corner.

The bank had a large revolving door system with well-worn brass plates to turn the doors. As a precaution against leaving prints Doc pressed with the side of his fist against the door to make it revolve. Walking directly to the guard station, he set his brief case down and pulled out a card introducing himself as an auditor. "Hello, I'm Daniel O'Connor from London. I'm here for a quiet audit of the Amalgamated Insurance Technology Company. This audit's for Her Majesty's Auditing, and must be discreet. The manager is about to be promoted to a very prestigious post in the London office, but an audit must be preformed first per government regulations. Due to the discreet nature of the post, I must do the audit after business hours. Because of that I'm presenting myself to you so that you may confirm my identification, or whatever is necessary so that I may complete the audit with all due haste."

"What exactly are you talking about?" asked the heavyset guard.

"I'll return at closing time in order to do the audit. I've a key to the office from company headquarters; however, I need you to not alert any of the employees. Also please have the cleaning crew do that floor later, so I'll not be disturbed.

"I don't like auditors," commented the one guard.

Smiling, Doc replied in a truthful tone, "I don't like being one either."

"You 'gotta' do what you 'gotta' do," commented the taller guard.

"Would you be kind enough to call the 800 number and confirm my identity as a matter of protocol," Doc said.

"For protocol, anything," said the heavyset guard and he picked up the phone. He dialed '9' for an outside line then dialed the 800 numbers on the card. A few seconds later, he punched the four-digit extension into the phone. "Damn that sounds just like you on the phone," he said, looking at Doc.

"It's. If you needed to do a voice print identification for comparison you could do it to confirm my identity."

"All right, for good old protocol, What's the password for the week?" asked the guard.

"Popsicle," replied Doc.

"You really are detailed," commented the guard.

"As auditors we must be certain that all possibilities are covered, but I've made an error that perhaps you can help me correct."

"What can we help with?"

"My body is out of sync with the transatlantic flight. In short, I'm hungry. Where can I get something to eat until I've to do the audit?"

"Go out the main door and turn left for about one and a half blocks. There is a little diner next to the newsstand. Tell the waitress that Charlie sent you and she will take good care of you."

"Thank you." Doc picked up his brief case and left the building. He stopped at the newsstand and picked up a paper. He went into the almost empty restaurant. Doc sat at a table near a window so that he would have enough light to read the newspaper and also be able to watch traffic. Old habits still prevailed and he made sure his back was to the wall so that no one could sneak up behind him.

"What's your pleasure?" asked the cute waitress who sauntered up to his table.

"Charlie, the guard, said to say hello, and that you could fix me up with something to eat. What's good on the menu?"

“Everything is good, but the fish sandwich is fresh today,” she said giving him a wink.

“OK, make it a fish sandwich and coffee,” said Doc as he winked back.

“Broiled or fired?”

“Broilcd”

“Do you want fries with that?”

“No. Just the coffee, black.”

As she left to get the order, she put a little extra wiggle into her walk. Perhaps it was because there were only two other people in the place. Doc smiled to himself. Tonight would ***not*** be a night for pleasure. He opened the paper and read the local news in Toronto. The waitress brought his fish sandwich and coffee. Charlie was right; this was a good place to eat. Unfortunately because of the nature of his business, he couldn’t afford to be a repeat customer anytime in the near future. After he was done eating the fish sandwich, Doc used the men’s facility and washed the smell of the food from his hands. When he returned to the table, the waitress had filled his coffee cup. He checked his watch. It was almost time to move. He drank the coffee as he figured he might need the caffeine to keep him going. He put a five-dollar bill under the empty coffee cup. He went up to the cash register to pay his bill. Doc again assumed the formal attitude of an auditor.

Doc went into the lobby and waited by the row of phones until 5:10. He walked over to the guards and asked, “Is everyone down from the insurance company?”

“Yes, that brunette who just left was the last from that office. She is the head clerk. Is she the one you’re going to promote?”

“I don’t really know. The home office only referred to the person as the office manager. You know how it’s to be politically correct when referring to genders these days.” Doc straightened his tie, again using the glass door of the fire hose reel. Sure enough he could see the emitters and also the beams where the dust in the air caused them to occasionally sparkle.

“I’ll be going up now. Please see that I’m not disturbed. If you need me, please ring the phone twice and hang up then call back otherwise I'll not pick up." With that, he turned, strode to the elevator, and pressed UP.

The chrome plated doors whisked open and he boarded the elevator. As they were hissing shut he heard one of the guards mutter, "Royal bastard if you ask me."

Doc smiled to himself when he heard the remark. He had given the impression he wanted to be anywhere else. The guards would avoid him like the plague. *Plague.* A poor choice of words, considering he was on the trail of anthrax. The elevator continued to the 10th floor. He snapped open the valise and pulled out the radar/laser detector. He pushed the switch ON and set the volume for MUTE. Doc had just clicked the snap on the valise when the elevator came to a stop on the tenth floor.

The doors opened. Doc took one step off the elevator then stopped. He listened for any sound. The lights were off in the insurance office. He watched the radar detector for any alert lights, but none showed. He slid the detector into his coat pocket, and waited a full 30 seconds before he moved to the door. His right hand went to his pants pocket for the little Clippet knife. He swung the blade open with his thumb. He set his valise on the carpet in front of the door, grabbed the handle with his left hand, and set his shoulder against the door to cause a torque on the latch mechanism. The little knife blade caught the night latch. The follower bar had not engaged. Thank God for sloppy workmanship, he thought. The latch moved back an eighth of an inch. He released the pressure against the door to reset the knife blade against the latch. On the third try the door opened. Doc set the lock open using the inside catch and went into the room. He pulled out the radar detector. As he made an arc from left to right, the signal lights flickered. Somewhere close was an infrared laser trip, but not in this room.

Doc snapped on the overhead lights. If someone came up he could look busy. He went to the secretary's desk farthest from the door and opened the valise on top of the desk so that anyone coming upon him couldn't see what he was working on. Next he opened the towel and the deodorant spray can rolled into the bottom of the valise. Doc picked it up and snapped off the cap. He pulled the radar detector out of his pocket and held it out in his left hand, swinging it back and forth. The aerosol container was in his right hand.

Doc walked back through a hallway lined with private offices. Only one office caused the lights on the alarm to glow. In a sadistic way, he felt grateful for the person to mark where to look by adding the extra security on only one private office. Whoever fit this door knew what they were doing. The lock's latch was tight. There was no room to fit the knife blade between the lock and doorframe. It was, however, a Weiser lock. Reaching into his right coat pocket he retrieved the lock pick and wire wrench. He knelt on the carpet, and placed the radar detector and aerosol can beside himself. *I hate picking locks.* After about 3 minutes the latch swung as the pins released. Unfortunately it went the wrong way. It had inadvertently gone to the locked position. It was another four minutes until he got the pins to release and this time he had the wrench set the opposite direction so the lock would open. The metal of the flat wire spring was bending at an exaggerated angle as he forced the rotation of the lock. *Damn maintenance ought to lubricate their locks.* It was better to work a stiff lock, than to lubricate it and have someone aware that the lock had been tampered.

The door opened inward. He pushed it in about 6 inches and moved the detector into the opening. The light display was fully illuminated. There was definitely an alarm somewhere just inside the door. Doc inched backward, grateful to stand. His knees had started to ache after kneeling so long. He picked up the aerosol, held it near the top of the door opening, and triggered a burst of spray. As it drifted, he saw two beams. One was level with the floor about 18 inches above the carpet. The other veered off at a 30-degree angle back across the opening. Both were at least four feet into the room. Evidently someone wanted to be able to activate the alarms and still leave the door open. Doc opened the door a little wider and checked behind it with the spray. No other beams were visible. He spritzed the air close to the beams and then went into the room. He saw the emitter. It was between some books at the bottom of a bookcase to his left. The beam crossed the room completely and was reflected from a little mirror mounted on the wall. A third mirror, mounted on the light fixture reflected, it back to the emitter to complete the circuit.

Doc moved like a limbo dancer, stepping over the bottom beam while avoiding the overhead beam. Now that he was done with the preliminaries he wanted to get down to work. He sat at a desk chair and turned on power to the computer. It was time for answers. The screen came up and wanted a password. He hit enter. It still wanted a password. He looked about the room. On the bookcase he saw a picture of an Irish setter. He typed RED. *Enter password* repeated. He tried SETTER. 'Enter Password' was displayed again. He went over to the picture and turned it over. The back was part of the upright stand so he slid the stand off and there on the back of the picture was the notation *Flame's first hunt*. He went back to the computer and typed *FLAME*. The hard drive kicked on. The diagnostics of the machine checked directories, and it came up with a Windows 98 desktop full of icons.

Doc noticed that one of the diagnostic programs was Norton Utilities. He let the computer do a search of all files for several key words. First he tried Anthrax, but it came up blank. Next he tried the name of the airline, which also came up blank. He tried the flight number and got his first good response. The flight number was the code for an entire directory of files. He started through the files and found claim forms for death claims of the passengers. The odd thing was that all of the documents contained supposed scanned policies that the passengers had taken out prior to the flight. However, the written signatures were similar. On a piece of note paper, he made tick marks as he looked through the file. Four upright marks and then a crossbar for the fifth number. He counted 18 people on the plane with the same trust in Pittsburgh Pennsylvania as the beneficiary on their life policies. The Vaught Trust was in receipt of $750,000

He used the search function to look for *Vaught*. The search brought up three different files. Cargo owned by a J.M. Vaught was destroyed on the plane. A separate cargo claim was filed for $500,000 of computer supplies. John M. Vaught was also a resident of Allegheny County who personally insured 3 Lear jets with the company.

Doc searched several different patterns but came up blank. He tried the Daytimer Organizer program to check appointments. He entered the program without a password problem. Whoever had this computer didn't password protect that program. He backed up two weeks and found several cryptic notes about appointments and shipments. One item struck home: JV – terminate Pearl with job.

There seemed to be a lot of notes just prior to the airplane crash date. Places noted included Munich, Paris, Pittsburgh, and New York. Doc did a directory search of programs and found a CAD, computer aided design program. He couldn't fathom why an insurance company would want this type program, so he opened the file last used. It was a three dimensional map. At first he thought it was a map of train stops. Actually it was a type of train. He recognized some of the stops as being the New York subway system. There were notes about insertions and times of flow. Suddenly a horrifying thought clicked home in his brain. They were going to release the gas on the New York subway system. The flow rates were the times to contaminate entire sections of the city.

Flipping to another CAD screen, he found a similar system for the Washington subway, turned on the Hewlett Packard printer and printed the map of Washington DC overlaid with the insertion points. He did the same with the New York subway system. He knew that CAD programs were proprietary and even if he copied the program, it would take a number of and even then it might not work. A print of the map would have to do. Next he thought about the Daytimer program and decided to print a listing of all appointments for the prior, current, and next month. He could always look at it later to match dates with events.

One thing gnawed at him. Why would someone want to do this? He held his hands cradling his face while he was staring at the computer screen. He leaned back into the chair shaking his head left to right as though saying no the terrible plan; no, to the mind that conceived this destruction. *Why*? A small voice in the back of his mind said, "Follow the money." It was a basic training system. Look for the money. So he opened the Norton Utilities and searched for files having the words, *finance, stocks, investments* as well as other key words. There, buried in the system was a Microsoft Excel chart of drug company holdings with values. He printed a copy of that sheet because it neatly listed a lot of details of the company at the bottom of the chart. Next he searched by the name of the company, Vaught Pharmaceuticals, and hit pay dirt.

Listing of shipments of chemicals to and from Europe as well as future deliveries to the cities of New York, Chicago, and Washington scrolled down the screen. He printed that listing also.

Doc had not paid a lot of attention to whose office he was in, only that it was the only one with the laser security. As he pulled the copies off the laser printer he noted that the Daytimer listed the owner as Marty Williams, Senior Vice President.

Doc turned off the Hewlett Packard printer and reset the keyboard to its original position. He exited the computer, and shut down the system. He stuffed the laser prints under his shirt. Double-checking the desk to be sure it was exactly as it was when he came in, he used a linen handkerchief to wipe all of the things he touched. He crawled between the still active laser alarm beams. As he pulled the door shut, he checked the room one last time. The door was set to lock as soon as it clicked shut. He checked the door to make sure that it was locked. It was only then that he noticed a few hairline scratches on the lock. Not scratches that he had made, but by someone else who probably had made it into the room and probably had the information he had just retrieved. Could it have been the red headed shooter he had seen on the moor?

Doc went back to the outer office and put the aerosol back into the towel with the radar detector. He placed the papers into the upper compartment of the case, turned off the lights, and walked out of the office.

As the elevator descended, he tried to take on the composure of a pain in the neck auditor. When the chrome doors opened, Charlie was sitting in a chair reading a book while the other man was on the phone. The guard said, "Call you back later honey."

Doc walked up to the desk. "Everything passes with flying colors. Thank you both for your help." Doc turned and went out the door. Although Smythe and Carrie were to his left he turned right and walked for two blocks just to be sure no one was following him. He stopped at a phone booth and dialed the 800 number he had used on his fake business card. As soon as the recording came on, he pressed the pound sign twice and then pressed 7824. The phone beeped twice as a confirmation and disconnected. He redialed the number and to his satisfaction a recording came on announcing, "Pete's Bar and Grill, Pete died so we are closed until further notice." The phone then disconnected. If either of the guards ever tried the number again they would get the new recording.

Doc left the phone and walked further down the street, making three more right turns, effectively walking around a six-block loop. He walked up to the car as Smythe rolled down the window. Carrie leaned over and said, "Need a lift sailor?"

"Yes, if you don't mind," said Doc, as he opened the rear door and put in his case.

"Did you find anything?" asked Smythe.

"A lot. We need to get to your field office as soon as possible."

"We are on our way," stated Carrie as she engaged the engine.

Chapter 13

Rain had started to drizzle as they drove through the dark toward the field office. The rain coated everything with gloss of moisture that turned the asphalt into a black reflective mirror. Night reflected the darkness of the thoughts going through Doc's mind. Movement of the car, the bounce of the car springs over the uncertain pavement, and the lack of light prohibited him from looking at the papers he had printed. He wanted to look again at what he had seen on the computer monitor, but he had to endure the patience to wait until he could share the information with his companions.

Carrie stopped the black Saab along the curb in front of a maroon brick building, and pressed a garage door opener. The 14-foot security fence gate slid open. Chain link fencing surrounding the private lot had strips of vinyl threaded through the links to provide a semblance of privacy. As she had the only car in the lot, she parked near a back doorway. Smythe started to open the door when Carrie warned, "Wait!"

Carrie had unhooked the seatbelt and leaned extremely forward in the. She reached behind her waist and pulled a small 9mm Walter automatic from the small of her back.

"Is this a bad neighborhood?" Smythe inquired.

"Not really, but some of the visitors are really bad," she replied grinning at her two companions. She then got out of the car holding the automatic at her side. "It looks okay."

Smythe and Doc walked to the building. Carrie followed, keeping a watchful eye for anyone who might be interested in the group.

After they were inside, she slid the little automatic back into her waistband holster. "We did have a problem three weeks ago. It may have been nothing but a stray shot from a drug deal, or maybe something else, but one of the agents was hit in the arm when he was coming into the building late one night. We don't know any reason for the attack, but I would rather be safe than sorry."

"What makes you think that it was a stray bullet?" asked Smythe.

"I hit what I aim at. I'm sure that you do too, and I've never aimed at hitting anyone in the arm," she said with an air of conviction.

Doc asked, "Do you've a conference room with a large table and a computer?"

"We're headed there."

Carrie led the way to a large room about eighteen by thirty feet, with a large oval conference table in the center. To the left of the table was a series of corkboards with multi colored pins in a tray at the base of each corkboard. Doc pulled out a chair and put the valise on it so that it faced him when he opened it. He pulled out the prints he had made from Marty Williams's computer in the Amalgamated Insurance Technology offices.

"Carrie, if you would rather not be here, we'll understand. This is our problem," Doc said.

"Like hell. If someone is going to use a biological weapon I want to help fry his ass."

"OK, you're in. Everything that we find here must be confidential, even from your superiors in this office. Do you agree?"

"Yes I agree. Now what did you find that is making you so jumpy?"

Doc started by putting down the maps of the Washington DC and New York City subways. "I think they are going to use the subway system in several cities to disburse the toxin. See, the maps show insertion points and rates of flow." He pointed to the marking on the print. Fingering through the sheets he came upon the shipping invoices and put these sheets down next to the maps. "The other cities also have subway systems or mass transit systems of major proportions. The one thing in common is that all have international airports. I think this isn't a terrorist attack on a city or even the United States. This is a deliberate spreading of a biological toxin throughout the major commerce areas of the world. I think that it was just convenient to start in the United States"

"Why would anyone want to kill people in some of the largest cities in the world?" asked Smythe.

My guess is that they don't want them dead, but incapacitated, or at least susceptible."

"Susceptible to what?" asked Carrie.

"I'm not sure. At first I thought it was terrorism for money. Then I thought it might be blackmail. Now I think it's a combination of power and money. I feel sure that the Vaught is the center of our problem." He produced another paper that showed Vaught Pharmaceuticals had done a lot of shipping. "Smythe can you cross reference any of these shipments with possible locations for the importation of the biological toxin?" Turning to Carrie he said, "Will you look up anything and everything you can about John M. Vaught on your computer? Also check out the Vaught Pharmaceutical Company."

Carrie sat down at the computer screen and started typing. Smythe took a yellow legal pad and pen from the walnut cabinet and started referencing the dates. Doc paced twice around the table then he too took a yellow legal pad. However instead of referencing any listing, he started drawing.

Beginning with a circle in the center of the pad, Doc put a smaller circle at 12:00 on the paper. In the smaller circle he labeled it *stolen Iraq Anthrax*, at the 3:00 position he put another smaller circle and labeled it *Plane – cover-up*. The circle at 6:00 he labeled *Toronto-funding center*. Finally at the 9:00 position he put *targets-quick dispersion.* He stared at the paper trying to make sense out of whatever was going on.

Carrie interrupted his thought; "I got a biography and some financials."

In a tired voice Doc said, "Tell us the quick version."

She read parts of the screen. "About 50 years old. Single. Very rich. Not directly into politics, but bought and paid for a good portion of senators and possibly the President of the United States. He also contributes to several *charities* in France and various countries in Africa. He owns Vaught Pharmaceuticals as a private solely owned company. He lives on a converted farm outside Pittsburgh, Pennsylvania."

Smythe had stopped his correlation of dates and looked up. "Does he have any branches of the Pharmaceutical Company overseas?"

Carrie replied, "Munich, Paris, and London."

Doc asked, "Anything in Greece, Turkey, or anything in northern Africa?"

"I'm reading, I'm reading, give me a little time," returned Carrie. "It looks like they are doing drug trials in Africa. No real office, but more like temporary clinics set up for short times."

"Oh great, he just does tests on people instead of animals," replied Smythe.

"From what disease is he saving humanity?" asked Doc.

"Give me time," Carrie complained.

"I got something," said Smythe. "It looks like this guy shipped a load of French pine bark into the United States about the same time the VX gas would have come in. The shipment was coded for manufacture of some vitamin substance like Pycnogenol. The odd thing is that there was a lot of refrigeration equipment to keep the maritime pine bark cold. I wonder why they didn't just import the extract directly?"

"How did it come into the States," asked Carrie.

"It didn't. It came into the Saint Lawrence Seaway to be refined here in Canada at a plant nearby," stated Smythe.

"Here. Do you mean here as in Toronto?" asked Doc.

"Yes, the ship arrived here three days ago," said Smythe looking at the computer screen.

"Where is the refining plant?" asked Doc.

Carrie, looking over Smythe's shoulder, answered, "About a half hour's drive from here."

Doc leaned forward with his elbows on the tabletop, his fingers interlocked and the thumbs of either hand holding his head at the temples. He eyes were closed as he thought out loud. "What if –
1. Vaught found out about the VX gas and anthrax from his polit-

ical connections in Washington. 2. He makes arrangements through his African medical testing friends to find out about the transport of the toxic material and then pays someone to steal the toxic material. 3. He pays for the *merchandise* out of borrowed funds, and then uses insurance connections to arrange a disaster for the dual purpose of a cover-up of the theft and to create liquidity to fund phase two. 4. Phase two would be the transport of the toxins to France and then load them on the ship to be brought to North America. 5. I'm willing to bet that this vitamin processing plant is being used to break down the toxins to smaller delivery systems that will be used to hit mass transport systems throughout the United States."

"Why would he kill thousands, maybe even millions of people?" asked Smythe.

"I think that he wants – panic, and a few deaths, but most of all --," Doc stood up, never completing his sentence. He walked to a global map that was hanging on the far wall. "Here, and here," he repeated pointing on the map. "Smythe, can you get a listing of all pharmaceutical outlets he deals with worldwide?"

Smythe pushed a series of keys, and in a few minutes a spinning globe appeared on his screen with little flashing yellow stars where the distribution plants were located. Smythe looked up, grinning, as Doc continued his restless pacing and said, "How is this for fast service with nice graphics?"

Doc stared at the screen for three rotations of the graphic illustration of the earth spinning on its axis. "That son of a bitch," he exclaimed as his eyes gleamed with anger.

Carrie interjected, "What do you see? He has a lot of plants, but I don't see a pattern."

"I think that he is after money- pure and simple."

"What?" asked Smythe and Carrie simultaneously.

"Follow this – he dilutes the toxins and puts them into an aspiration device to use on subway systems. This will infect large areas of cities quickly so that it will appear that a plague has broken out."

Smythe interjected. "It would be a plague."

"Think back to your War College training. If you kill a soldier you eliminate one enemy. If you injure an enemy you eliminate seven to ten people to care for that wounded person." Doc continued, "I think he wants to spread a plague and sell the cure. I know that ever since Desert Storm we have been working on antidotes for both VX and Anthrax. I'm fairly sure that Vaught Pharmaceuticals was one of the providers for the military. If you look at the locations that I stole from the insurance company against the locations of the distribution outlets, they correspond. He is also going for a double play."

"What are you talking about? I can't picture him playing baseball while people are dying," commented Carrie.

Doc continued, "Remember, he collected on insurance from the plane crash to fund the theft of the toxins. I think he is going to let certain areas of the country die to enhance his political influence, and also eliminate competition from other pharmaceutical companies. This is speculation, but lets go to the supposed vitamin processing center and find some concrete evidence and stop this bastard."

"Slow down, how do you dilute VX or Anthrax? I thought that either would kill," stated Smythe.

Doc replied, " VX is a poison. In very small dosages it kills almost any living animal. All you've to do is dilute the dispersion to less than the minimal kill dosage and it damages the nervous system but doesn't kill. If treated, the effect can be stopped. Anthrax is a different killer. It kills the first host on exposure. The second and third sequential host exposures may also die, but then for some reason the anthrax mutates and becomes survivable. I guess at that point the anthrax strain is mutating. Some people proposed doing gene re-mapping to restructure the Anthrax so that it will only debilitate, not kill. If inoculated early, this effect is negated. If left unattended for 24 to 30 hours the debilitation is permanent."

Carrie flatly stated, "Time to stop this."

Doc and Smythe nodded in affirmation. Doc closed his case and all three walked out of the building into the dark, rain-soaked night.

Chapter 14

On the way out of the field office Carrie grabbed three night binoculars to conduct surveillance on the 'vitamin factory' and find out what was really going on at the facility. The trio got into the black Saab, and traveled across town to a warehouse laboratory built near the ship's dock. There was no ship at the pier.

"Do you think we are too late?" asked Smythe.

Doc tried to ease the tension by saying, "To catch the ship, yes. To find out What's in the building, no. We still have some time if they are keeping to the original time table."

Carrie put the car in park and brought the binoculars up to scan the scene. " No ship, boat or anything on the dock. There are only a few lights on inside the building. My guess is everyone went home for the night."

"Do you think they already moved out?" asked Smythe.

"Maybe, but there is only one way to know for sure," said Doc as he opened the back door and stepped into the chilly damp night air. He unbuttoned his shirt and rolled it into a ball then put it back on in a rumpled state with his shirttails out. "Smythe, do you've a condom?"

"What?" replied Smythe incredulously.

Doc was ruffling his fingers through his normally neatly combed hair. "I would appreciate it if you've a condom."

"Here, said Carrie as she reached into her purse. Smythe was looking at her in a questioning way yet keeping his mouth shut. Answering his unasked question she said, "A girl has to be careful. Besides, they are good at keeping detonator timers dry in wet weather."

"Sure," muttered Smythe under his breath.

Doc took the condom and opened it, unrolled it and stuck it into his pocket so that it hung out slightly. He then turned out another pocket. Leaning against the car, he took off his right shoe and removed his right sock. Turning to Smythe he asked, "How do I look?"

"Like hell!"

"Good," Doc responded. "Wait for my signal."

"What signal?" asked Carrie.

"You'll know when you see it."

Doc started down the private drive toward the concrete complex. A haze from the cool lake water combined with the yellow cast from the sodium lights to form cones of illumination surrounding the complex. Ahead of him a guard post blocked the road. He couldn't see the guard from this distance, but he did see the flicker of a cigarette lighter indicating that a guard was in residence. When he got within 20 feet of the guard post the security man came out of the block building and started toward him.

"This is private property, you must leave at once," announced the guard in a deep crescendo.

"I would like to leave. In fact I was hoping you could call a tow truck. I had an accident about a mile back the road, and ran into a ditch."

The guard's eyes took him in, noting the disheveled condition including the lack of one sock, the shirttail and other improprieties.

"You would not believe what happened. I left the key on. Never leave the key on. I wanted to keep the air circulating so that the windows would not steam up. Dropping his head he repeated, "Never leave the key on."

"What in the hell are you talking about?" asked the guard.

All the while Doc had been moving closer to the man. "I left the key on and the motor running. We were doing it and in the throws of passion her foot kicked it into gear and we went into the ditch." He moved another step closer. "Damn it was worth it, but never leave the key on." Just then Doc stumbled and started to fall. The guard reached forward out of normal reaction to help a fellow human being. His thoughtfulness was rewarded by a snap punch to his larynx causing him to gasp for breath. Doc quickly cupped his hands and clapped them over the guard's ears.

The guard's eyes rolled back showing only white as he lapsed into unconsciousness.

Doc picked up the guard's feet and pulled the limp body back into the block building. The guard station was more that just a guard post. It had surveillance camera displays on three monitors. Doc watched as they cycled through a series of locations around the plant. He didn't see any other person so he clicked the post's overhead lights on and off twice. He found the video recorder saving all of the displays. He backed up the tape so that he would not be seen approaching the guard post. On second thought he removed the tape completely from the machine.

Carrie's car approached the block building and Doc opened the door. "Catch", he said, throwing the VCR tape to Smythe. Just then a red blinking light came on at the top of the warehouse and a mechanical voice said, "Security bio purge on 30 minutes"

"What the hell was that," exclaimed Carrie.

"I think we now have a time limit," said Doc. He reached down to the unconscious form on the floor. He snapped the ring of keys from the man's belt, and started for the building.

"How long do you want him to stay out," asked Carrie as she opened a little black kit she had taken from the trunk.

"Make it an hour," said Doc over his shoulder.

Carrie pulled a new needle from the elastic band, pulled the plastic sterile seal from it and fitted it onto the syringe. Twisting off the plastic safety shield, she plunged the point through the seal on a little vial to fill the hypodermic needle. She adjusted the dosage by squirting the residual onto the ground. Next she put a rubber tube over his arm, tightening it to cause the veins to stand out. She injected him with a dosage to keep a two hundred-pound man out for one hour. She watched his body relax and his breathing improved as the muscle spasm that Doc had caused, released. She looked up in time to see both Doc and Smythe enter the building.

"Where are we going?" asked Smythe.

"I've never been here before. Look for a large room that looks like a laboratory. Until we find it let's go straight ahead."

A mechanical voice warned "Bio purge in 20 minutes. Please proceed to level one and leave the building immediately."

Doc pulled open the stairwell door and started up the steps. "I thought you didn't know where you were going," said Smythe.

"We're on level one now. Whatever we want to see is above us." Doc raced up the steps. Level two had a normal looking door so he continued up the steps. Level three had a flashing warning light on it. Doc opened the door and could see down a corridor where plate glass windows gave a view of some type production line. The mechanical voice came on again, "Laboratory lock-down in 3 minutes."

"What are we looking for?" asked Smythe.

"See the aerosol cans in the hallway," said Doc, pointing to a wooden pallet.

"Yes."

"Why would they need a whole pallet of air fresheners?"

"Maybe they work on garlic."

"We have less than three minutes. Let's get back to the stair-well."

"Lockdown in thirty seconds."

"Run!"

As they ran through the fire door and started down the stairs, they could hear the click of the mechanical lock on the door behind them. .

They were sprinting for the door as the warning voice came on the speaker. "Electrostatic grid to be charged in 1 minute."

They raced out the door and ran toward the guard post. Carrie saw them running toward her and opened the guardhouse door. The guard, still unconscious, rolled in his sleep so that his steel-toed shoe blocked the door from closing completely. As Doc and Smythe approached, she pointed to the top of the building. The men slowed, looking back over their shoulders. They saw a blue cast of electrical sparks dancing between thirty stainless steel perforated plates that were arranged like a huge air filter.

"Bio purge ignition in two minutes," announced the mechanical voice.

"Grab the other tapes," Doc yelled above high-pitched hiss being emitted from the building.

Carrie grabbed the VCR security tapes from a stand and threw them into the back of the car. Doc and Smythe reached her as she started back into the guard post. The mechanical system of the door kept automatically trying to close the door against the guard's foot.

" I'll hold the door. Pull him out," said Doc.

Carrie and Smythe each grabbed a foot. As soon as the body was clear of the door it snapped shut and there was an audible click as it locked. A hiss came from gas being vented into the little building.

"Get the car going and pop the trunk." Smythe got behind the wheel. Carrie opened the front passenger door for Doc, then tumbled into the back seat with the tapes. The automatic trunk release on the vehicle opened and Doc used a fireman's carry to lift the unconscious body of the guard and dump it unceremoniously into the trunk. "GO!" he shouted slamming the door. Smythe was spinning the tires as he pealed out of position and headed down the road. Suddenly there was a roar. A roar they felt as much as heard. A turn in the lane allowed them to see a massive plume of fire coming out of the electrostatic grids. A second or two later the guardhouse roof flew up into the air like a champagne bottle popping its cork. A plume of fire and smoke streaked into the air, meeting the roof before it started its descent to the ground.

"What was that?" asked Carrie as Smythe reduced the speed of the vehicle to normal levels. Doc answered," When we were in the building, I noticed pipes marked for propane as well as oxygen. I figured that they really do purge the laboratory, by fire. They must vent the oxygen and propane into the laboratory area to purge it by fire to kill any microbes that may escape. Then they vent the fire through a chimney to the electrostatic filters in the roof. The filters would hold the microbes until the fire killed them. Or more probably vaporized them."

"What was with the guard house?" asked Smythe.

"Probably a staged accident. Whoever is behind this needed to have security until the last minute, and one-second later to have no witness. What better way to do it than kill the guard and destroy the tapes in the ensuing fire? Carrie, do you've any connections to keep this guard *dead* for a few days."

Carrie reached for the cell phone and started to make a phone call when Smythe grabbed it, "Is that secure?"

"It's a digital phone with an encrypter. Now let me continue."

"Sorry."

Carrie arranged for a cover story of a body being found but whose identity was being withheld until notification of relatives. She also arranged for someone to meet them to pick up a package for a health resort. When she was done there was an uneasy silence in the car for about two minutes. She ended it by a simple question. "It wasn't there was it?"

"No, it must have been sent out. The fire destroyed evidence as well as sterilizing the area. I do think we've got something," said Doc.

"The only thing I got was out of breath," exclaimed Smythe.

"Remember the air fresheners in the hall? I think they broke down the main load to a lot of smaller dispersion units disguised as those air fresheners," Doc said.

"Shit, how can we find everyone with an air freshener?" stated Smythe in disgust.

"Don't be so hasty. I think they just broke down the delivery system. I didn't say they shipped it to different areas yet. Probably we'll be looking for one shipment of many air fresheners. For their own security and safety they are probably keeping the toxins as one load until the last minute."

"Where do you think the shipment is now?" asked Carrie.

"Headed for the United States. I'm hoping the VCR tapes in the back or the guard will be able to tell us by what means."

"Damn needle in a haystack," commented Smythe.

"Not really, we know that it was here, and we know some of the places they're going to use it. All we have to do is intercept it and destroy the toxin before they can disperse it. The security tapes may give us an idea or two."

Carrie was already pulling up to the security gate. She pressed the release button and the gate rolled open. Another car was parked in the lot with two men standing beside it. She pulled her vehicle along side theirs and rolled down the window. "Our friend is in the trunk," she said as she popped the trunk open. "He needs a rest for a week with no visitors." The two men lifted the unconscious body of the guard into their back seat. They propped the body upright, then took the precaution of putting handcuffs onto their prisoner. The cuffs were connected to a chain bolted into the floor of the vehicle so that a prisoner couldn't use his cuffed hands to throttle the driver or passenger in the front seat.

"See you later boys." Carrie waved goodbye.

Only after the gate rolled back into locked position did Smythe and Doc open the doors and get out of the vehicle. Doc picked up 7 tapes, stacking them in his left arm. "I hope that your machine has a fast forward."

"Now that we're almost back to normal, please explain. What was the deal with the condom?" asked Smythe.

"I wanted him to look at the condition of my clothing, but not me. He was so busy seeing but trying not to say anything about the missing sock and condom that he let me get close enough to take him out. I'll be willing to bet money that he can't identify me if he had to save his life." Doc smiled and put a tape into the VCR. "Now if we only had some popcorn."

Chapter 15

The VCR was hooked to a television in the conference room where Doc, Smythe, and Carrie had worked just hours before. Doc arranged the tapes to play them in the order they had been marked with the day of the week. The first day showed the arrival of a sea-going ship. The camera angle and the constant rotation of camera positions were irritating. White-suited men removed something from the ship. Whatever it was, it wasn't heavy enough to change the waterline weight of the ship. Day two showed the ship leaving. Evidently it was no longer needed to carry the cargo. Late in both day one and day two, there seemed to be shifts of five technicians who worked inside the facility for 12-hour shifts. Day three showed a tanker truck refilling the oxygen supply tank along the side of the building. About 3 hours later a propane truck refilled that tank. Day four offered a lead. A delivery truck from a local quick color copy service pulled up and delivered a package. Two hours later a stake bed truck arrived with three wooden pallets on the back sealed in clear stretch wrap. The pallets were aerosol canisters without labels.

It was in the early morning as they watched the tape, and Carrie was making notes of the truck's plate so she could make inquiries when offices opened later that day. The tape showed a limousine with tinted windows drive up to the door. A man got out but had his back to the camera, almost as though he knew the positioning of the surveillance. He was in the building for about two hours, and then returned to the limousine, which drove away. "I would surely like to know who he is," said Smythe, as he sipped his third cup of coffee.

"The limousine looks like the ones at Toronto National Airport. I'll run the plate but it may not show who the man is, only who rented the vehicle," responded Carrie.

The second shift didn't show up that day. Instead, a panel truck from a rental company came to the front gate. The truck driver loaded 6 medium cardboard boxes and drove off. About an hour later the remaining employees left, with exception of the guard. The next event was Doc walking toward the guard post. Doc clicked off the tape.

"First, can you get an identification on the panel truck, the limousine, and make blowups of faces of the workers and run them for identifications? Second, where can I lie down for some rest?" said Doc, as exhaustion overcame him.

Carrie motioned, "Come with me. You too, Smythe." She led the way down a hallway to two little rooms with cots. "The shower is through the connecting door. Leave your clothes outside the door; I'll have them laundered. I can't have you going around smelling."

"Thanks, wake us in four hours," said Doc.

During the time the two men slept, Carrie made several phone calls and got three technicians into the office. First she assigned one of the guys to launder the clothes. Then she directed the remaining two men to capture the images off the videotape and digitize them into the computer. Next she had the one technician run license plates. Another ran a photo match for 12 of the worker's pictures that were suitable for identification. They had identification hits on three workers. Both vehicles were registered to rental companies. She sent an agent out to get copies of the rental agreements. She figured, probably correctly so, that a face-to-face confrontation with an agent would be the best way to get the information quickly. Perhaps she was slightly sadistic in sending out an agent who used to be a goalie for a semi-pro hockey team. He was 280 pounds of muscle with several scars that showed. For some strange reason people seemed to open up when he asked questions.

In tracing the identification of the workers, she found the ones she could confirm who were research scientists specializing in either microbiology or disease transmission. All three of those identified had credentials including PhD's from prestigious universities. She ordered the technician to print out college records, as well as any work records for those individuals.

Four hours had passed and she felt like she had run a race. Sweat ran down her spine in spite of the air-conditioning. Her agent had not yet returned from the rental facilities, so she decided to let Doc and Smythe continue to sleep. Suddenly she had an idea. She called a friend at the air defense system and asked if, by any chance, any satellites were mapping the location of the plant at about the time the 6 boxes were removed. "I'll have to call you back," was the reply. "What's you fax number?" She gave the number for the fax in the conference room.

"When will you know?" she asked.

"Know what?" the voice replied, and the line went dead.

She smiled. It must be one of the better imaging satellites, the type that no one admitted to having. "Hope it got some good pictures," she said to herself.

The agent returned from the rental companies. His news was no surprise. "The limousine was rented at the airport by the Vaught Corporation. They had it for ten days and returned it yesterday. The clerk on duty said that there were five men with the driver, but only the driver signed any of the forms. From their appearance she assumed they were company executives. The Vaught Corporation also rented the panel van and in conversation the driver said he had to move furniture between offices. He bought 10 of the blue moving blankets to cushion the furniture. The van is still out for another week."

"Do they have locator transmitters in the panel trucks?" she inquired.

"No, only the cars. The manager said they have never had a problem with the trucks not being returned at that location."

The fax line started ringing. On the third ring the sensor sent the telephone transmission to the fax. Carrie walked over to the fax and watched as images came off the machine. The third sheet showed something she had not expected. The dock at the back of the warehouse had a medium sized sailing craft docked. It looked like six boxes were being loaded onto the deck. Goosebumps raised on Carrie's arms. She realized there were two shipments that have to be stopped. Turning away from the fax machine she walked down the hallway to the sleeping quarters and knocked on the door. "Time to get up sleepyheads," she said.

"OK," came Smythe from behind the door. As she waited she heard water from the shower.

Carrie returned to the conference room, and started to figure travel times to determine how far the toxic cargo could have traveled. She was counting hours and multiplying them by 60 miles and started with a red circle around Toronto. "My God, they could be almost anywhere," she muttered to herself.

"Not necessarily, " said Doc as he looked at her circle. "North would not be logical. They need a dispersal system like the subways. There are no major cities with subways this far north. Have someone check the US border patrol and see if the truck crossed over on any of the major highways. Now What's this?" Doc said as he picked up the fax of the watercraft.

"They have some boxes onboard a sailboat," explained Carrie.

"Shit!" muttered Smythe as he came up behind Doc. "Those bastards are making it harder. I'll be willing to bet they will spread out each of the six cardboard boxes to different targets. If they do that we are in *Deep Do*."

"Is there any way to get a satellite view of the lakes to determine where that sailboat is located?" asked Doc.

"We're trying," answered Carrie.

"How many cans fit in a cardboard case?" asked Smythe. "It can't be that many. Maybe twelve on the bottom and twelve on top, -- possibly?"

"That would be my guess," responded Carrie.

"How potent can a can be?" asked Smythe.

"It could kill millions of people with the contents of each case," said Carrie in a furious voice.

"That's not what I mean. The volume of the can could possibly fill a large room or possibly the first floor of a home. The cans look like the insect bombs people use to fumigate a home. If I were going to use a device like that I'd use one on each floor of a building, or a lot of canisters spread throughout an airline terminal, or several along subway tunnels. They need to infect a lot of people quickly in order to get this plague rolling. They would need massive immediate exposure to flood the hospitals and morgues." Smythe pulled a piece of paper in front of him and started to make notes.

"Smythe, you really are a sadistic bastard talking like that," spat out Carrie.

Smythe continued, "24 aerosols times 12 cases, that would be a maximum of only 288 targets."

Doc interjected, "I think he has something. As of now we only have two targets One by land and the second by sea."

"Who do you think you're, some reincarnation of Paul Revere?" harassed Smythe to relieve the tension.

Doc continued, "We have two lots of 6 cases each. Assuming that you need 12 to 24 aerosol containers to infect an area, we are looking at only 12 to 24 targets. Where is that listing of places I copied from the insurance office? How many places are on that list?"

Carrie looked at the listing, "In the United States we have many possible targets, but actually several are in each city. It looks like they are going to infect several sites in each city for maximum panic."

With a look as sober as an undertaker Smythe asked, "Which cities?"

As if she were reading a eulogy, Carrie slowly read, "New York, Washington and Boston on the East Coast, Chicago in the Midwest, and San Francisco and Dallas in the West."

"I'll bet on the boat heading over the Great Lakes and ending up in Chicago for the first delivery and the truck is headed for Boston for the first drop." If we can stop them before the first delivery maybe we can stop this entire madness." Doc reached into his pocket and pulled out a coin. "Heads by land tails by sea." Looking at Smythe he said, "Call it," then flipped the coin into the air.

Smythe stared at the spinning coin. "Heads, I hate the cold water."

Doc snatched the coin out of the air and slapped it onto the back of his hand. Looking at it, while partially shielding it from Smythe he said, "Heads it's, you get to stop the truck. I'll get the boat." Turning to Carrie he said, "Can you arrange for a HALO (High Altitude Low Opening) drop for a night drop intercept?"

After a second Carrie gasped, "You've got to be crazy. HALO is hard enough in daylight over land."

Doc looked directly into her eyes, "Can you make the calls for tonight?"

"Ycs," she said, as she swallowed.

"I'll also need night vision goggles for over the face mask, C-4 igniter cord, and a recovery balloon."

Smythe asked, "Are you going to try to destroy it or recover it?"

"Whatever is necessary. I'd like to recover it so it can be destroyed in a controlled circumstance, but I'll incinerate it and everything else if necessary while at sea."

Carrie turned to one of the agents and ordered him to get a car ready to take Doc to a private airport. She turned to Doc, "I'll probably not see you again, but good luck anyway. Smythe and I'll get the truck."

"Promise me something?" asked Doc.

"Yes."

"Order both napalm and phosphorus bombs for 7:00 in the morning in case I fail."

"That will kill everything."

"Exactly."

"Including you, if you're even close."

"Then I better not let it get to be 7:00 without capturing or destroying the cargo."

"Break a leg," said Smythe.

"I sincerely hope not," responded Doc, as he started out the door following the agent assigned to drive him to the airport.

Smythe turned to Carrie saying, "If the truck is going to any of the targets in the United States on the east coast, we'd better get in the air ourselves to be closer for our own intercept."

"I'm still assigned to the Toronto office. I can't just leave," replied Carrie.

"Only for the next five minutes," responded Smythe, as he picked up a secure phone and dialed to an unlisted number in London.

Chapter 16

A fine mist was coming down as Doc walked from the building. It was a thick mist; so thick that walking through it dampened his jacket. The cold penetrated clothing to the point of chilling one's bones. The drive to the military airport took about 45 minutes. As they went through security at the main gate, the driver showed ID that gave permission for him, as well as any passenger, to enter the base. They drove past the barracks and across to the far side of the airport where there were three hangars. Approaching the far-left hangar, the driver blinked his lights from normal headlight to high beams and then back. The hangar door raised about 10 feet to let the vehicle drive in next to the only aircraft in the building. The driver got out, probably with intentions of opening the door for Doc, but Doc was out and standing beside the car by the time the driver made it around the vehicle.

At that instant another man appeared, approaching the vehicle. He started, "Mac, who lost their mind getting me out of bed for a simulated HALO drop in the middle of the night?"

Doc answered, "It's no drill. Were you given a list of extra equipment that may be needed?"

"Yes, but I don't understand. Are you the maniac going to do the HALO?"

Yes, I'm the maniac. Did you get any information as to the locations of the intercept?"

"No intercept coordinates yet, but I do have the equipment. It just arrived. Mind if I ask a question?"

"Ask away. I may not be able to answer, but I'll if I can," Doc responded.

Exerting his authority, the commander stated, "First, are you currently certified to do a HALO?"

"In answer, I've done them before. If I fail and die, this mission never took place. I never existed. In short you're not to blame and are not responsible in any way,"

Taken aback, the commander asked, "Second, I've the oxygen mask and tank, as well as the wet suit, but I didn't get a request for a mask and fins so I added them on to the list myself, especially if you want to go swimming."

"I'll not be needing the mask or fins. You can leave them here. Did you get the helium and pickup balloon?"

"I've that on the plane as safety precautions, for search and rescue."

Thoughtfully Doc said, "I forgot to ask, but I'll now. Do you've any pistol cross bows with a fine grappling line?"

"Yes, but those are used by Special Forces."

"Get one," Doc stated.

"Yes sir," replied the commander as he realized that Doc wasn't going to acquiesce to his authority.

"How many men are scheduled for this flight?"

"Only two. I'm flying and I've a navigation officer to find our target," replied the commander.

"Is he here?"

"She is onboard the plane checking equipment." The commander smiled. Finally he had one up on this usurper of his authority.

"Is there a place where we can talk, just the three of us?" Doc asked.

"Well I've got to eat. There are some frozen meals in the back with a couple of microwaves," replied the commander.

"Good, I don't want any tension, at least not what I'm feeling now"

Gathering a small flight case with charts and maps the commander called up the ladder into the hull of the plane, "Brown, get down here."

A voice from the interior of the plane responded, "Just a sec."

As they waited, a beautiful brunette backed down the ladder to the deck. Because of Doc's presence she straightened and saluted, "Sir?"

"At ease Brown," said the commander. "We are going back to the ready room for a little talk." The commander lead the way, followed by Doc. Brown brought up the rear. The ready room was very well equipped. Both a computer and fax machine were at one end. A long conference table sat in the middle and four microwaves were at the other end of the room with two drip coffee makers. The commander took the end chair at the long table. Doc sat to his left and Brown took the chair to his right.

"Permission to speak freely?" asked the commander.

"I'm not military, so speak your mind. I'll need cooperation up there not conflict," answered Doc.

"Who the hell are you to get me away from my family to fly a stupid test scenario in this freezing weather?" stated the commander with more than a little irritation in his voice.

Doc steadied his eyes on the commander. The weather was cold, but his eyes were colder. "This isn't a test. This isn't a drill. This is very God damn real. Terrorists have a biological weapon out on the open lake for delivery to somewhere in the Midwest, probably the Chicago area. I'm going to intercept the boat at sea. If an accident happens, the entire area can be fire bombed to keep it from spreading. I'm going to get on board that ship, and capture the cargo. If I can't capture it, I'll rig a shaped charge with the C-4 flash cord to contain and kill as much as possible of the biological toxin. Your jobs are to get me to the ship and then monitor at a safe distance. If it gets to be 7:00 in the morning then you'd better be away from the area because that is the time for the scheduled fire bombing."

Undaunted, the commander returned the gaze. "You know that a HALO has a poor rate of survival. A front is moving through and your intended target is somewhere below a snow front. The temperature up there is about 10 degrees below freezing. With the speed of your fall, the wind-chill will probably make an ice cube out of you before you hit. Why not order the fire bombing and be done with it."

"I'm glad you're understanding my problem." Doc smiled, "I want a wet suit not for swimming but for heat. I'll wear it as insulation. I'll have the chute over the wet suit and a blizzard suit over that when I start the jump."

Brown interrupted, "With that much clothing, how are you going to work the chute?"

"I'll watch the altimeter on the way down. "I'll take off the blizzard suit and drop the air tank before I open the chute. I'll have to glide the chute to intercept the boat. I'm counting on you to monitor my glide with your instruments to make sure I get as close as possible with the drop, then I won't have to do a lot of correction in the glide."

The commander interrupted. "Why not just do a flyover and drop a squad of Seals on the deck and end this."

"Two main reasons. If we take the cargo, I don't want the people on the mainland to know I've it. Second, if it isn't destroyed in a laboratory environment, some of it may escape and still cause a disease breakout. The best option is to recover it. Do you've a pickup hook, or will we need an additional plane later?"

"I can do a balloon pickup with up to a ton on the end," answered the commander.

"It won't be that heavy," replied Doc. Looking at the computer and fax machines he said, "I guess we wait."

Almost as if the machine was psychic, the phone rang and the fax started printing out. Brown walked over to the fax and picked up sheets. "We have a location."

"Show us," responded the commander.

Brown walked over to a large map of the area. "They are on open water at these coordinates," she said pointing to a spot of blue on the map.

"Any shipping lanes in that area?" asked Doc.

"Nothing on the map, but that doesn't mean anything in that area," said Brown.

"How long until they get close to a normal shipping lane?" asked Doc.

"At least six hours on the present course," replied Brown.

"Let's get something to eat, then get airborne," stated the commander. He got up, went over to the freezer, and took out a couple of frozen dinners. Turning to Doc he said, "Turkey okay with you?"

"Fine."

Looking at Doc, Brown asked, "What should we call you? I don't think 'hey you' works."

"Call me Doc." Smiling he said, "I answer to it."

"My name is Samantha Brown, just call me Brown. It's quick and military. I've gotten used to it."

While Doc and Brown engaged in polite conversation, the commander went to a locker in the main area of the hangar and brought back a blizzard suit with a hunchback area on the spinal region to accommodate the parachute. He also brought a pistol crossbow with the grappling line hook on the end. He placed these on the opposite end of the table from where they were seated. "Anything else you can think of?" he asked Doc.

Doc thought for a minute then replied, " Duct tape, scissors, and a parachute switchblade with the hooked blade."

The commander reached into his pocket and pulled out a fluorescent orange knife. He pushed the button on the side, and a hooked blade sprung out. He flipped it in his hand so that the butt of the knife was toward Doc. "Will this do? It will cut through the canopy."

Doc took the knife, examining the blade. He closed and opened the knife several times. "Your personal knife?" he asked.

"Yes. You can return it later."

"Thanks for your confidence. I will."

The bell on the first microwave chimed. The LED displayed the greeting *enjoy your meal*. The commander retrieved two plastic trays and slid them across the table to Doc and Brown. He went back, got his own dinner tray, and brought it to the table. At the same time Brown went to a drawer for got plastic utensils. "We use plastic for hygiene. No one wants to do dishes, and sometimes we are too rushed to take time to clean up."

They ate in silence. Each person was considering what must be done to make the mission work and how to prevent an unseen problem from wrecking the mission. When they finished eating, they disposed of the utensils and trays into a food waste container. Doc broke the silence by going over to the blizzard suit.

"Do you've scissors?"

Brown nodded toward the cabinet behind him. "Third drawer down."

Docs found the scissors and duct. He placed them on the table, and then laid the blizzard suit out so that it faced down. He took the scissors and slit both legs and continued the slice up the back of the suit, even severing the elastic band at the neck.

The Commander and Brown watched curiously.

Doc taped the slits in the material with long lengths on duct tape. The tape was positioned so that the ends of the long strips terminated in the front of the suit. Lastly he folded about a half inch of the tape back on itself to make a pull tab.

"You've done this before," smiled the commander.

"Yes, but the last time I didn't bring the tear-off starters to the front and I almost didn't get it off in time."

Brown asked, "Where did you figure this out?"

"I learned it from a magician friend who is an escape artist in Vegas."

Doc looked up. "Ready?"

"Ready," said the commander. "The wet suit, oxygen, GPS (Ground Positioning System) and other equipment is on board."

They boarded the plane. The commander pushed a button in the cockpit and the hangar door opened. "Just like the garage door at home, only bigger," commented the commander. Doc was watching from a rear seat in the cockpit. They taxied to the end of the runway. They held position for a few minutes and downloaded the latest meteorological data into the onboard computer. Finally the tower permitted take off. The commander gave full power and the engines hummed. In a moment they were airborne. The commander flipped on the green, low-light cabin lights. Doc and Brown left the cabin and went to the back of the plane to prepare for the jump.

Chapter 17

Without any display of deference to his modesty, Brown said, "I'll get an update on the location from the commander while you get into your wet suit."

Doc couldn't find a groin support with the suit, so he opened the first aid kit and pulled out a roll of flexible fabric bandage to wrap his groin area. The sudden jolt of the chute opening could cause considerable stress on his testicles. If he didn't give additional support in that area, he may be in such pain as to bc nonfunctional when he reached his target. He put on the black rubber suit. It was slightly cold so he dropped to the floor and did twenty push-ups to start building body heat. Next he put on the parachute harness making sure it was cinched as tightly as possible. Brown came back just as he started to put the altimeter on his wrist.

"Give that back," she said pointing to the altimeter. "I've the coordinates of the target and want to download them into the altimeter."

"What are you talking about?" asked Doc.

"I'll put the intercept coordinates into the altimeter, and it will show a red dot on the watch face to show the direction to control the chute."

Brown took the watch-like device and snapped it into a little three-inch holder on the end of a cord attached to the serial port of her computer. She keyed in a location and handed it back to him in less than two minutes. "There is a GPS built into the altimeter. It will get you to the target, assuming the craft continues on the same course at the same speed."

Doc had taken the fluorescent knife out of his pants and placed it on the tabletop when he began suiting. Now he put the knife in the left sleeve pouch of his wet suit for easy reach.

As he started getting into the blizzard suit Brown helped because of the bulk. "How are we doing with the flight?" he asked.

"Fine, we're following in a standard flight pattern. We're actually under a commercial flight. If someone is watching our profile they may think we're a shadow, or a commercial charter. The flight path will take us within 2 miles of your target. Your glide slope should be able to compensate if you open up a little early." With a glance at the open bandage box, she said, "It will also be a little easier on your body if you open early."

Doc wrapped the flat ribbed bungie cord from the pick-up balloon around his waist. It would act as support for his lower back on the way down during the sudden opening of the chute. It would also act to absorb the shock as the plane snapped the rescue balloon from a motionless float in the air to a sudden speed of flight. He also put on soft rubber-soled jump boots that were a dark camouflage mixture of leather and black nylon.

Doc snapped the pants closed, but in getting into the top of the suit, he split open the seat of the pants where he had slit them with scissors.

"Hold on while I duct tape your butt," laughed Brown. She pulled out two smaller strips of the tape and put them across the bottom of the suit at ninety degrees to the cut. "They should pull off when you pull the main strip," she said.

She handed him a ten-inch tube of oxygen. "This will give you up to fifteen minutes. You should actually need only 4 minutes. Pitch it to the side before you open the chute. I don't want it hitting you on the head and messing up the mission."

"Don't worry, I plan to get rid of the oxygen and the suit so that I can move."

"This is an interesting device," Brown said, as she handed him the pistol crossbow. "It has two steps to make it work. First it comes folded flat. You must rotate the bow and snap it into place. Next, when you cock the bow, the back of the bolt automatically aligns with the bolt for firing. You must arm the tip of the bolt." She clicked a little slide on the forearm of the pistol. "This slide extends the grappling hooks as well as a tungsten carbide barbed arrow tip. This will have enough force to penetrate a pine tree so that the barbs of the point will hold in case you miss with the grappling hooks. You'll only get one chance. Finally, after you shoot, and it hits, release and pull the trigger a second time and the miniature winch spring in the handle will re-roll some line to take out the slack. A clutch will lock the line solid."

Raising his eyebrow, Doc asked, "Have you ever seen a pine tree in the middle of the water?"

With a disgusted look Brown responded, "No but it will have enough force to shoot through a wooden door. Now lets get on with the briefing. Surface temperature is about 52 degrees. The drop in temperature is about three and a half-degrees per one thousand feet. If we are cruising at…"

Doc finished, "The temperature will be a drop of 63 degrees or about eleven degrees below zero at 18,000 feet."

"Yes. You've done this before, haven't you?"

Doc continued doing the math in his head, "The acceleration of the drop will be sixteen feet per second squared. If my math is right 8000 feet divided by 32 comes up to about 250 seconds or 4 minutes and 17 seconds to breathable air."

Brown was working with the calculator. "How do you do that so fast?"

"Practice. I've done it before. If I figure it correctly, the temperature will still be only seventeen above zero at 10,000 feet. I'll try to slow with arm and leg spread, but stay on the oxygen until about 8000 then get rid of the blizzard suit and oxygen. I'll try to hit the chute at about 6,500 to 6000 feet. That will give me enough time to find and steer the chute to the boat. Besides, at about 5,500 I should be above freezing."

"Damn. You're good with numbers. I hope you're good with a chute. That little boat will be a trick to hit in the middle of the water."

"I'll get onboard the boat," answered Doc without even cracking a grin.

"Ten minutes to jump," voiced the commander over the intercom. "I've a friend in the air flying a U.S Navy E-2. I had him do a check on the target with infrared for practice. He told me there is probably a diesel running hot for the power unit and two adult subjects on board."

"That will help," replied Doc.

"Here, put this over your chest," said Brown, as she handed him a square of eggshell foam. "It will cushion the oxygen and the crossbow."

"In a second," said Doc, as he tucked the phone pen into the sleeve on his right arm.

"Just send a signal from that digital device for four seconds. I'll know that you succeeded and will come back to pick you up," said Brown.

"How did you know?" asked Doc.

"I'm also doubling as the flight engineer on this flight and my systems monitor all the electronic frequencies. I don't know your phone number, but I do know your frequency."

"You're good."

"And you'll never know how good, until I see you again," she said in a flirtatious voice. Changing to a business tone, she said, "Here is a second altimeter for over your coat."

Doc zipped his coat and put on the second watch-like altimeter over his gear. Brown gave him the flight goggles. "These have illumination enhancing system built in for night drops. It's not as good as starlight, but you've less wind resistance. A starlight system would be ripped off by the wind and probably take your head with it."

"Time two minutes," spoke the commander over the speaker.

Brown opened the jump door and Doc backed up holding onto a handgrip by the doorframe. They waited until the red light flashed. Doc pushed away from the aircraft with both his feet. As soon as he was out, Brown closed the door muttering to herself, "Damn it's cold out there."

As Doc dropped, the difference in sound was a shock. He would never get used to the sudden change. Onboard the aircraft, the noise of the engines became a part of your thought. Now the silence was palpable. The heavy insulated suit kept the frigid air away from him. He took a breath of the bottled oxygen. So far, so good, he thought. Suddenly he felt a vibration in his right arm. At first he didn't realize what it was, then he remembered the phone pen in his sleeve. There was no way in hell he could answer the phone. It's probably one of those people wanting me to change my long distance, he thought.

He spread out his arms and legs to have a controlled descent. Glancing at the altimeter, noted that he had only dropped 3,000 feet. The air seemed to change. Suddenly he was falling through ice crystals. It felt as though he were being sandblasted. The ice cloud he was falling through was not that big, but it was causing ice to build up on the lenses of his goggles. He cleared the goggles and checked the altimeter. It was 10,000 feet and the ice had stopped. Suddenly the air got under the tape on his butt, and his trousers were flapping at his posterior. He took two deep breaths of oxygen then threw the oxygen tank away. He tucked into a ball reaching for the duct tape tabs on his legs. Pulling the tape, he opened the slits on the back of the suit. Wind got into the openings, and it literally ripped the suit from him. The legs and pants came off easily, but he had failed to slit the sleeves. The result was that the suit came off, except for the sleeves. Doc was caught in the suit and it was dragging behind him. Working like Houdini, he freed his right arm, but found himself spinning toward the lake below. Desperately, he worked out of the left sleeve. It was bitter cold, but he was sweating. Finally, twisting his left arm, he was free of the suit. Spreading out his arms and legs, he was able to stabilize the drop again. The altimeter with the direction finder was on his left arm. Checking it, Doc found that he was only about three-quarters of a mile off course. Everything was black. The cloud overhead blocked the moon and starlight. He thought, *I've got to quit doing this.*

At 6,000 feet Doc hit the chute figuring that he needed the height to make up the difference in ground distance to the target. He prepared himself for the sudden jerk as the chute opened. Nothing can explain the jarring a body goes through when a chute opens after a fall of 12,000 feet. It hurt. The harness held his torso but his feet felt like they were being ripped off his legs, his legs felt like they were being ripped from his torso. It hurt. His shoulder hurt worst. The canopy was fully opened and he was dangling from it. Doc flexed and moved his neck and head. He pulled off his gloves and pitched them to the side. He felt his neck. He felt his ankles. Everything was still attached. So far the mission was going well. Watching the altimeter he adjusted the guidelines so the chute would drift into the area of the target. While he floated to the target, Doc felt for the crossbow. It was still there, clipped to his harness. For a second he had doubts. He twisted the bow so that it clicked into position. He slid the arrow point out of the grappling device and the grappling hooks came out automatically. All it needed was to be cocked. To be safe, he waited to cock it. He watched the altimeter as it continued to drop. At zero he would be swimming unless he found that little boat. All he could see was black water. He thought, That little red dot better be right.

It was 2,000 feet and only black water was beneath him. At 1,500 he could still see only black water. Finally he saw running lights and a cabin light to his right. Doc pulled the guidelines to float in that direction. A surface breeze caught him. He put the chute into a steeper glide to catch up to the boat. Reaching down he pulled the levered cocking mechanism on the crossbow. If worse came to worst, he would try to hook the boat with the crossbow. After checking the safety, he left it dangle from one of the grappling hooks he had looped into the bungie cord around his waist. Doc was at 300 feet when he was hit with another gust of wind. Pulling on two of the guidelines, he twisted the descent so that he was headed directly over the boat. In spite of the steep glide path he was a little high. Doc unhooked the crossbow and held it in his left hand. With his right hand he kept tension on the two guidelines so he would hit the deck of the boat. Just then a man came out onto the deck and walked toward the edge of the railing. It looked like he was unzipping his fly to urinate into the water. Doc was going to hit the deck behind the man. Whether he heard, or somehow sensed something, the man turned and simultaneously pulled a colt automatic from under his coat. Doc pulled the 'D' ring, releasing him from the chute. Doc plunged feet first into the man, hitting him hard in the chest with the soles of his feet. The man fell back, snapping his head against the railing. His body slumped to the deck.

Doc rolled left and stood up just as a second man from the steering cabin came into the light brandishing a Mac-10. In a single motion Doc turned and shot him in the chest with the grappling hook. The hardened steel point went into the man's sternum and came out his back. The man looked down at the tines of the grappling hooks blooming from his chest. Doc snapped the trigger a second time and the spring took up the slack in the line stretching from him to the man with the automatic weapon. Reflexively the man continued to bring the automatic. The little clutch on the grappling line clicked with tension. Doc pulled the pistol and line toward himself as the dying man pulled the trigger sending a burst of shots into the air.

There was no doubt the man with the Mac-10 was dead. Doc checked the man he had hit with his feet. Confirming he was dead, Doc put the Colt in a loop of the bungie cord. Never wanting to take a chance, he went to the man he had speared and checked to be sure that he was dead, too. Leaving the bodies where they were, he staggered to the railing. Holding onto it, he stretched his sore muscles.

His left arm and shoulder were swelling and getting stiff. Doc dislocated it in the course of the jump. He was also having difficulty walking. He sat on the deck and felt his feet and ankles. One of the bones in his right foot was dislocated. The little bone couldn't take the impact of killing a man by landing on him. It didn't feel broken. He worked the little bone back into place. It hurt. The swelling had not started, so he put his boot back on and re-laced it tightly. Taking a few tentative steps he was satisfied that the bone was no longer dislocated.

Doc took off the bungie cord, Colt, and parachute harness. He put the equipment on the deck at the base of a footlocker bolted to the deck. Wearing only his boots and the black wet suit, he walked back and forth across the deck flexing his stiff muscles.

HALO drops have a tendency to dislocate bones all over your body when the chute opens. After the second trip across the deck, he figured that it was time to search the boat. He had already taken out two occupants; there should be time to do a proper search. Doc noticed a machine at the back end of the boat. It looked out of place. He took off the protective weather cover and realized it was a chumming grinder. Scrap or low value fish were put into the grinding device and shredded in order to bait the water for larger fish. Usually these machines were on salt-water shark fishing boats. Doc went to the steering cabin, found a flashlight, and returned to the chumming machine. He found the bent stem from a pair of glasses jammed into the edge of the grinder. He checked the exit chute of the device and saw a human finger. He realized what must have happened to at least one of the technicians they couldn't locate. Checking his watch, he still had time to find the toxins.

Doc headed below deck looking for the six boxes of poison. He searched two of the cabins and thought he heard something, possibly something shifting. Back at the steering cabin, he checked the course and couldn't see any vessels even close on the radar. The automatic pilot was set. He left it and headed below deck. He searched the storage cabin and was just coming out when a pipe wrench crashed into his left arm. It hit the sleeve pocket where the parachute knife took some of the impact. Doc rolled away from the assault. A very large man picked him up off the deck. Doc's body was hurt but his mind was working overtime. He recognized the smell of diesel fuel on the man who held him. Evidently this third man must have been working on the engines when the Navy E-2 did the scan of the boat. Diesel man must have had his body heat disguised by the heat off the engine. A lot of good it would do to know who your attacker was, if you ended up dead. Doc tried to fight, moving his arms, but the blow from the pipe wrench numbed the left one. The guy was big, very big. He held Doc from behind with his right forearm crushing against Doc's neck. Doc used every muscle in his neck to force his chin against his chest. If the man got the forearm against his larynx his throat would be crushed. As much as he tried, he couldn't touch the deck. This guy was so big that he was crushing Doc's throat against his chest while Doc's feet couldn't even touch the deck. Doc tried to kick. The big guy held on slamming Doc into the bulkhead. Doc's left arm was still not working, and he was slammed into the bulkhead on the other side. Doc rammed his right elbow into the man's ribcage to no avail. He jabbed three times with his right arm, but the counterattack wasn't working. The tension on his neck was continuing to the point that small points of light were flickering across Doc's vision.

Doc reached across his own chest and found the parachute knife. Praying that it still worked, he pressed the release. The hooked blade snapped open. He was slammed against the bulkhead again and held there. Doc couldn't even lift his right arm to strike at the man's face or the arm that was suffocating him. A red haze started to rise in his vision. Doc was suffocating. He clawed with the knife against the man's groin, the only area he could reach. The first try wasn't successful and the rounded hook slid off the man's clothing. The second try cut the cloth, and Doc pulled up with the remainder of his strength. The man's scream almost deafened Doc, but the man kept the pressure on Doc's neck. Doc twisted the angle of the blade and yanked again. The man screamed again and fell over backward, pulling Doc onto himself. Doc breathed. It took a second to realize that he wasn't restrained. Rolling off the big man who had passed out, Doc crawled on his hands and knees. He couldn't stand. He moved across the passage and leaned against the bulkhead. There was blood all over his right hand. He wiped this off on his pants then checked his neck and left arm. All the blood on his right belonged to Diesel Man.

Doc remembered a tool chest in one of the cabins he had searched. He went to that cabin and got nylon electrical ties and duct tape. Rolling the unconscious man onto his back, Doc used the electrical ties to bind his wrists together. Next he bound the man's ankles. Finally with the man rolled onto his stomach he connected the ankles and wrist ties behind his back.

Doc picked up the pipe wrench, holding it in his right hand and decided it would be best to secure the boat before he continued his search. He came to one of the cabins with a padlock on the door. He smashed the lock and hasp. The room was bare except for six cardboard boxes. He had found his target. The only problem now was to recover it.

Automatically Doc reached with his left arm for the pen phone in his right sleeve. He couldn't lift his left arm; it hung limp along the side of his torso. "Shit," he said out loud. Slowly he flexed his fingers. At least they worked. He grabbed the forearm of his left arm with his right hand and held it up to the sleeve pocket. The pain was excruciating. He was barely able to get the pen out of the neoprene pocket. As he lowered his left arm he noticed that it felt squishy and blood started to run out of the cuff at his wrist. "Dam," he said out loud, partially because of the blood dripping from his wristband and partially for dropping the pen phone on the floor.

He didn't want to take a chance that the metal of the ship would interfere with the transmission, so he forced himself to leave the boxes and go to the deck. He triggered a four-second transmission and hung up. Doc was exhausted and his arm was throbbing. That was a good sign. He sat on a footlocker bolted to the deck, the pen phone beside him as he sat. He started feeling the damaged arm with the fingers of his right hand. The wrist was fine as well as the forearm. His bicep was swollen but seemed fine. He forced the muscles to relax and felt the bone. It seemed intact. The tricep muscle was damaged. That was what took the impact of the pipe wrench. Something was still wrong. He felt the shoulder. Both collarbones were intact, but he realized that the shoulder was dislocated, probably the result of getting out of that blizzard suit. He was thinking, "Next time I'll have to cut the sleeves. Piss on that, I'm going back into retirement after I'm done with this."

The phone buzzed beside him. "Yes," he answered.

"Smythe here. Are you all right? Do you've them?"

"I can't use my left arm worth shit, but I did find the merchandise."

"Resistance controlled?" asked Smythe.

"Two down, one is tied up with some odds and ends. I do have a problem; I don't think I can get the boxes ready for pickup very easily with only one arm working. Could you call off the strike? I'm not fond of becoming a piece of toast."

Smythe smiled to Carrie. "At least he still has his sense of humor. I hope he keeps it after I tell him the news."

Continuing the conversation Smythe asked, "Why didn't you answer your phone?"

"When?"

"About an hour ago."

"I thought it was one of those idiots trying to sell me long distance telephone service. I had just stepped out of the plane, and was a little busy at the time. Why were you calling anyway?"

"Just that one of Carrie's people found that type of container and tested it. If you try for an aerial pickup the change in pressure will cause the containers to leak. Don't do the aerial pickup. I've a submarine headed your way. One of the subs is in your area for maneuvers out of the Great Lakes Navy center. They can retrieve you and the packages and return safely. Did you get all six?"

"Yes."

"You don't seem too talkative. Are you all right?"

"I'm OK, you just make sure the cookout is called off."

"That was my first call when Brown contacted me. You're safe. The fire drop was called off." Smythe hesitated for a second; "She did give me a message for you."

"Tell me she wants my body," Doc said smiling.

"Not really, she said that the plane was pinged twice. Someone was checking up on anything close to the boat. She doubts that you ever showed up on any tracking. The ping originated from the shoreline around the Chicago area. Probably our friends are watching. Try to stay on course and keep everything normal. You'll have help shortly."

"Were you able to find your target?" Doc asked.

"Tentative. We are planning the intercept in about another hour. I'll see you at Great Lakes tonight. Smythe out." The phone went dead in Doc's hand. He put the top back onto the pen-phone. Unzipping the chest of his wet suit, he slipped the digital phone into the top of the suit.

Talking to himself he muttered, "First things first. I've got to get this shoulder back into socket before it swells any more." He went into the steering cabin and rooted through a few boxes until he found some nylon rope. He looped it around a pipe railing and made a simple hitch knot. He fastened the knot around his left wrist and pulled. By pulling with his right arm, he was able to stretch his left arm. It hurt and he didn't feel stable enough to do this standing on his feet, so he sat on the deck. He pulled again on the nylon that was looped around the pipe, pulling his left arm even more. It was now straight out from his shoulder. It hurt. He eased up on the rope with his right hand looping a coil of rope twice around his right wrist to take up the slack. He took a deep breath and pulled. His eyes watered from the pain. He increased the tension on the rope until he felt the shoulder moving. There was a sensation, accompanied by a weird sound that reminded him of the sucking sound as a boot is pulled out of mud. The bone was now really out of socket. Next he had to seat it properly. He twisted his torso slightly while releasing the tension slowly. Doc felt it go back into socket. The intense pain stopped instantly and was replaced by a warm feeling and tingling throughout his arm. He released the rope and undid the cinch knot. His left arm was humming. Slowly he flexed his fingers. They worked. He bent his forearm in and out. He could feel the bruises. He had been through this before. He would recover.

Now he needed to check on the diesel man. He walked down to the lower deck where he had left the man. He was still there. His breathing was a little erratic, but he remained unconscious. Doc checked the nylon ties and returned to the top deck of the boat. He looked around for any sign of the submarine. Suddenly the water chop to the port side of the boat evened out and he could see the form of the cigar shaped hull matching his speed. The conning tower broke water and the sub rose out of the water still matching the boat's speed. The hatch came open and two men appeared on the deck.

"Are you the doctor?" the one man yelled.

Doc responded, "My code name is Doc, if that's what you mean."

"Permission to come aboard... Doc," asked the executive officer.

"Permission granted," responded Doc formally.

"Do we need any equipment… Sir?" asked the Navy man.

"Two body bags, a medical officer for an injured man and some sort of a bio-container. The container can wait until you see the parcels."

Two sailors worked the hydraulics of the tubular boarding plank. One scrambled across the streaming water between the two vessels and secured the plank on the other side. When this was done, the executive officer, two sailors and the ship's doctor came aboard.

"Nice boarding plank. Pirates wished that they had these with the handrails in the old days," Doc quipped.

The executive officer was very direct. "We have been ordered to put this ship, all of its capabilities and men at your disposal. Permission to speak freely."

"Permission granted," replied Doc.

"What type of shit are we in? Are my ship or crew at risk...Sir?"

"I don't think there is any real risk. For the most part you're the cab driver simply because you happened to be close," replied Doc as honestly as he could. "There are six boxes that contain a poison that we should handle carefully. You're going to transport them to shore for safe disposal."

"What was this about dead bodies?" asked the ship doctor.

"Come with me." Doc led the way to where the first man was dead with a broken neck and a cracked skull.

"Put him in a body bag and take him to the ship," the doctor ordered to the one sailor. "And there is another?"

"Over there." Doc pointed to the man he had speared.

"And you must be the one who needs a doctor," said the ship's physician looking at the blood dripping from Doc's left arm.

"No, there is another below deck. He is very big and should be kept under restraints."

The doctor motioned to the sailor trying to figure how to get a man with a grappling hook sticking through his chest into a body bag. "Leave him and come with me." The physician and sailors went below deck to see just how badly damaged Diesel Man was.

Doc and the executive officer remained on the deck. The one sailor started upchucking over the rail. The officer raised two fingers and motioned for them to come across. Two men instantly came across the plank and stood at attention. "Follow us," he directed. Then motioning to Doc he said, "Lead the way."

Doc took the three men below deck to the room with the broken lock. He showed them the six boxes. "Each box is loaded with aerosol containers filled with a bio-toxin. I would like these sealed in plastic bags then secured in a room until we reach the base. "

"Anything else?" asked the officer as he looked at the blood drops coming from the sleeve of Doc's wet suit.

"I found the stem of a pair of glasses in the chumming machine, along with a finger. I'll need a machinist to tear it apart and recover what ever can be had and put in a refrigerator for identification later. Last I'll need two of your men to keep this boat on course with the automatic pilot as a distraction until the rest of this mission is complete."

The executive officer said in matter of fact voice, "If that's all here, we can take care of it. Now I need you in the dispensary so you can have that arm attended. I don't want people bleeding all over my ship." With that Doc and the executive officer crossed the plank and climbed down the ladder into the submarine.

Chapter 18

The submarine was bigger than the last one Doc had been on. The passageway was wider, although not much wider than a Russian submarine. The executive officer led the and opened the hatch to the white walls of the dispensary. "Can you get out of that wetsuit by yourself?

"Afraid not," answered Doc. "I think it will need to be cut off around the left shoulder."

"I'll send the doctor in as soon as he gets back," said the executive officer as he closed the hatch on the way out.

Waiting for the ship's physician took time. Doc thought about being in a doctor's office, and the many hours of wasted time. There was nothing he could do until he had the wetsuit off and could determine the damage to his arm.

The hatch opened. "You certainly have created a stir. The two dead ones are going to the diving chamber. It will be our makeshift morgue. The other fellow will need surgery and some blood to survive." The doctor put his head into the corridor and grunted. "Johnson, get in here." Turning to Doc he introduced the man entering the cabin, "Johnson is a registered nurse. He will check you out while I try to save that other man's life … that is, if you need it saved?"

Doc answered, "Yes, I need to have him interrogated if possible."

Johnson picked up a white terry cloth towel and put it around Doc's arm to capture the seeping blood. "Lets take you to x-ray and find out how bad that arm is," suggested Johnson.

"Are you familiar with sewing?" asked Doc.

"If you mean stitching, yes," answered Johnson.

"Is there a shower area around here?" Doc inquired.

"Are you trying to change the subject?"

"Not really, I'll need a little help cutting this top off, and I know there's a lot of blood under the left sleeve. I was hoping to ask you to help me cut it off in the shower, that way the blood will go down the drain. Grab something to numb the muscle and a pair of right-handed scissors, then lead me to the shower stall," explained Doc.

"Okay, it sounds like a good plan to me," said the medic.

The next hatch down was the shower cabin. Doc went into the shower stall. Johnson set a portable medical kit on the bench by the lockers. He pulled out an angled pair of right-handed round-nosed scissors. "Here, these should work by lifting the rubber away from your skin as you cut." He held out the scissors to Doc.

"They look good to me," replied Doc. He started with the cuff of the left arm and slit it up to the shoulder area. He stood in the shower area and turned on the water, washing the old blood down the drain. He shut off the water and motioned to Johnson. "Can you cut the rest of the sleeve off? I can't reach far enough to complete the job."

Johnson obliged, "We might as well get the rest of the top off," he said as he slit the suit from shoulder to neck.

"You might as well keep cutting, I don't have the strength in my left arm to pull out of the neoprene. It's ruined anyway."

Johnson continued until Doc was free from the top of the suit. He pulled a plastic disposal bag from the wall dispenser and put the wetsuit top into the bag. "Now let's look at that arm. You'd better shower it off again."

Doc rinsed off more blood so that they could see the gash. "It doesn't look too bad," said Johnson. "What hit you?"

"Would you believe a pipe-wrench?"

"No, a pipe-wrench would have broken the arm, whatever did the damage split the skin away from the muscle for about seven inches running with the bone. From the impression and bruising it was about three fourths of an inch by about 6 inches long," explained Johnson.

"The guy hit me with a pipe-wrench, but the knife that I had in the sleeve pocket took the impact," said Doc.

"That explains it," said Johnson. He reached into the medical kit and pulled out a hypodermic needle and a little vial of clear liquid. "I'm going to numb that area so I can probe the muscle to see of it's torn." Johnson injected small amounts of the anesthetic in eight points on either side of the wound. Doc couldn't feel anything from his shoulder to his elbow in a matter of two minutes.

Johnson probed the swelling and then squeezed with both hands. A burst of blood shot out of the wound. "There, that should give you some relief. Some of the blood pooled between the muscles and bones causing pressure on the nerves. You should get a lot of movement back shortly. You would have been is a world of hurt for months if we had not relieved that pressure by getting out the pooled blood."

"Hand me a towel," said Doc.

Johnson did, and Doc wiped the splatter of blood from his face.

Johnson held Doc's shoulder with his right arm and grabbed the forearm with his left hand. "Now let me move it. Don't you try to move anything at all, I want these muscles relaxed." Johnson flexed Doc's arm through a complete range of motions. He felt the wound area again and daubed a little blood that had seeped out. "That should do it." He reached into the medical kit and swabbed the area with distilled water and then with a benadine solution. "Plastic or paper?" he asked.

"I'm not in a grocery store," replied Docs with a quizzical look on his face.

"We have plastic and paper closures for wounds. Some people are allergic to the plastic so we use paper on them. We also use paper if we seam the wound."

"Use paper and seam it," replied Doc.

"You know what I mean?" asked Johnson.

"Yes, the French Emergency Medical Technicians have been using the seaming for years. I've even had it done before. Usually there is little or no scar."

"OK." Said Johnson as he used butterfly closures to hold the skin together. He was very careful and aligned it perfectly with four of the butterfly closures. "I think these are better than stitches, but you should be careful." Johnson put a strip of porous paper lengthwise along the split skin. Finally he reached into the medical kit and pulled out the Super Glue ®. He puncturing the top, and directed the flow onto the paper. It penetrated the paper and glued the edges of skin together as well as bonding the paper to more of the injured surface.

"Whew," said Doc.

"I know it burns, but it will be over in about a minute." He blew on the shiny wet surface for a few seconds and it started drying almost instantly. The surface became a shiny gloss as it dried. "After it's dry, your wound will be waterproof. As it heals, just cut off the loose sections. For God sake, don't just pull it off. The edges should start to lift and be healed in about a week, but the center might take two to three weeks. Just give it time."

"I wish I had time," responded Doc. Looking at his arm he commented, "Good work."

"Now, did you come in doing a HALO?" asked Johnson.

"Yes, how did you know?"

"You were not on radar, and you were not on that boat for very long. The only option is a high altitude jump."

"OK Sherlock, you've me."

"Now we'd better get your joints back to normal. I want you to get in the whirlpool. The jets of water will relieve the damage you did to your joints. After about an hour you should be as good as new. That arm should be dry enough to shower off the rest of the blood. Strip off those pants and I'll fill up the whirlpool."

Doc lathered then showered off. He stepped into the stainless steel whirlpool. The water was warm and the jets of water felt like a massage on his muscles.

"Put this towel over your head," instructed Johnson. "It will catch the moisture of the water and help rehydrate your sinus. I'll be back in an hour."

Doc was very relaxed in the whirlpool, enjoying the action of the jets massaging his sore muscles when two sailors came into the shower cabin.

"Damn, there was blood all over. It was a massacre. Whoever was up there must have been one mean dude. He smashed one guy's skull open and shot another with a grappling hook. You don't even want to know what happened to the third guy."

"I give, what happened?" asked the other sailor.

"You know that big guy. Well the other one cut his balls off. He must have been really pissed off. He literally castrated him. He must be one bad-ass dude."

Just then the two sailors noticed Doc in the whirlpool with the towel over his head. "What happened to you?" one on them asked.

Doc responded, "I had a rough fall. Johnson wanted to alleviate the bruising with the whirlpool."

"Yea, Johnson is good." The sailor started getting out of his clothes to shower. "You new? I don't think I know you," he asked Doc.

"I'm new, just got onboard at the last stop."

"We haven't had a port since we left … aw shit," said the sailor. He had his pants down around his ankles. Suddenly he yanked them up as though they were on fire and he headed for the hatch. His other companion had the hatch open and was already in the passageway.

Doc muttered to himself, "I guess this makes me the bad ass dude." He chuckled to himself.

Meanwhile over a rural area of New York State, Carrie and Smythe looked down at a panel truck from a MH-60K Nighthawk Helicopter. The helicopter was the new stealth machine with a whisper mode for the rotor and more ordnance than some small countries.

"There's our baby," said Smythe to the pilot of the stealth-killing machine.

"Sir, madam, how close do you want to go?" asked the pilot.

"We want to stay back from the action. The intercept will be up the road around a curve. Can we set this down in that cow field?" asked Carrie pointing to the left.

"Whatever you want. My orders are to do anything possible to assist you," replied the pilot.

Smythe interjected, "Actually the State Police are doing all of the work. They controlled the traffic so there was a roadblock after the truck went past. The highway was also blocked ahead.

Our target will be the only truck on this section of roadway. They have staged an accident with a policewoman in civilian clothes acting as the victim. Two officers are hidden in the trees to take down the driver and passenger of the truck. The main idea is to separate them from the truck so that the bio-toxin isn't released. They will arrest the men and we transport the boxes to a military base for destruction. It should be a piece of cake."

Shaking her head, Carrie said, "I wish you had not said that. Every time you say that, things turn to shit."

The rotor of the helicopter was on whisper mode. There was still a wash of air surrounding the machine as it touched down in a farmer's cow field. In the distance they could see a gray Chevrolet with the hood up and driver's hatch open. A shapely lady in a short skirt talked on a hand held radio.

"Do you've a long rifle?" asked Carrie of the helicopter pilot.

"In the back, matte black case behind the jump seat."

"I'm going to get a better view," said Carrie as she reached for the case. "Smythe's remark has me spooked. Do you've it set point of aim point of impact?"

"Yes madam. The range is set dead on at 500 meters. It's a 300 Weatherby magnum, and it does kick."

Carrie took the case and went out the door. She went left about 50 feet from the bird and opened the case. Inside she saw a beautiful rifle. She snapped out the bipod and rested the gun on the ground. She picked up four shells from the case and loaded them into the rifle. As she locked the bolt, she muttered to herself, "Better safe than sorry." She settled down behind the scope to watch the scene. Reflexively Carrie checked the distance to the target with the laser range finder. She focused on the driver's seat of the vehicle and bounced the little red dot off the upholstery of the gray Chevy. The digital display in the scope registered 469 meters. She backed off the magnification to better watch the entire scene.

Smythe and the pilot watched the scene through a video screen above the control panel. "This is nice," said Smythe. "You don't have to go traipsing around avoiding cow pies and you get a zoom picture of the action. All we need is popcorn."

Just about then they noticed the woman ditch the portable radio under the driver's seat of the car and trigger a smoke device in the engine area of the vehicle. Next, she bit a blood capsule and sprawled on the ground as though she had come out of the driver's seat.

The panel truck came around the curve in the road and the driver saw the accident. The helicopter pilot adjusted a tubular directional microphone from the knobs on the overhead console. "This should give us sound with the picture."

The driver pulled the panel truck to the edge of the roadway about thirty feet from the vehicle. He was wary of the smoke coming from the motor compartment. Both the driver and passenger opened the doors and ran toward the woman on the ground. Each man grabbed an arm and both pulled the feigned unconscious woman away from the vehicle. "So far, so good," said Smythe.

Two uniformed officers came out of hiding holding automatics. "This is the State Police. Drop the woman and put your hands in the air." The woman rolled and started to stand up between the driver and the policemen. Suddenly the passenger from the truck dropped on his right knee as he extended his arm. His hand held a pistol. His fluid motion caught the policeman slightly off guard. Both men shot within an instant of each other. The cop was hit in the lower abdomen. The officer hit the gunman's firing arm. The second policeman turned and fired. His shot caught the man in the left shoulder, throwing him back onto the pavement.

In that instant of distraction, the driver of the truck caught the female officer as she was getting to her feet, pulled a gun out and held it to her head. He started backing with his prisoner to the truck. The policeman had his weapon trained on the remaining gunman. Neither said a word. The gunman took another step toward the truck, dragging the woman with him.

Carrie watched everything through the sniper scope. She focused on the gunman. Suddenly she spotted movement from the woman. The lady cop held her free left hand open with all fingers and thumb extended down. Suddenly her thumb snapped toward the palm. Carrie took off the safety of the rifle. The forefinger snapped toward the palm. Carrie whispered "four". The middle finger snapped closed…'Three' The ring finger was next, and Carrie's finger started to tighten on the trigger as she thought 'two'. The little finger snapped to make a closed fist and the lady cop dropped to the ground. Carrie had the man's head in her crosshairs. The center of the crosshair was the base of the man's skull. She knew that if she blew out that section of his brain, the signal from the brain would never reach his hand to tell it to squeeze the trigger on his gun. What happened was a blur.

The lady cop had not even hit the ground when Carrie's shot exploded the man's skull. As Carrie watched through the scope it appeared to be in slow motion. The man no longer had a head. There was only a fine pink mist in the air surrounding his torso. The body stood for a second then fell to the side. The policeman reflexively shot the man's headless torso. He ran to the woman to make sure she wasn't hit. After a minute they both went to the policeman who had taken the shot in the abdomen.

Carrie worked the bolt, removing the remaining three cartridges and put them back into the holder with the one spent round. She snapped the bipod closed and put the gun back into the case. Latching the hold clasp she returned to the helicopter, and handed it to Smythe. "I should make you clean that rifle for jinxing this operation with your 'piece of cake'."

The pilot had the rotor going and in two minutes they were airborne, headed for the panel truck. The pilot commented, "I guess I should have told you, the cartridges had exploding tips." Carrie just glared back. As his wheels touched the blacktop, both Carrie and Smythe jumped out of the helicopter causing it to rise in the air due to the sudden loss of weight. The pilot compensated and finished landing the machine.

The male uniformed officer walked to Smythe. Holding out his hand he said "Thank you."

"Not me mate," he said, nodding his head to Carrie. "She is a better shot than I am."

Carrie had already started walking to where the policewoman was kneeling beside the downed officer talking on his radio. "Yes, we have one officer down, conditions under control. We need an ambulance," the policewoman said into her radio.

"Do you want us to take him in our helicopter?" asked Carrie.

"No, he's losing a lot of blood. The medical team should be able to stabilize him with an IV." The woman was covered with blood and bits of skin and bone from the exploding skull. "I'm really a mess. I don't think I can take this to the cleaners," she said through the tears of released tension. "Were you the one who did the shot?"

"Yes."

"God that was close."

"Not really, even while he was holding you, I had a good eight inches of clearance," responded Carrie in a matter of fact voice.

"Christ!" said the woman as her face went ashen.

Carrie turned away from the crying woman and joined Smythe as he started for the truck. Smythe saw that the truck was still running. He reached into the truck, turned off the engine, and removed the keys. They both went to the back of the truck. After unlocking the padlock, Smythe worked the steel locking bar to open the door. Inside they could see the cardboard boxes. "Is that it?" asked Carrie in disbelief.

"Yes. Let me lift you up and you bring them to the door."

"Okay."

Carrie unfastened the tie-down netting holding the cardboard boxes and carried them to the back door of the truck. As she brought the last box back, she said, "I think we have a problem."

Smythe looked into the truck. It was empty except for the tie-down netting. He only had five boxes on the ground. "They must have already delivered one box. We'd better find out where."

Smythe went over to the downed gunman. The policeman had already taken the Colt as a precaution. The man was prone on the blacktop, moaning. Smythe looked down at him. "You're going to live. The medical team has been called. But before they take you, I need to ask a few questions."

"Go to Hell!" replied the gunman between winces of pain.

Smythe went over to the policeman holding the colt 45-caliber automatic that he had taken from the gunman. "May I borrow that?" he said as he put on surgical gloves used to preserve evidence.

"It's evidence in a crime scene," replied the officer.

"Let me rephrase that. Hand me the weapon," said Smythe, with a determined look that made the veteran officer think twice.

"Here you're sir," he said, as he handed the weapon, butt first, to Smythe.

"Thank you, now perhaps you should go over to the side and take a smoke with the young lady."

"Sir, I don't smoke," replied the officer.

Smythe glared at him. "Learn."

Smythe walked back to the gunman. Standing over him, he asked, "What did you do with one of the boxes?"

The gunman just spat a mixture of blood and spittle at Smythe. Smythe pulled the action back putting a round in the firing chamber. He aimed between the man's legs and fired. Blacktop sprayed as the 45-caliber bullet dug a hole into the asphalt before it ricocheted off into the woods. "Oops… I missed," said Smythe as he started to aim again.

"NO, MAN," the gunman screamed.

"I'll ask another time. Where did you drop off the other box?"

"I've got rights."

Smythe aimed and said, "You've the right to die. You've a biotoxin that can kill millions of people and you talk to me of rights. You're a terrorist who got killed in a gun fight with the police." Smythe fired another round into the road surface next to the man's thigh. As the slug ricocheted it tore some of the skin causing the man to scream.

"Erie, I gave it to a man in Erie. It was at a truck stop. A man in Erie took it."

"Where was he going with the package?"

"I don't know."

"What was he driving?"

"A dark blue Chevy station wagon, maybe two years old."

"What did he look like?"

"Maybe 35-40 years old. Clean cut normal looking."

Under further questioning the gunman revealed that the man had joked about going somewhere warm, and that he was glad that the kids had been to it the past summer.

Carrie remained in the background as Smythe conducted the questioning. Now she voiced her opinion, "Do you think the target is Williamsburg, Bush Gardens, or Disney World?"

Smythe just shook his head. "I don't know. If I were a terrorist, I'd know that Disney had an entire city underground. With the air circulation system, that would be the best bet."

"But they will kill children," Carrie protested.

"What better way to start a panic. The kids would spread it faster than an adult."

Smythe walked over to the uniformed officer. Sirens were coming in the distance. "You'd better take your evidence back." He handed him the Colt. Motioning to the helicopter pilot, Smythe went back to the truck, picked up a box, and walked to the helicopter. "This is the poison. We have to get out of here and get this back to the base before it gets crazy."

The pilot nodded and picked up a box, as did Carrie. They loaded the three boxes into the back of the helicopter. "I'll get it started if you get the last two boxes," said the pilot. He touched the ignition and the rotor started to whine.

Smythe and Carrie ran back to the truck and got the remaining boxes as the sirens were getting closer. While they secured them in the back of the helicopter, the uniformed officer came over to the machine, "I'll need your names and information. You can't leave."

"I'll get back to your commander. Right now I've to get this toxin out of here for everyone's safety. I want you to keep this incident totally quiet for 48 hours," ordered Smythe.

The officer nodded his assent as the blade whirled, and the helicopter lifted off.

"You're going to call and explain how we killed a man and illegally interrogated another?" asked Carrie.

"Sure, about the time hell freezes over. My report will show that the officer, at great risk to his own life, killed one perpetrator and wounded another."

"That's how I saw it," confirmed Carrie.

"Me too," said the pilot as they flew to Great Lakes Military Base.

Chapter 19

Doc was enjoying the whirlpool. He had been working on flexing his knees and rotating his ankles to relieve the stress to those joints from the sudden jerk of the chute opening during the HALO jump. Everything seemed to flex properly. He spotted a set of octagon hand weights that were strapped down in a little stand at the side of the cabin. He stood up, got out of the whirlpool, and retrieved one of the eight-pound dumbbells. Easing himself back into the warm water and holding the dumbbell, he flexed his right arm. It felt good to get his muscles working again. He did thirty curls and let the arm dangle for a count of ten, repeating the exercise with ten more curls. Doc wished he could have exercised with both arms, but the left one would not be ready for flexing with any power for about ten days. He didn't want it to break out bleeding again.

Just as Doc started another set of repetitions with the dumbbell, Johnson stuck his head in the hatch. "The ship's doctor is almost done with your big friend. He should be in to check on you in about ten minutes. I was able to get some clothes for you." He put underwear, slacks and a shirt on the bench. "What size shoes do you wear? Your boots had blood soaked into the lining."

"Size nine, either a 'D' or Wide," answered Doc.

"I'll be right back." Johnson waved as he shut the hatch.

Doc set the dumbbell beside the tub and got a towel from a stand. He dried off, went to the bench and started to get dressed. He put on the boxer shorts and slacks. Next he pulled on the crew socks. He was dressed except for shoes and shirt so the physician could look at his 'repair job' on the left arm.

"Here you go," said Johnson as he returned with a set of Navy issue rubber soled shoes. "The rubber will be good on steel decks. It's a non-slip sole."

"Thanks," said Doc.

"Our doctor will be here in a minute, he's washing up now." Johnson left and Doc was finishing tying the lace on the second shoe as the doctor came into the cabin.

"You certainly are looking a lot better than the last time," said the ship's physician.

"Doc looked up from the laces and said, "Johnson did a good job patching me up."

"Johnson is good enough to be a doctor himself. On the other hand, you my friend, are lethal. Another quarter of an inch and you would have severed that man's femoral artery. If that had happened we would have another corpse. He's sedated now and resting. You can question him when he wakes."

"The oath you took for your profession said you would do no harm. My oath is quite the opposite," said Doc.

Just then a steel tray slammed into the physician's head, knocking him sprawling onto the deck. In a split second Doc looked up and saw the man who had almost strangled him just over an hour ago. Doc rolled to the deck and behind the whirlpool. The large man looked comical as he picked up the steel tray and started toward Doc. He was naked except for bandages wrapped around his groin covering his wound. He almost looked like a street beggar from Calcutta wearing a loincloth, only he was a lot larger and mean.

Doc picked up the octagon dumbbell in his right arm as he squatted behind the shelter of the stainless steel tub. Diesel Man still had an odor of the diesel fuel as he came forward. Doc had his weight on his toes and balls of his feet as he sprang up using the full force of his legs to add momentum. He brought his right arm, holding the barbell, up in a right jab. In the instant before he connected he twisted the barbell so that the octagon side of the steel was what impacted the large man's jaw.

Blood, teeth and bone sprayed across the cabin, but the large man kept coming toward Doc. He slammed the steel tray against the whirlpool, denting the stainless steel frame. Doc twisted and rolled, avoiding any blows. He sprinted for the hatch. The soft rubber sole shoes gave Doc an edge in the race, compared to the other man's bare feet. Diesel Man was right behind him. Doc went down the corridor and through a watertight hatch. He ducked behind it, ahead of the large man in the loincloth. Bracing himself against the wall, Doc waited behind the three hundred pound hatch until Diesel Man was just entering the opening. He pushed the hatch closed with all his might. It slammed into the large man's body knocking him to the deck. The man was stunned but started to get up. Doc grabbed a carbon dioxide fire extinguisher from the bulkhead holder and discharged it into his opponent's face just as he stood up. The CO2 froze the large man's eyes in a frost. Diesel Man then made a fatal mistake. He wiped his eyes. His hands damaged the frozen corneas causing him to lose his vision. Doc slammed the half-discharged extinguisher against his opponent's skull. Diesel Man collapsed to the deck as a pool of blood seeped from the back of his skull. Doc slumped against the bulkhead, trying to catch his breath. He heard the ship's alarm going off. He didn't know if it was triggered by the CO2 discharge or if someone had found the physician.

Doc bent over to check the downed man's pulse. He didn't have any. Doc rolled the body over and the eyes stared fixedly at the overhead. Frost and blood combined with the dislocated broken jaw to make the face frightening. Through the alarm, Doc heard footfalls coming down the passageway. Johnson had a nine-millimeter browning in his right hand as he ran forward. Doc held up his hand. "It's over."

Coincidentally two of the sailors who followed closely behind Johnson were the same ones who helped remove the bodies on the boat. One of the sailors couldn't restrain himself, "What did you do to his face?"

Doc smiled from relief, "I punched him in the mouth."

The sailor just muttered, "Shit. Oh shit."

Doc explained, "I was holding a dumbbell at the time I hit him."

Johnson ordered the sailors to get a body bag to take the dead man to the dive chamber with the other corpses.

Just as the sailor started down the passageway to retrieve the body bag, the captain strode down the other end of the same hall. The sailor stiffened at attention as the captain passed. He looked down at the scene, and then at Doc. "You even dented my extinguisher." He then addressed Johnson, "Our doctor is Okay, but nursing a huge lump on the back of his head. I want you to watch him for a concussion."

"Yes sir," replied Johnson. He left immediately, heading for sickbay.

"The sailors will take care of this," said the captain, motioning toward the dead body. "You've a call." Narrowing his eyes, "It seems that I've been promoted to the position of your private secretary."

Doc was disturbed, as he didn't want to usurp the command of the captain. Evidently it showed on his face.

The captain broke into a smile, and Doc realized that the captain wasn't serious at the affront. "Someone named Smythe called on a secure line and asked me to let you know that he only got five out of six containers. He said that he would be out to pick you up in a copter, and that I should wake you. He seemed to think you were just loafing about, enjoying a cruise."

Both the captain and Doc broke into laughter at the same time.

***

Smythe and Carrie arrived at Great Lakes with their toxic cargo. As a precaution before they left on the mission, Carrie had suggested they notify someone who could dispose of the biotoxin. Smythe agreed and used his pen phone to contact Shelly. She agreed to take care of things in a discreet manor. As the helicopter landed near a high security area of the base, Smythe could see special trailers with Centers for Disease Control marked plainly on the side of the vehicles.

A man in a bio-isolation suit that looked like Marshmallow Man in a space helmet approached the helicopter. He motioned with his hand that they should stay were they were. He used a portable meter device to check air samples.

He had little devices in plastic containers that he handed to Carrie, Smythe and the pilot. "Open the foil container." They did and it held a hard blue plastic device with a white handle. "Pull out the white paddle and wipe it against your tongues," the man ordered. He watched Carrie and Smythe as they very gingerly did what he asked. "Do it again. We need a good sample of your saliva to see if you're clean, or have been infected." All three wiped the paddles again against their tongues. "Now place the paddles back into the blue sleeves." They complied. Handing them marking pens, he told them to print their names on plastic bags and put the pen and the blue containers into the plastic pouches.

Smythe thought that the substance on the paddle was slightly citrus in flavor. Whatever it was sucked the moisture out of his tongue. All three were given white disposable suits with self-contained breathing apparatus attached to each. The men from the CDC insisted they put on the suits immediately.

They were transported to one of the trailers and ordered to disrobe, take chemical showers, and scrub with very stiff brushes, which stripped their outer layer of skin. They were then given simple scrub clothes and put into an isolation room. A nurse in bio-protective garb took blood samples.

"Do you think we were infected?" asked Carrie.

"No, they're just being protective," answered Smythe.

"I never had anything like this in Desert Storm," interjected the pilot.

"Just relax. We brought back a mixture of VX and mutated anthrax in convenient spray aerosols. They just want to make sure that nothing leaked," explained Smythe.

The CDC was nice enough to provide a television outside the glass of the confinement area. It was tuned to CNN. Nothing of any importance was mentioned dealing with the United States. Smythe prayed they would not get wind of the New York highway shutdown. The 'official' cover story was that there was a bad accident, which needed to be cleaned up. Actually, that wasn't too far from the truth. Smythe started to doze off.

A doctor in his white smock and tie came into the room carrying a clipboard. "You two are fine," he said gesturing to the men. "Young lady you've me puzzled. Your saliva sample came back with high nitrates, but you blood doesn't show the high levels. Were you eating bacon within the past hour or two?"

Carrie grinned, "No doctor, I don't even like bacon. The high nitrates are probably due to inhaling gunpowder smoke," she explained.

"Were you out on a shooting range?" inquired the doctor.

"No, I was just trying out a rifle. It made a horrible bang and it kicked. I don't think I like guns."

Smythe and the pilot had simultaneous coughing spells to the point of their eyes watering. Carrie remained the essence of prim demure self-composure.

A clerk came up behind the doctor. "Pardon me sir, but is one of you named Smythe?"

"I'm Smythe."

"Sir, you've a phone call from a Senator. He is mighty mad and wants your, well let us just say he wants you on the phone now. Follow me, please," implored the clerk.

He spoke politely, "Smythe here."

"A New York State Policeman called my constituent and informed him that a truck rented by his firm was stolen and recovered. He said that he wasn't allowed to release any other information. Now son, I'm a United States Senator and I demand to know what's going on. I called the governor and he got me this number. That son-of-a –bitch would not tell me squat, but then again he is a member of the other party. Probably just wants to jerk my chain. What happened with the truck? Did these thieves car jack the truck and kill any of the employees? I want to know what happened to the medicine that was in the back of the vehicle. Did you know that it was going to save lives in some third world country? My God man, say something. My constituent needs that medicine back. Did you find it? One of the troopers remembers you and another man putting boxes from the truck onto a military helicopter."

"Slow down Senator," Smythe said as he started to concoct a lie on the spot. At least the Senator didn't know about the CDC or he probably would have said something. "Sir, the employees who rented the truck were not found yet." He crossed his fingers for the next lie. "The thieves may have thrown out the cargo. At this point we don't know." The Senator breathed deeply at that news. "They were carrying cocaine and small arms in the back of the truck. That is all that was recovered."

"Are you sure son? There were some aerosols with a high tech antibiotic in the back of the truck. Are you sure you didn't find anything like that with your cocaine?"

"No sir, only the cocaine and an Uzi." Smythe was enjoying leading the bureaucrat down a series of lies. He might as well make it good. "Sir I should tell you, there was a lot of blood in the back. In fact the employees may have been put into the back of the vehicle and then shot."

"Christ, where did this happen?"

"We apprehended them in a rural part of New York. I'll be glad to fax you a copy of the report after the State Police have examined the truck. Funny thing though, the one officer collecting the blood samples got sick at the scene and ended up with cramps and vomiting. He had to be taken to a local hospital. Probably ate too many doughnuts. We ordered the truck to be taken to storage until he is able to finish the work. Supposedly he is the best blood man in that part of New York. We didn't want to drag anyone from the city. They have enough crime to deal with. Anyhow, we have the dope and guns." The seeds were planted. Now he wanted to get a reaction from the Senator. "Do you want me to fax you our report? What's your private number, we don't want just anyone to see a report in an ongoing investigation."

"Son, are you with the DEA or some such organization?"

"Sir, I'm with the British government working on a joint effort. The bad guys were British Nationals." Smythe could hear the relief on the other end of the line.

"Well son, you just fill in your reports and have your superiors forward a copy when this business is done. I've to be away on business for a while. Just send it to my office, I'll get it eventually."

"Thank you for your concern Senator, I wish all politicians were as concerned as you're about your constituents. My office will be in touch." Smythe hung up the phone and turned to the clerk. "Was that phone call recorded?"

"Yes sir. We are under a stage five alert. All communications are monitored."

"Make me a tape and bring it to me," he ordered.

In a panic the clerk saluted and said, "Yes sir, right away sir."

Smythe walked back to find Carrie. She and the pilot had left for the cafeteria to get something to eat. Smythe decided to join them.

Smythe picked up a tuna salad sandwich and a cup of coffee. He found Carrie at a table in the corner. "We have a situation," he began. "The CDC has all communications monitored. Someone at the State Police let Vaught know about the takedown of the truck, and we don't know where the other box of toxins is."

"Nothing like light conversation to help digestion," Carrie said ironically.

Smythe continued, "Carrie, I would appreciate your working with the CDC here to check out the submariners. I'm going to fly out and pick up Doc. I'll leave it to you to play with the computers here to find out anything you can. Try to reference driver license photos and compare them to the names used to rent the vehicles. I don't think we have much time left." Looking at the pilot he asked, "Are you ready to fly?"

The pilot grinned, "I had the crew refuel and check out the machine as soon as I was released from quarantine. The only thing not done is cleaning the rifle."

The clerk approached the table. "Sir here is your tape. I took the liberty of getting a battery player so you could listen to it." He handed the tape and player to Smythe.

"Sit down and join us," suggested Smythe.

"Sir I've to get back to work," responded the clerk.

Smythe looked up, "Sit down now."

The clerk pulled out a chair beside Carrie and sat down.

Smythe started, "I need an office with computer links for Carrie. I mean a private office where no one sees what she is doing. I'll also need to call her, so I need a direct number to that office."

"No problem sirs and madam. There is a communication room just a doorway from my office. It has a computer with a T-1 line for communications. No one uses it but me. He pulled a business card out of his pocket and wrote on the back of it. The extension for me is 8651; the extension for the computer room is 8652. Just call the main number, then press the extension and you'll ring that desk." Smythe nodded and the clerk left for duties elsewhere.

"Good. Now since that that is settled I want you all to listen to this tapc. I licd to mislcad thc scnator." Smythc playcd thc tapc. The pilot shook his head and Carrie pointed her tongue and played with her front teeth as she listened to the Senator's reactions.

The tape ended and Smythe clicked the machine off. Carrie was the first to speak, "He knows. He knows that it was toxin in the aerosols, and the dumb bastard thinks that when the thieves shot the Vaught people in the back of the van, they must have hit a container. The leakage is what would have infected the cop you invented. Damn Smythe, you lie like a rug." She continued, "If I can find out where he goes on his vacation we'll know that the target is in the opposite end of the country."

"We'll have to pick up Doc in the chopper. You find out where we have to go."

"I'll tell you where you're going Smythe," said Carrie as she giggled. "You're going straight to hell for lying, at least that is what my Sunday school teacher would say."

Smythe and the pilot finished their sandwiches and went to the helicopter. The pilot used the onboard system to bypass any communication traps on the base and placed a transmission to the submarine on a secure channel. As he finished the settings on the radio he handed the microphone to Smythe. "Press to talk, release to listen. It's an old system, but extremely secure."

A gray BMW sped along the Route 22-West parkway outside of Pittsburgh Pennsylvania. It turned off onto Route 79 for about a quarter mile, then slowed as it approached a fortress style office building. The architect must have designed bunkers for Germany in World War II. Allen Murphy steered the vehicle into a private drive that led to the underground parking area. Murphy was the head of security for the Vaught Corporations. His true job was simply to keep the money stream flowing. If there was a problem, eliminate it, or them, and finally, keep secret what was secret, by any means.

As Murphy's car approached the security door of the garage entrance, a laser scanner recorded the barcode attached to the back of his rear view mirror. The computer referenced his access and the steel door raised automatically. He pulled into a parking space reserved for Chief of Security. He never wanted his name on the parking spot, he just wanted the title. As Murphy left the car, he waved at the camera to acknowledge the security guard who would be watching. He proceeded to a private elevator. The elevator only had three stops: the garage level, Vaught's private office, and the helicopter pad on the top of the building. It was a small carriage made for four people maximum. He pushed the button for Vaught's office.

When the doors of the elevator opened, Murphy walked out of the elevator past Vaught's private secretary and opened the door to Vaught's very private office, going in unannounced. Vaught was behind his desk working on some papers. As Allen Murphy approached the desk, Marty Vaught looked up. "How is our little project coming?" he asked.

"It's a shame about the plant in Toronto. There was an accident when we did the purge and a guard was killed," answered Murphy, grinning.

"Good then our little extra piping did work. Send flowers to the widow. Send our deepest sympathy."

"I already did. I also sent a man over to confirm the identification of the body. The body was so badly burned that the mortician said he had to have a closed coffin. He said the little they were able to find was already almost all cremated, so that'is what they did with the remains they found."

"Your mixture of oxygen and propane was an excellent idea," said Vaught.

"It must have worked better than I thought. It blew sections of the guardhouse roof over 400 feet. The tapes must have been destroyed in the heat. I did find some blackened plastic. I would have liked to have an identifiable body. I just don't like it when they are blown to pieces."

"Calm down, dead is dcad. Other cops and his wife identified the remains. Our witness is gone," muttered Vaught with a wave of his right hand. He opened a desk drawer and flipped a Toronto newspaper to Murphy. "The newspaper is calling it an accident. On the other hand, how is our cargo coming?"

Checking the date on his Rolex, Murphy said, "Everything should be in place in another two days."

"Any word on the truck?" asked Vaught.

"They met the truck at Erie and your special New York project will have it's own box. The others will be delivered to my men at different locations," answered Murphy.

"And how about the two chemists who had second thoughts?" asked Vaught.

"We told them it was understandable and we would give them transportation back to the Chicago area on the boat. They accepted our offer. I did get a radio transmission that there was a boating accident. They became fish food," said Murphy smiling. "I had a friend at the coast guard check the location of our boat a few times and it appears they're making good time."

"So far it looks like we can coordinate both the East and West Coast releases. I do want to take care of my friends here in Pittsburgh at the same time, "he said reaching down and patting a briefcase on the floor. "May their souls rot in hell," he said with a smile.

"Remember that the vaccine only works on secondary exposure. Initial exposure to the vapors will kill anyone regardless of the anti-toxin in their system," cautioned Murphy. "That VX kills the nerves even in micro-dosages and lets the anthrax get a good hold on the victim. Death is certain."

"Don't worry, I'm not going to dirty my hands," smiled Vaught. "It's up to you to get a person to trigger the device."

Just then the paging system for the building came on. "Allen Murphy, you've an important call. Please contact the operator." The operator repeated the message.

"May I?" asked Murphy as he motioned to the phone on Vaught's desk.

"Of course."

"Murphy here. Transfer the call to this extension."

The man on the other end of the phone identified himself as a New York State Police officer. He wanted to inform them that one of their rental trucks had been hijacked and recovered. Murphy was polite on the phone and thanked the officer. He then turned to Vaught. "We may have a problem."

Vaught answered, "We do downtown tomorrow."

***

A blue Cavalier sedan pulled into the parking lot of an office building just down the road from the Vaught Corporate Headquarters. A woman in her mid thirties with long blond hair got out of the vehicle and pulled an aluminum attaché case from the trunk. She placed the case on the passenger seat and opened it. Withdrawing a pair of binoculars, she took a close look at the Vaught building. Mueller had been right. It was a fortress. He said that there was an American agent with a British partner also looking for this murderer. He would let her have a 24-hour advance notice on information, but he also said he had an obligation of honor to notify them as well.

From her vantage point, she watched the gray BMW turn into the parking garage. She knew that the driver would be Allen Murphy, the same Allen Murphy who made the arrangements in Germany to kill her sister, Pearl. He would die by her hands. He would be made to pay for her sister's death. His death would not be easy. His boss, the mysterious Mr. Vaught would also die. He was the bastard who ordered her sister's death.

Ruby studied the building. It was a massive concrete structure. The windows on the first and second floor were long and narrow from floor to ceiling. They were coated with a reflective material that made them look like golden mirrors. The third floor windows looked different. The windows didn't have the same reflective material over the glass. They were of similar architecture, long and narrow from floor to ceiling. As she studied the building she noticed a window cleaner's truck. A large framed black man got out a bucket, rag, sponge, squeegee and pole. He methodically washed each window on the first and second floor, then squeeqeed the glass to a pristine shine. For about forty-five minutes she watched as he took care to clean every window except the ones in the top floor. Finally, he assembled an extension ladder and started on the top floor windows. He did these differently. He used a lot of water then a spray on the glass. Finally he used a clean cloth on each window.

It came to her in a flash. Quite literally it was a flash of light reflected from the side of the building. The bottom windows showed the beam of light in a straight reflection. The reflection from the top windows was slightly distorted. The windows were not perfectly flat glass. The windows were made of a clear plastic that was slightly distorted. Probably they were Lexon ®, a bulletproof glass that wasn't really glass.

The idea of shooting through a window would not work. The steep angle of the shot would ricochet off the bulletproof glass. Even if it were normal glass, the target would have to be standing next to the window to be seen by the person trying to take a shot. She had to find another way to get at these men. Besides, a bullet would be too easy a death. She decided to try to find out anything she could. She put on headphones and assembled a small parabolic device that sensed sound at long distances. She pointed the device at one window, then the next of the third floor. She heard something. Adjusting the dials on the sensor she was able to discern that the speaker was a woman. She heard a phone ring and then a muffled voice. Since she couldn't understand the words of the conversation, she aimed at the lower windows of the building. The first window gave no sound. Finally the third window worked as an excellent conductor of the voices in the room. A page went out and she heard clearly, "Allen Murphy, you've an important call. Please contact the operator."

Suddenly she noticed movement in her rear view mirror. It was a man in a brown uniform with an insignia on his arm. He was walking directly toward her parked car. Quickly she snapped apart the three sections of the parabolic microphone and put it into the aluminum case on the passenger seat. She patted the blond wig to make sure it hid her red hair, hiked up her skirt so that it showed a lot of thigh, opened her purse and removed a tube of lipstick. She made an excessive act of being preoccupied primping herself in the mirror as the guard approached.

Rapping his knuckles on her window to get her attention he said, "Madam, this is a private lot. If you don't have business with someone inside the building, I would appreciate it if you would park somewhere else."

First she batted her eyelashes at the guard, and answered in her best imitation southern dumb blond accent. "Mr. officer, sir, I've to keep watch on my boyfriend. I think he's cheating on me." She played with her knee and his eyes went immediately to her white thighs. He never even got a good look at her face.

"Madam, it would be a shame for someone to cheat on a fine woman like yourself, but this is an office building, not a motel. People work with computers here. There is no time for them to fool around."

"He's not acting like himself. Well, I just know he's having an affair on me. I think he's meeting her here and they may very well go to a motel. I wanted to be sure."

"Do you know which woman your boyfriend is cheating with?"

"His wife. I think he wants to leave me for his wife."

The guard's face fell. "Madam. You're going to have to leave."

She turned the key to the ignition and the guard walked back to the office building, "Ditzy blond!"

She smiled and waved at him as she pulled out of the parking lot. As he waved back at her, she muttered, "Men are so easy."

Luck was on her side. The BMW had also left the Vaught building and was on the same roadway. She waited until it passed, then pulled into traffic and followed it. She knew the vehicle belonged to Allen Murphy, the head of security. Whatever phone call he had received catapulted him into motion. She intended to find out what was going on.

Murphy's car was on Route 22 for only a short time, until it turned down a side road. She allowed a good distance between the vehicles so he would not be aware he was being followed. At one point he turned into a dirt lane. Ruby continued driving the asphalt roadway until it rounded a small knoll. She pulled off and parked at the edge of the field. Where she changed into a dark blue jogging suit and running shoes. She locked the car and started up over the little hill to see what was going on.

In a field below Ruby saw an old apple orchard, a wheat field, and a barn with the BMW adjacent to the open doors. From her location she couldn't see inside the building, so she carefully worked her way through the orchard to get an angle to see into the barn. Inside the barn she saw a white panel van with the back doors open. The sign on the side of the van read, Stand Pipe Testing Service. The truck had tanks of compressed gas chained and locked into a special stand built into the sides of the truck bed. Two young men practiced attaching a device onto a pipe, then running a hose from the truck to the device. Allen Murphy held a stopwatch in his hand as he watched the speed of the operation. They repeated the drill ten times. Murphy ended the practice and headed back to his car. The two men closed the panel truck doors and locked the barn.

Ruby carefully made her way back until she was over the crest of the hill, and then jogged back to her parked auto. She changed back into her skirt and blouse and got into the car. She pulled the car slowly to a point in the road just short of the curve, so that her vehicle couldn't be seen as the BMW left the farm road. The BMW came out the lane and started toward the parkway. She engaged the gears and started to pull out when she saw the two young men pull out of the same lane in a beat up Ford truck. On a whim she decided to follow them.

They turned onto the parkway and headed towards Pittsburgh. She followed at a safe distance. Continuing on Route 22 they went through a tunnel and came out with the Three Rivers Stadium visible on her left side as she crossed the high bridge. Traffic was heavy and she barely made it into the right lane to follow them. They took the Grant street exit and went into the center of the metropolis of Pittsburgh. Bumper-to-bumper style of downtown driving was nerve wracking. The truck pulled alongside the curb behind a skyscraper and one man got out, holding a Polaroid camera. He snapped a photo of the back of the building. No person or entrance was there. The loading dock was off to the side. The man raced to the car and jumped in. When she pulled her vehicle alongside the building, she saw the standpipes of the fire system.

In the event of a fire in the tall building, the fire department could attach the hose from the pumper truck to the standpipe. Water would be pumped up the metal pipes built into the building so that portable hoses on reels on each floor could be used to put out a fire.

Ruby didn't understand the significance of the incident. As she looked up, the boys had turned into traffic again. She wheeled the car into a turn, just making it in front of a panel truck. The driver gave her a one-finger salute. She closed on the boys so only three cars were between them. The boys whipped the vehicle into a student parking lot of a Duke University. Ruby continued in traffic to the bottom of the lot, and then turned up a street. Se double-parked on the side street and watched the boys get out of the car and go into a dormitory. No wonder they looked young, they were college students.

Chapter 20

As soon as Smythe was done talking to Doc, the pilot started the rotor blades. Two of the men with the CDC came from one of the trailers and motioned with an extended finger to bring the helicopter down. Instead, Smythe waved goodbye. An instant later, the Nighthawk was airborne. The pilot's voice came over the headset that Smythe was wearing. "Radar damping is now on. We'll go inland for a little while, then go out and meet up with the sub."

"Sounds like a plan to me," replied Smythe.

The low ride over the chop of the water was tedious. No crafts were spotted on the way to the sub. Finally, thirty-five minutes into the flight they spotted the 25-watt red flashing light on the conning tower of the submarine.

Onboard the ship, Doc had the Captain's ear. "Are you going to honor the order you received placing your ship and crew at my disposal?"

"It was a lawful order. I intend to follow it as best I can," answered the Captain. Squinting his left eye from nervous tension, he wondered what Doc was up to, and what he really wanted.

"I need a favor, due to a change of plans. I promise your ship will not be put into jeopardy. I found out from Smythe that they're going to quarantine this ship and crew to be sure that the toxins haven't escaped by accident. I need to delay that. I want you to go back to the boat you took me from and have your men set up a Mayday call. I need for them to set the ship afire, as though it were an engine fire. I want lots of smoke and fire, but I need that boat sunk to hide the removal of the cartons containing the toxins. I want to take them from the ship and watch for whoever responds. I've a feeling that such a maneuver may be a key to cinch this problem. Just stay at periscope depth and watch from a distance. If they try to do any diving to recover the canisters, I want you to surface and offer assistance to search for bodies. I don't want anyone recovering the boat for at least a week. Since all hands would have been lost I want you to then return to base and go through quarantine."

"Is there a chance that the toxin has leaked?" asked the Captain.

"There is always a chance, but if it did, we would all be dead now," said Doc with a fixed look. "There is a component to the toxin that is VX gas. If even a little escaped, everyone on this ship would be dead. I want you to leave the door secured to the dive compartment as a safety provision. Let men in special suits remove the boxes from the ship, just in case."

"So far what you said is reasonable, I've no problem following those instructions," said that Captain.

"The favor I ask is that you don't obey any orders to go back to base prior to completing the sinking. Someone of high authority will order you to return. I need your radio to malfunction," said Doc. "I'll also need to know who issues that order."

"Your ride will be here in a few minutes," interjected the Captain. "I'll walk you up."

Doc was very aware that the Captain didn't reply to his last request with any answer. He followed the Captain up the steel ladder that led to the hatch on the conning tower. As they were outside the sub watching for the helicopter, the Captain said, "I can't disobey a direct order from command, but we did experience some sort of anomaly causing uncanny static, or will as soon as I get to the radio room."

"Thank you," said Doc, as the Captain turned and pointed at the horizon.

"It looks like your ride is here." The Captain saluted, then opened the hatch and went into the sub.

From onboard the helicopter, Smythe lowered a rope ladder with wooden steps. Doc grabbed it and climbed into the Nighthawk. As he swung onto the seat, Smythe pulled up the rope ladder, and then closed the door. Even with the door shut, the motor noise made it difficult to hear onboard the helicopter. Smythe handed Doc a helmet and motioned where to plug in the cord that made the built in microphone and speakers work inside the helmet.

Doc spoke first. "Well, how did you make out with the truck?"

"We only got five of the six boxes. One box was transferred to another vehicle. So far we haven't found it. The CDC has taken up residence at Great Lakes to check the toxin. Finally, Carrie is on base with a clerk who is a computer geek, trying to find out anything she can regarding Vaught and where the last box is going to be used." Smythe continued his fast-paced summary, "We took the truck down with the help of the New York state police, but one of the officers called Vaught's company for information about the drivers and Vaught pulled connections. He had a United States Senator call me. The politician knew my name. He called me and wanted to know what was going on. I lied like a rug. The Senator thinks I'm with the DEA. I've a tape of the conversation. You've to hear this politician."

The pilot interjected, "Pass the tape and I'll put it over the intercom." Smythe unzipped his jacket, pulled the cassette out, and handed it to the pilot. The pilot inserted it into the player and in a few seconds Smyth's voice and that of a Senator came over the headsets. Doc listened with an intense concentration. He listened, but also checked out the inside of the Nighthawk. When he was climbing onboard he had noticed a full complement of rocket ordnance, strapped in pods underneath the frame. The inside was modified to accommodate several extra surveillance toys. The pilot was wearing an old leather bomber jacket with no name patch.

After the tape ended, Smyth said, "What do you think?"

Doc didn't answer the question, but instead poised a question of his own. "Pilot, I hate to just call you 'Pilot', what is your name?"

"Call me Gabe," the pilot responded.

"Gabe, where are you stationed?"

"Great Lakes."

"Nice up there. How soon till we can set this down on a beach?" asked Doc.

"About another five minutes."

"Land it on a deserted beach area or farm field," instructed Doc.

Smythe looked at Doc strangely. "Are you Okay buddy?"

"I just have to get my feet on land, my head is swimming," replied Doc.

Five minutes passed quickly. The beach area was full of rocks, but a dairy farm offered a meadow less than a quarter mile inland. They landed there and Doc got out of the helicopter. As he disembarked, he snapped a flare pistol from the side of the rear door. Smythe noticed and after a minute, he told the pilot that he better check on Doc. "What's up?" Smythe said as he approached Doc.

"Follow my lead."

Doc went behind a rock outcrop and feigned dry heaves. Between the retching he asked, "Do you know this pilot?"

"He seemed all right when we worked on the truck take-down in New York," responded Smythe.

Both men walked back to the helicopter. Doc walked around to the pilot's door, and stood there. The pilot opened the door and asked, "Are you feeling better?"

Doc then feigned a stomach pain. He bent forward. One hand grabbed the snap release of the harness releasing the webbing holding the pilot in his seat. At the same instant he pulled the startled man from the seat, flipping him onto the ground. The pilot rolled and came up in a fighting stance. Doc was holding the flare pistol on him. "Move and you'll burn here and in hell."

Doc started, "I've been in Nighthawks, and this isn't a normal bird. Who are you working for and where are you stationed?"

Gabe answered, "You've a good eye. The bird has been modified for anti-terrorist surveillance and attack. It isn't yet released. When it's finally approved, the Company will control it. It's stationed out of a CIA training facility to the north east of Durham."

"So you're a Company man?" asked Doc.

"They write the paycheck, but I'm on a weird loan. Treasury is giving me the assignment to check out the bird under various conditions. They are the ones who ordered me to be prepared for a takedown at the New York site."

"What exactly were the orders?"

"If things went bad and my gas monitor went off, I was to blanket the area with incendiary devices. I was then to get out and fire every rocket I had into the conflagration."

Smythe asked, "What about the police? Were you to kill them?"

"Sir, I was to monitor and offer assistance. I'm not supposed to act on United States soil. I could offer Carrie the rifle but I wasn't permitted to fire the shot. However, if the gas monitor went off I was to incinerate everything and everyone not in my bird."

Doc stared at him, "Why is your code 'Gabe'?"

"Someone has a sense on humor. It's Gabe, for Gabriel. I'm to blow the horn. Either the all clear, or call in the troops."

Smyth asked, "The CDC was there as a result of you?"

"No, my control had ordered them to Great Lakes. They have been on standby for several days. I just signaled that we had the material onboard, and were on the way."

"Who gives you the orders," demanded Doc.

"It was a two star who handed me the keys to this bird. He introduced me to a lady with long legs, and a body that wouldn't quit. She introduced herself as Shelly. That was all, just Shelly." I was ordered to do whatever she said. Since then I've only heard her voice. I never saw her again."

"What are your orders now?"

"I've two orders. First – Shelly had two devices sent to me at Great Lakes. I gave one to Carrie. I'm to give the other to you." Gabe slowly raised his right hand. "If I may?" asked Gabe.

"Slowly," ordered Doc.

Gabe did move very slowly. He unzipped his jacket and pulled a pen from his inside pocket. "She, Shelly, said that yours must have been damaged. She couldn't reach you," he said as he held out his palm with the pen-phone as a final proof of his story.

"You said two orders?" questioned Doc.

"I'm to take you wherever you need to go and do whatever you say. Finally, the pen will open. Press the button on the inside and it will send out a homing signal. If I receive that signal in my bird, I'm to incinerate the source of the homing signal as quickly as possible. If it's a building or vehicle, all land surrounding it must go. All animal and plant life must be incinerated. Evidently the stuff on the loose is really bad."

Doc handed the flare pistol to Smythe. "Hold this on him." He then triggered the pen phone. On the second ring it answered.

"About time you give a girl a call," teased Shelly on the other end.

Doc was formal, "Describe Gabe," he ordered.

Shelly described Gabe and confirmed that he was one of the good guys. She added, "The CDC has confirmed the toxin. It's a mix of VX and Anthrax. The problem is that it takes 3600 microbes of anthrax to infect a host animal or human under normal circumstance. The additions of the VX and possibly a mutation cause it to infect the initial host at only 114 microbes. Ebola infects at 4 to 7 microbes, so isn't as bad as Ebola, but nearly as bad. The good news is that the secondary infection is at 2700 microbes and the tertiary infection is back to a normal 3600 microbes."

"So that explains the incineration orders."

"If the toxin gets out, we must destroy as much as possible to contain the infection," explained Shelly. "I got a phone message for you. Mueller wants you to call."

"Thanks. Any other good news?"

"No, but did you get your boxes?" questioned Shelly

"All five are on their way back to Great Lakes, shortly."

"Shortly, what do your mean shortly," said Shelly with a degree of frustration.

"I've the submarine doing a chore for me. They'll be home soon. Talk to you later." replied Doc.

Doc looked at Gabe. "She confirms you're Okay." Now can you shut down the rotor and get me a digital phone line?"

"Yes sir," saluted Gabe as he climbed back into the pilot's seat.

Smythe climbed into the rear seat. He leaned forward and asked the pilot, "Would you've killed Carrie if your gas detector had gone off?"

Gabe turned in the seat to face Smythe, "Only if she were outside the cabin when the detector went off. If the door was open and it goes off, I've 10 minutes to do my job, then the auto-destruct takes over and destroys everything in a three block area, including me."

"Shit," was the only response that Smythe could come up with.

Doc got into the navigator's seat and put on the helmet with the headset built into it. Gabe pressed a release switch and a numerical touch pad slid out from the control panel. "Press 'DS2" for a digital satellite connection, then press the country access and number."

Doc nodded, and dialed the number he had committed to memory. A woman answered the phone. "This is Mueller's friend from the States," Doc said.

"I'll get him. Please hold," she responded. It took about two minutes then Mueller came on the line.

"Hello, are you in control of this line?" asked Mueller.

"Yes, it's digital. Watch your line monitor for safety. If it jumps signaling that someone has tapped the connection, just break communications," answered Doc.

"I found out a few things that you should know. Vaught used an Insurance company to fund his plans by having insurance pay for planned losses."

Doc interrupted, "Which of your people were in the offices in Toronto?"

"You know?"

"I saw those scratches on the inside door lock."

"Jade, she is probably the best with locks. She could be an excellent cat burglar," said Mueller with a high degree of pride. "Did you find the Washington connection?"

"No, I was looking for the deployment of the gas, not the funding," responded Doc.

"Well she was looking for the people responsible, all of the people behind the death of my beloved Pearl." Mueller started to choke up with emotion.

"Tell me about Washington." said Doc.

"Vaught is very interested in politics. He wants to control your federal government. He buys politicians. Those he can't buy, he blackmails. Finally those he can't control he plans on killing with that gas you're chasing. He can make it look like a terrorist act or an outbreak of a disease. Either way Vaught's opponents will die. He doesn't need to assassinate individuals. That is his way. He plans to gain majority control of both parties to go forward with his own agenda." Mueller continued, "You've a major problem if the United States is destabilized."

Doc asked, "Where did Jade go after she left Toronto?"

"To Washington. She visited a lawyer who lobbies in Washington for Vaught's causes."

"She actually visited the lawyer?" questioned Doc.

"Well it was late and he didn't happen to be there at the time," laughed Mueller. She borrowed his photocopier. If your country survives this next week, there will be a package delivered to the Attorney General that should cause the lawyer to take a leave of absence permanently. She did find one document that led her to another office. There is a Senator down there who will do anything for sex, money or drugs. The man is an idiot. Why do you elect people like that?"

"I can only answer that we are a free country. Free to elect idiots of our own choice. Too often votes are bought by how much federal politicians can steal from the federal government and bring back to their local communities. I wish they would work for the good of the country as a whole, but in times of peace, personal greed takes over," said Doc soberly. "Why did you want me to call?"

Mueller answered, "Ruby is in Pittsburgh and has been watching Vaught's office. Jade is flying into Pittsburgh tonight. They found out something that disturbers me. I think Vaught has some gas and intends to use it in Pittsburgh. Additionally the girls intend to kill Vaught and his men. Jade has never killed before. You and I've killed. You know as well as I do, that each life we take taints our soul a little more. I don't want the girls to become tainted by Vaught's murder. I want you to use the girls as bird-dogs, but I don't want either of them to pull the trigger."

"Don't bullshit me, I personally saw Ruby kill several men in cold blood on a moor in England. If you trained them, they are as capable as I," stated Doc. "Also, what makes you think Vaught is going to use gas in Pittsburgh?"

"Ruby called me less than a half hour ago. She told me of an incident where she followed Vaught's head of security. I suggest that you get the details directly from her. She will be meeting the Washington shuttle in two hours. I think those girls will be a handful even for you." Mueller hesitated, then said only one word before the phone went dead, "Monitor."

Doc looked at Gabe. Gabe answered, "The line background noise did increase just before the connection went dead."

"How long would it take to get from here to Pittsburgh International Airport?" asked Doc.

"Between forty five to sixty minutes," responded Gabe. "I want to put some identification numbers on the fuselage. I don't want to take any chances since we'll be going in high traffic civilian air space."

Gabe got out of the seat and went to the back of the Nighthawk. He opened a small compartment. Inside were peal and stick numbers for the identification of the helicopter. Within four minutes he returned to the cabin. "Now we look legit. Even FAA inspectors couldn't tell the difference unless they get within 10 feet of the machine."

Looking to Smythe in the back seat, Gabe said, "Buckle up, we're going to make time." The actual flight took thirty-seven minutes until he set the Nighthawk down on the military section of the old Pittsburgh airport. "We have to take ground transportation to the new airport. "Leave your weapons here. They have pretty good detectors.

A sergeant drove up to the parked Nighthawk and asked for authorization papers. Gabe did the talking, and in short order he had the sergeant drive them to the main terminal were they entered through an employees door.

They had entered the main terminal. The sergeant pointed them toward the commuters at the far end of the terminal. Gabe waved goodbye. "We'll have your bird refueled when you get back." The sergeant and Gabe went back toward the helicopter.

"Just my luck," muttered Smythe when he realized the distance they had to travel across the terminal.

Doc led the way down an escalator toward a two-car subway shuttle. They boarded the shuttle and the doors whisked shut. Four minutes later the doors opened again and the two men stepped out onto a corridor that had another escalator, leading up this time. They went up and checked the monitors on the wall, listing all the recent incoming flights showing which gates are used for each flight. There was a refreshment area with a number of seats where people could wait for friends or relatives while watching television. They walked to the side of this area and down a hallway to the left where the flight would be disembarking. No one was in the hallway; it was too early for the airline personnel. They walked back to the snack bar. Doc ordered coffee. Smythe said, "Make it a double."

They sat nursing their coffee and waited. It didn't take long. Fifteen minutes before the flight was due to arrive, Ruby showed up. She walked directly to the hallway leading to where the flight from Washington would disembark. "How do you want to do the approach?" asked Smythe.

"You stay here, I don't want to scare them." Doc took a cocktail napkin and wrote something on it, then walked down the hallway carrying the last dregs of his coffee. Doc walked down the hallway and sat one seat away from the redhead known as Ruby. He put his coffee on the seat between them with the napkin beneath it. He took a swig and finished the coffee. "Damn, I need a refill," he said out-loud. He stood up and took the empty cup with him under the pretense of getting a refill.

In disgust of a litterbug, Ruby looked down at the cocktail napkin and saw the writing. "R –M said to meet you and J. Call if you need to confirm – I'll be at snack bar."

She looked at the man walking down the hallway. "Shit," she said under her breath. He knew her name and her sister's name. He knew the flight, and about Mueller. He was probably legitimate, but she never took chances. She stood up and went down the hallway, following the man. She saw him sitting on a chair sipping a fresh coffee. He was watching her. She went to the ladies room. Bending down she checked each of the stalls. She was alone. Now if Mueller were just home she prayed silently. She used one of the pre-paid phone cards so that no one could trace the user, in case this was a setup.

On the second ring Mueller himself answered, "I've been expecting your call Ruby. Don't talk. I want you and your sister to work with two men who have the exact, I say EXACT same goals."

She uttered only one word, "description?"

"One saw you in England; ask him to describe the circumstances. He also was in my study and basement; ask him to describe it to you. You may have to trust these men with your life. If you've to trust anyone, trust the man who was in my house. His nickname is Doc. Goodbye and good luck."

Ruby was shaken; she didn't like trusting someone she just met. The ladies room was still empty. She opened a stall closed the lid on the commode and sat down to collect her thoughts. After two minutes she opened the stall door, went to the mirror, straightened her skirt, and patted her hair into place. If the man in the hall wanted Vaught dead, that was a good thing. If he had a friend who also wanted Vaught dead, that was even better. Once Jade arrived, the four of them could coordinate their efforts and shortly Pearl would be revenged. She walked from the ladies room and back to the waiting area.

Doc stayed in the snack shop. The plane came in and Ruby's twin, Jade, was the fifth person through the gate. Both women hugged and Ruby whispered into Jade's ear. They sat down in the waiting area. Other passengers raced off the airplane. The flight attendants directed the last of the passengers to the luggage claim area, and then left, leaving only Ruby and Jade in the gate section. Ruby looked down the hallway and could see Doc sitting in a chair still sipping his coffee. She extended her right arm, the palm up and open. She then pointed to Doc and made a curling motion with her forefinger. It didn't take Doc anytime at all to realize a come-hither motion from a beautiful woman.

Doc thought to himself, "Mueller was right. These women are going to be a handful."

Chapter 21

It is not often that two beautiful women beckon Doc to sit with them. Under other circumstances he would be flattered, but due to current conditions, he felt like he was about to step into trouble. On the bright side, trouble with these two would be fun. As Doc walked down the corridor, the ladies separated so that there was a seat between them. Ruby patted the empty chair, offering it to Doc. Doc thought, *divide and conquer* these girls were good. There was no way he could watch both at the same time while sitting between them. He took an empty seat across from them.

"Don't you want to sit with us?" questioned Jade is a coquettish voice.

"In order to enjoy both of you at the same time, I need a little distance," he replied.

Ruby started, "Mueller said that you're probably real. Can your describe his home?"

Doc described everything including the steel gate, the mahogany finish of the library room, and the bulletproof garage door.

"Have you ever been down in his basement?" asked Jade.

"Yes, it's an interesting laboratory for dissection of the human mind complete with recording equipment and two way glass for observation."

"Ok, you're real," said Ruby. "Mueller said there are two men. I take it that you're the doctor. Where is the other man?"

"I'm not a doctor. My code name is Doc." He motioned to Smythe who was eating a sandwich at the bar. "That is Smythe. He will be here as soon as he's done eating. I didn't want to scare you by having two men approach you."

Ruby looked surprised, "You think that you would be a threat?" She laughed.

"I was afraid for us." Looking directly at Ruby, "I saw you work in England. You're not someone I would want to surprise."

Smythe finished his sandwich and walked up to the threesome. "May I join you? My name is Smythe."

"Have a seat," said Jade, as she patted the area between herself and Ruby.

Smythe fell for it. Ruby distracted him in conversation and Jade had his wallet without his even being aware that it was being taken. She slid it alongside her thigh, opened it by feel, found a card, and removed it from the wallet. Under the guise of smoothing her skirt, she looked at the card. Satisfied, she deftly replaced the card in the wallet. Then, with the help of Ruby, who was straightening her stocking over her calf, Jade replaced the wallet.

Doc watched the entire incident with interest. He asked, "Satisfied?"

Jade nodded 'Yes.' She then turned to Smythe and asked, "Commander Smythe, of the British Foreign Service, is your office on the third floor?"

Smythe looked startled. At that instant Ruby gently lifted his hand off her knee and let it fall into his own lap. Ruby said, "Let's get down to business. What do you know?"

Doc summarized the theft of the anthrax and VX gas. He discussed the Toronto plant where the mutated anthrax and VX combination was put into pressurized containers. He estimated that there were six boxes recovered from a ship and five of the six recovered from a truck in New York. "One box of 36 canisters is missing. It was off loaded shortly after the original truck passed from Canada into the United States. We have a team working on finding that truck."

"Close, but you missed some details," responded Ruby. "Vaught originally sold both the VX and anthrax to Sadam. Sadam's people accidentally found the mutation by inadvertently exposing the anthrax to an old VX container. They were changing the contents of warheads when the accidental discovery occurred. The four technicians were killed, their co-workers were the secondary exposure and they became very sick but the antitoxin did work to save all but one of them. They tried twice again, deliberately exposing people with the antitoxin in their system. Their immunity didn't work. They all died. Because the antitoxin didn't work, Sadam decided not to use it initially. That is the reason it survived Desert Storm. Vaught wanted the mutated virus back and tried to buy it from Sadam. He eventually let the United Nations inspectors in on where the toxin was hidden so they would find it and destroy it, since he was afraid to use it himself. He was also worried that he couldn't neutralize it safely. After that it was easy to steal from the United Nations."

Smythe was listening intently. "Do you mean he actually stole what he originally made?"

Jade answered for her sister, "Yes, but he made a profit at it. He blew up the airliner to collect the insurance, then arranged to sell the toxin again. This time for something he desperately wants, political power."

Doc asked, "Could you explain?"

Jade answered, "When I examined a few offices in Toronto and Washington, I found out that Vaught is blackmailing politicians. He sets them up with a DUI, driving under the influence charge, or a prostitute and then blackmail them for votes on his interests. Unfortunately, some politicians are hard to blackmail. Sometimes he buys them by paying for most of their re-election campaign expenses. Some of these have voted their conscience rather than repaying the favors to their benefactor. Vaught gets very upset. He literally freaks."

Ruby continued, "Those whom he feels betrayed him, he wants dead. Not just politically, but physically. The man is good at covering his tracks. He makes sure the reason for the death can't be connected to him. One of his competitors for government contracts died in a store holdup. The man went out for milk. Two gunmen robbing a corner store shot him. For some reason the cameras in the store were not working, and the police never found any leads."

Jade continued, "I found over thirty inconclusive deaths. Two people died in boating accidents, eight by hit and run, nineteen health related problems, and one fell down a flight of steps and fractured his skull. Our man uses strong-arm tactics. The man who arranges the accidents is probably Murphy, his head of security."

"I saw Murphy today," said Ruby. "He drove to a farm and had two college students go through some sort of a practice drill."

Smythe became alert, "Where was this? Was it here in Pittsburgh?"

"Yes, the farm is just a few miles from Vaught headquarters. When the boys left the farm, I followed them downtown where they checked out the back of a building," answered Ruby.

Doc looked at Smythe. "Why the sudden interest in Murphy?"

"Murphy was working toward conflicting goals when my partner died suddenly of lead poisoning, the nine-millimeter kind. Murphy was responsible. I think he was the one who pulled the trigger. I would not mind returning the courtesy."

"I've first shot," said Ruby.

Doc interjected, "We have priorities, first we stop and destroy the poisons. Murphy and Vaught are second. I think we are missing something important." He looked directly at Ruby, "Tell me everything you saw when you followed Murphy."

Ruby described the farm, the standpipe truck, and the building downtown. Doc questioned her on details a few times, nodding when he thought about the implications of the answers. After she told them about following the two college students back to the dorm, Doc cradled his head in his hands. Silence ruled the situation for a full three minutes. Finally Smythe spoke, "Are you thinking what I'm thinking?"

"I think we have more than one box of thirty-six canisters on the loose. If he's planning to use it here in Pittsburgh, he's doing it for a purpose." Locking his gaze on Ruby, "Do you've a car available to show us the barn and the building?"

Ruby answered, "We all go. My car is in the short-term parking."

Just then Gabe came walking down the corridor. He was carrying an overnight bag over his shoulder. He walked up to Doc and flipped the bag off his shoulder, onto an empty seat. "An officer named Brown said to give your clothes back." He was having a hard time restraining a smile. "Two thing came up. We need to talk."

"So talk here," said Doc. "These women are as involved as the rest of us."

Gabe reached into his jacket. "Carrie is trying to reach you." He handed a brick cell phone to Doc. "This has a descrambler and coders built in. The second thing is that Vaught Pharmaceutical has a Lear jet in their hangar here. The plane is being fueled now for an early flight out."

"That cinches it," said Smythe as he stood up. "We have to stop whatever is going off tomorrow, and then arrange to have Vaught arrested."

"I wish it were that easy," responded Doc. We'll need proof, and even then an arrest will not be easy." Doc asked Gabe, "Do you've any homer built into this thing," he asked as he weighed the brick phone by bouncing it up and down in his hand?

"Yes. Press #998 and it will activate."

Doc pressed the numbers. "Smythe, you go with Gabe and take Jade with you. Jade, do you've any luggage?"

"Only my carry-on," she responded.

"Ruby and I'll go to the farm. Gabe, I want those fancy gas detectors of yours to make sure there is no toxin in the barn before we go in. After we check out the barn we'll go downtown and check out that other building. I want you to see if there's a good place to monitor it from, just in case. Gabe, have your sergeant keep an eye on the Vaught jet. I want to know who gets on that plane and when it takes off."

Gabe turned and went back the long hallway. Smythe asked Jade, "May I carry that for you?" referring to her overnight bag.

"Thank you, yes," Jade smiled back. Together Jade and Smythe followed Gabe down the hallway.

Doc asked Ruby, "Mind if I change?"

"Who is Brown?" asked Ruby. "And why did she have your clothes?"

"Brown was the flight navigation officer on a flight I took from Great Lakes to the boat carrying the toxins to Chicago. I left my clothes on the base when I got into the jump suit," Doc explained. "I'd better change clothes."

"Do I get to watch?" Ruby said with an impish smile.

"I'll be back in a few minutes." Doc headed toward the men's room. Four minutes later he re-emerged as a businessman, complete with silk tie in a full Windsor knot. He gallantly held out his arm to Ruby, "May I escort you to your vehicle?"

"Thank you sir, it's this way," she said as she motioned with a wave of her arm.

Doc and Ruby walked down the long hallway without further conversation. Finally onboard the shuttle from the commuter aircraft to the main terminal Ruby asked, "Did you really see me in England?"

"Not in great detail, but enough to recognize you. You're an excellent marksman, or should I say markswoman."

Ruby slowed her step. "Are you going to arrest me after this business is over?"

Doc actually laughed out loud. "Of course not. First, I don't arrest people. Second, I watched the entire incident through a sniper scope myself. Besides, the world is a lot better off with the likes of those men dead."

"Thank God, I don't want to go to prison," said Ruby with a sigh of relief.

They continued out the entrance and located the car. They got into the car, and Ruby was ready to start the engine when Doc asked, "Wait a minute. I want to make a call to find out what's going on elsewhere."

Doc pressed the code for the secure number to Carrie. On the third ring she answered. "Can you talk freely?" asked Doc.

Carrie answered, "Yes. I've no problem talking, but we all have another problem."

"What problem?"

"You know that Smythe and I got part of the land shipment."

"Yes."

"Well it seems they off loaded one box of thirty-six canisters to another truck. That truck was being traced, but somehow they must have found out something was amiss. They left the empty truck at a road rest. Evidently they changed vehicles to continue the journey and we don't have a clue as to what they are driving."

Do you know where they're going?"

"I've got it narrowed to two targets. One is the T, the mass transit system in Boston. The second is the New York subway system. I've tried everything that I can to figure out which one is the target, but so far I've no clue."

Doc then questioned, "Does Vaught have offices in both places?"

"Yes."

"Are both offices at full staffing?"

"I think so, at least as of today."

Doc explained that there might be extra canisters that Vaught may have in Pittsburgh. He told her about the plane being readied for tomorrow morning. "Probably we'll have an incident here tomorrow. Send someone to Vaught's offices at both New York and in Boston. I want them outside, counting employees. Check the local airports for any personnel from Vaught enterprises leaving either city. I think one of your cities is going to have a problem very soon. I'll talk to you shortly. Goodbye."

Looking at Ruby he said, "Let's take a look at that farm."

Ruby pulled out of the parking space and wove through the airport maze until she turned onto Route 22. She drove in silence for about ten minutes then said, "We're coming up on the turnoff. I hope we can find it in the dark." They continued for a few more minutes. "There it's on the right. I'll pull in around the bend in the road like I did last time."

Doc triggered the send button on his brick phone connecting to Gabe. "Do you've us?"

"I've been following you ever since you left airport parking. Is that the farm?"

"Yes. Do an infra red scan for any life forms inside the buildings."

"Clear, no one home."

"Can you check for any sign of the gas?"

"That monitor is always on. I can't shut it off. No sign of any bio-toxin," said Gabe.

I'm going in to take a peek at what's in the building," said Doc.

"We're going in, "corrected Ruby.

"Fine," said Doc nodding in agreement to Ruby.

Ruby reached into her purse and pulled out a little pencil flashlight. For some reason Doc wasn't surprised when the overhead light didn't come on when he opened his door. They left the car and crossed the field. Ruby led the way and Doc held the brick communicator so that Gabe could be in touch.

Gabe's voice came over the communicator; "I pulled up to 800 feet so that I can monitor any traffic approaching your position. So far so good, no one in sight."

When they reached the building, it had a padlock on the door. "Hold this," said Ruby, as she handed the flashlight to Doc. Reaching into her pocket, she retrieved a lock pick and a lock wrench. Deftly she worked the devices into the lock pins. After cursing under her breath twice, she was relieved when the lock finally released. Inside the building they looked around but couldn't find anything other than the truck. The building probably had not been used for twenty years for anything other than storage, as evidenced by the state of disrepair. They couldn't find any sign of recent garbage in the corners of the building. They turned their attention to the truck.

Within the confines of the building they could detect a faint trace of paint fumes. The vehicle has been painted in the last couple of days. The truck doors were open, so they looked inside without having to resort to the lock picks. The odometer was over 100,000 miles. The inside was retrofitted as Ruby had described. There were several tanks of compressed air.

"This is interesting," said Doc.

"What do you see?" asked Ruby.

Doc pointed, "The fitting on the air hose is for something like a canister. It looks like it would fit nozzle first into this injection fitting. A protection cap would enclose the entire canister. This plunger would activate the release of the gas from the canister.

The end of the fitting would connect to the fire protection standpipe. The compressed gas from these tanks would disperse the toxin throughout the fire protection system built into the building."

Ruby questioned, "How would they get the gas to the people inside the building?"

"The easiest way would be to disconnect the fire hoses from the wall fittings and open the valves. The system is normally dry. No one would notice the disconnected hoses or the gas release," explained Doc.

They searched the rest of the vehicle, but found no evidence that could link Vaught Pharmaceuticals to the van. As they were getting ready to leave, Doc triggered the communicator to Gabe. "Are we clear to return?"

"No one in sight. Come on home."

"Do you've a tag homer?" asked Doc.

"Absolutely," responded Gabe.

They left the building and crossed the field. The helicopter whispered to a landing in front of them. Doc went to the pilot's door and Gabe held out a miniature homing transmitter. "This is good for three days. It holds by magnetism. There is a sensor for electrical changes that can detect when the vehicle is started."

"Thanks, I'm going back and put this on the truck. How about keeping watch?"

Ruby went to the car while doc went back and planted the transmitter under the back bumper. He locked the padlock and headed back to Ruby's car, being careful to walk on the gravel of the driveway so he would not leave any trace of footprints. As he slid into the passenger side of the car, Ruby started the engine.

Looking at Doc with a smile, Ruby asked, "Ready?"

"Ready," replied Doc.

Ruby drove from the farm lane to the intersection of Route 22 and headed for downtown. She passed Greentree going down a long hill to a tunnel. Doc got on the radio. "Gabe, pick up on the other side."

"Roger that. I'll not fit in those tubes with this bird," laughed Gabe.

On the other side of the tunnel they came out onto a bridge. The Three Rivers stadium was to the left. Ruby took the Second Street exit and headed downtown. Ruby pulled up to the back of the building and pointed to the standpipe connections. The brass fittings were marked, FIRE DEPARTMENT ONLY on a plaque fitted into the brick adjacent to the standpipe fittings. The brass caps on the pipes designated which floors were fed by the piping in the event of a fire. The pipes could be pressurized with air to test them instead of using actual water to test for possible leaks. Doc triggered the radio. "Gabe, do you've our location?"

"We are directly above you. Is that the target?"

"Probably. Can you find a place to set the bird down and still watch?"

"We'll check it out," answered Gabe.

Doc looked at Ruby, "Let's find a parking place and check out the inside."

Ruby found a long-term parking spot by the Greyhound station. They left the car, and returned to the building on foot. "Let's do a walk-by first to see what shows up," suggested Doc.

"Good by me."

The main doors to the lobby were comprised of two sets of revolving glass doors and three sets of hinged glass doors. The nature and amount of doors revealed that this was a place that held conventions and had a need to get many people in and out at the same time. They looked in the doors and saw a security desk with a guard watching television. They saw banks of elevators to the right and left down a short hallway behind the security station. To the right of the security desk was an escalator. The lobby had several signs in place listing which of the convention rooms would be used for each of the political special interest groups.

"I think we'd better find a newspaper to find out What's going on here tomorrow," suggested Doc.

"There will be one in the bus station, "said Ruby.

They walked back the way they had just come and found a newspaper stand in the bus terminal. "This is a big paper. You take half and I'll take the other half."

They looked through the paper, scanning each article for any mention of the building they had just examined. Suddenly Ruby said, "Bingo. It's in the section called *Pittsburgh This Week*. They're having a political meeting with a lot of big wigs tomorrow. The guest of honor is the Vice President's wife."

"Do you mean the wife of the Vice President of the United States?"

Doc studied Ruby. She looked into his eyes and realized that he wasn't actually looking at her, but through her. He started, "Lets suppose that the Vice President and his wife meet later, after she is exposed to the toxin, but before it breaks out."

"It says in the paper that she will give the speech at 11:00 am then attend the luncheon. Afterward she will return to Washington. My guess is that they will be in the sack having sex tonight," commented Ruby with a discreet smile.

Doc continued, "If they infect her, and she infects the Vice President, it would be probable that the President and possibly other high ranking politicians would become infected. Our government would be compromised."

"What's our next step?"

"Follow my lead, we're going into the building and at least shut down the pipe system. Then we wait and stop Vaught's men when they try to disperse the virus. First I want to check in with Carrie."

Doc pressed the automatic dialer code on the phone Gabe had given to him. Carrie answered on the second ring. "Carrie, I want you to check into possible motivations of Vaught. If we can understand why that man does things, and make sense of his motivation, we can make a pattern and catch him."

"What exactly do you want me to do?" asked Carrie.

"I want you to cross reference political votes in which the Vice President voted against projects sponsored by Vaught. Since the Vice-President only votes in the event of a tie vote in the Senate, and that doesn't happen very often, we should be able to find what ticked off Vaught. Our current suspicion is that he is going to spread the toxin in a convention center where the Vice President's wife is going to give a speech in a few hours."

"Why would he want to kill her?" asked Carrie.

"That's what I want you to find out. Call me back when you find anything. I've to get moving now, I'll talk with you when you find answers." Doc terminated the call and immediately pressed the code to contact Gabe. "Did you see the building we walked around?"

Gabe answered, "Absolutely. The convention center would be an excellent target with the Second Lady giving a rally there tomorrow."

"Are you psychic or what?"

"When we saw you two scope-out the building, I started to look for a good landing spot. There's a hospital across from the Civic Arena that has a helicopter pad for emergencies, so I landed. An emergency team greeted us. I assured them that I needed a temporary parking space for this bird. They assumed we were part of a special security detail for the Vice President's wife. We encouraged those assumptions. Their questions turned to asking if the Vice President himself was going to make a special appearance. Let's face it, this bird doesn't look like an emergency bird."

"What did you tell them?"

"I just asked for permission to park it for a few hours. Your buddy Smythe then asked if they had any coffee. He and Jade left to go to a cafeteria to get something to eat."

"Any movement on the homing signal as of yet?" asked Doc.

"Nothing yet. I'll let you know when it moves."

"We're going in to check the piping system and shut it down. Can you contact Shelly and get her to call security and confirm identities for Ruby and me as part of the security detail?"

"That is easy, but you do realize if the gas is released I've to shoot an incendiary rocket?"

"That is why I need you to try to get Shelly to stop the Second Lady from coming to this meeting. If possible try to call it off," requested Doc.

"Chances are slim to none, but I'll ask. By the way, Carrie downloaded the driver's license photos of all of Vaught's people in the Pittsburgh office. Smythe, Jade and I are going to be watching so that you've some warning."

"I appreciate any help we can get," replied Doc. "Call Shelly first, we're going in the building in 5 minutes." With that remark, Doc ended the conversation.

Ruby looked at Doc and asked, "Do I've time to use the little ladies room?"

"We move is five minutes. I think we should both get some relief, I don't know when we'll get a chance again."

Returning from the restrooms, Doc gave a quick nod to Ruby. "Ready?"

"Ready," Ruby confirmed.

Doc and Ruby walked out of the bus terminal, continuing down the street. As they entered the targeted building, Doc held the door for Ruby. She stepped through, then waited for Doc. He looked directly into her eyes once they were in the building, and then flicked his eyes in the direction of two men playing a game of chess to the side of the lobby. She responded by a quick up and down motion of her eyes without moving her head. Instead of walking to the security desk, they walked directly toward the two men and the chess game.

Doc asked, "Did you get confirmation of my identity?"

"What are you talking about?" answered the older man.

"You're wearing soft body armor and keeping both hands free to reach for your weapon, you've all the symptoms of being Secret Service. Now, did you get my confirmation?" demanded Doc.

"Yes, we received a phone call asking us to assist you if requested. Are you military intelligence or something like that?" asked the older agent.

"Something like that is the best description." Doc paused and asked, "When does the Second Lady get here?"

"She's due at the airport at 10:00 and here at 10:30. Is there a problem?" asked the agent with a look of worry on his face. "She's stubborn, I doubt she'll let us wave off this conference."

"If I were to guess, she will either continue without a problem or there won't be a convention center here when she shows up."

"Are you talking a bomb, because if you're, we already had the dogs go through the entire building. Everything is clean," said the younger agent.

"Just stay alert here." He motioned toward Ruby, "My partner and I'll check out our information. By the way, do you've local police here to hold any suspicious persons?" asked Doc.

"We have them on alert, but no one will show until about nine o'clock."

"Good." Doc and Ruby walked across the lobby to the building security desk. Doc addressed the rent-a cop, "We are doing a check for the Second Lady's security and we would like to know if there is to be a fire system check today? Could you check your log book?"

The security guard was a young smart mouth. He made the mistake by asking Doc, "Second Lady, do you mean that the president's whore is coming instead?"

Doc reached across the countertop with his right arm. Grabbing the tie and collar of the man's uniform he pulled the man off his feet, across the counter and held the man about an inch from his face. He then whispered, "You'll address the lady as a lady. You'll address any female as a lady. If you ever make another smart remark like that, I'll put your head up your ass where it belongs."

Still not deterred, the young man croaked, "It's impossible to put my head up my ass."

"Wrong. What's impossible is for you to remain alive when I do it," responded Doc, holding eye contact.

The young security guard gulped once and croaked hoarsely, "Okay man, I was just kidding. No harm no foul."

Doc released him. “Now check your log and tell me when the test of the fire system is scheduled.”

“They’re due here in about a half hour. They’ll be gone by the time things get cooking,” answered the man, swallowing several times trying to get moisture into his mouth.

Doc and Ruby walked back to the two Secret Service agents. “We’ll be checking each floor. Please radio any of your men on the upper floors so we don’t have to explain anything.”

The older agent smiled and said, “Thanks, I would like to have done that to the young punk, but it would have cost me my pension if he pressed charges.”

Doc smiled, “I don’t think he will be pressing any charges. He did piss his pants, he was so scared.”

Doc and Ruby went to the elevator. Once inside Ruby pressed the button for the top floor, “Might as well start at the top and work down.”

Chapter 22

Doc and Ruby took the elevator to the top floor of the convention center. They exited the elevator and went down the long hallway. At the far end, a cubical was inset into the wall, holding a fire hose on a reel. The end of the hose should have been connected to the massive brass valve. It wasn't. Doc checked the valve and it was open. "They were going to flood the entire center with the gas, not just the floor where the Vice President's wife will be giving the speech."

By the time they had worked their way down to the third floor, the brick communicator that Doc was carrying chimed. Gabe's voice came over the communicator, "Heads up folks. It's show time. The van just started moving."

Ruby held the elevator door open for the last floors while Doc raced down the corridor to close the last three valves. When they finally reached the main floor, Ruby asked, "How do you want to handle it?"

"I'll come at them from the other side of the street. I'll use the van to shield my approach. You distract them. I think you could distract even a Benedictine monk," said Doc as he smiled at her. He called Gabe on the communicator. "Give Smythe the rifle. There's no way they're going to release the gas. I need a backup."

"Smythe isn't here. He spotted Murphy and figured that he was bringing the gas to your location."

Ruby asked, "Doc, may I talk to Gabe?"

Doc handed her the communicator. "Gabe, is Jade there?"

"Right here beside me."

"Jade, remember what we did in St. Petersburg?"

"Russia or Florida?" giggled Jade.

"Russia, silly"

"Yes, I remember."

"We're going to do the same thing here. Doc will try to stop them but under no circumstance let them put the canister into the stand pipe," instructed Ruby. "Be careful to place the shot so as to protect the canister."

"You mean a kill shot?" asked Jade. "They are bloody and messy."

"Not nearly as messy as what would happen if Gabe starts shooting incendiary rockets," commented Ruby.

Gabe interrupted, "I'll get her set up from a window of the hospital."

Gabe took the long case from the back compartment and also a second smaller case. He held a small locking device in his hand. After they exited the helicopter, he pressed a button on the locking device. The helicopter blades continued to rotate in a slow idle, but the doors all locked. "That should keep for a few minutes until I get you set up. Together he and Jade went into the hospital through the emergency doors. "I need an examining room facing downtown." The floor nurse guided them down to an end room.

"Will this do?" the nurse asked.

Gabe went over to the window. Seeing that it opened, he said, "Yes. Please see that no one enters. We are setting up an acoustical monitoring device."

"All right, I'll make sure that no one enters, but could you get me an autograph?" requested the nurse.

"Whose autograph do you want?" asked Gabe.

"The Vice President's wife naturally, although I would really like one from the First Lady if you're offering," the nurse said in a pleading voice.

"How do you want it made out?"

"My name is Judy, Judy Webb. Would you really do that for me?"

"Consider it done. It may take a few days, but I'll get it for you," promised Gabe.

Jade looked him in the eye. "Did you just lie to that nice nurse?

"I'll make a call when I get back into the helicopter. She will get both. Now we have only a few minutes to set you up." Gabe opened the little case and took out a tripod stand. He set it in front of the window. Next he opened the aluminum case and took out the sniper rifle. "Do you know how to use this?"

"How is it sighted?"

"Point of aim, point of impact," he answered.

Jade deftly assembled the rifle. She put the suppressor on the end of the barrel and checked the scope. Next she opened the action, pulled the bolt and checked the barrel. "It will be a long shot, can you give me wind speed and direction from that fancy helicopter?"

"Affirmative, here you go." Gabe handed her an earpiece and lip microphone. "Keep in touch." He winked at her as he left the room.

He jogged back to the helicopter. When he was ten feet from it he pressed the locking device and the door on the pilot's side clicked open. He jumped into the seat and put his helmet on, pulling down the heads-up targeting visor of the helmet. He triggered the radio. "Doc, they are two clicks away."

Doc looked at Ruby, "Two thousand feet away. I'm crossing the street. Just hold tight until we see the aerosol container. Vaught would not trust just anyone with the gas, so Murphy will probably give it to them. We have to let them get it, and prevent them from using it. If they do, we'll be toast."

She gently reached up and kissed him. "Don't worry, Jade will be watching. She won't let anything happen to either of us."

Doc crossed the street and pretended to be interested in something in the window of a shop. As he was looking in the window he was watching Ruby's reflection in the glass. Just then a young blond prostitute sauntered up to Doc. "You got the time?"

Doc's mind was racing. He opened his wallet.

"Hey man, not here in the open. We can negotiate after we go in," she said, motioning to a building two doors down.

"I'll give you $20.00 to just stand here and talk with me for five minutes. I'm waiting for a van. I'm on a stakeout."

"Are you going to bust me?" she said, starting to back up.

"No, I'm not going to bust you, but I've to stop the men in the van that will be coming."

The communicator clicked, then Gabe's voice interrupted them. One hundred feet from your location."

Doc asked, "Gabe, any sign of Smythe?"

"No I should have planted a homer on that Brit."

"Jade?"

"She's in position."

Doc spotted the van turning the corner at the end of the block. "It's show-time," he said into the communicator. As he watched, the van did the unexpected. It turned the other way and pulled in front of a coffee shop. Doc relayed the information to Gabe. Ruby stared at the van in disbelief.

Ruby shrugged her shoulder and was adjusting something at her elbow. Doc watched in disbelief as she pulled her bra out of her sleeve. She saw Doc watching and motioned with her hand as though she were cradling her breast.

The prostitute was watching Doc and the show that Ruby had just put on. The prostitute offered, "I'm not even wearing a bra or panties."

"Calm down young lady." Motioning toward Ruby, "She's with me."

Doc looked up the street. The two boys were returning to the van carrying cups of coffee and a brown paper bag. They got into the van and then did a U turn, heading for the conference center. They pulled the van into the curb so the back doors were adjacent to the standpipes.

It truly was show time.

In his position in the helicopter, Gabe watched the van pull in next to the curb. His heads-up visor was in place and he put the pale green cross hair onto the panel section of the van. He released the safety catch on the firing button. Next he said a silent prayer, hoping that he would not have to fire the rockets. His scanners swept the area and registered negative for any trace of the toxin.

In the hospital room, Jade watched the van pull in and she backed off the magnification of the sniper scope so she could get a wider view of the action. She watched her sister, Ruby, leaning against the building bracing herself with her foot against the marble facade of the building wall. Ruby deftly undid another button on her blouse with her left hand. Jade smiled to herself thinking now we'll get a real show. She watched the driver get out, go around the back of the van, and open the double doors. The occupant came out of the passenger side gingerly holding a brown bag. He walked around the back of the van, putting the bag on the floor of the van, adjacent to the hoses. Jade swiveled the scope so she could look up the block to the donut shop. A couple was just coming out of the shop holding a bag of pastries. The bag was white. Swinging the scope back into position she flipped off the safety. There was no way anyone was going to release the contents of the brown bag. If they did her sister would be history.

When the van pulled into the curb Doc turned to face the prostitute so that the men in the van couldn't see his face. He handed the communicator to the woman saying, "Hold onto this until it's over. Here is an additional twenty. I'll give you a hundred when you give this back. Now look behind me and tell me when the driver gets out and goes around the back of the van."

The prostitute hugged him as she looked at the van. "Good luck, he's going around the back of the van now."

Doc hugged her back, "Thank you." He crossed the street, keeping the van between him and the men at the back of the vehicle. From this advantage he could see Ruby making her approach.

Ruby feigned drunkenness as she moved toward the men at the back of the van. She dropped her purse and then bent over from the waist to pick up the purse. As she did, she controlled her shoulder muscles and breathing so that her left breast flopped out. The one fellow who had just put the brown bag onto the van's floor nudged his buddy to watch the show.

Ruby tucked her left breast back into her blouse and tried again to pick up the purse by bending from the waist. This time her right breast fell out. She tucked it back into her blouse. The two young men were now laughing.

From her view in the hospital room Jade mouthed. "And now fall down, just like you did in St. Petersburg."

On the street below, Ruby bent forward a third time and ended up falling onto the sidewalk. The way she landed was carefully positioned so that her left leg bent and her foot was underneath her butt. The right leg was forward and bent at the knee. "Could you please, please help me up?" she asked the two men.

"Sure lady," said the driver.

She held her hand up, as one of the men reached down, offering his right hand. She grabbed the man's wrist. She levered her body by lifting her body with her left leg. The effort pulled the man off balance. At that same instant she kicked her right leg forward sweeping it against the man's legs, knocking him to the ground. She twisted and rolled her body around his falling frame so that she ended up sitting on his back as his face slammed into the concrete. Next she twisted his arms behind his back, pinning him to the sidewalk.

Doc had come around the van at the same time Ruby fell to the walkway. The driver was distracted. Doc got into position behind him. As Ruby swept the legs out from the one man, Doc slipped a chokehold around the other man's neck with his right forearm pressed against the man's larynx. Doc held the pressure so that the larynx closed the trachea. The lack of oxygen caused the man to black out. As the man slumped in Doc's arms, he maintained pressure to make sure he would stay out. "You okay?" He asked Ruby as she sat on the other man's back.

"I'm okay. Get security to take these two," she suggested.

Doc left the unconscious man on the ground and went fifteen feet to the door, and yelled in, "We need some help out here."

Jade was watching through the scope. Ruby was still sitting on the man's back. Two men in suits carrying nine-millimeter weapons came out the door to assist. Everything seemed to be going fine. The operation was going to be a success. Just then a Yellow Cab came down the street. Jade was focused on the security men coming out of the building and didn't think twice about the cab stopping in traffic. Doc was handed a pair of handcuffs to put on one man, while the two suits put and cuffs on the man Ruby was holding down. Movement caught her eye. The cab door was open and a man had started toward the back of the panel truck. The man grabbed the brown bag, and sprinted to the waiting cab.

Smythe came jogging down the middle of the street. He was almost hit by a delivery truck backing up. In the middle of traffic he stopped, stood with his legs spread wide, and held a pistol out with his right hand, cradling it in his left for a steady sight picture. It was a classic Cup and Saucer stance. He fired at the man sprinting back to the waiting cab. Doc had just looked up as the gun went off. The bullet passed within several feet of Doc. Doc turned to see what Smythe was firing at. Murphy was the man trying to take back the aerosol of toxin. The slug hit the Kevlar vest Murphy was wearing, knocking him backward. At the same time Smythe had fired, Jade also let go a round from the sniper rifle. Smythe's bullet threw Murphy backward an instant before Jade's round would have hit. The result was that Jade's bullet impacted where the street met the curb. A piece of concrete exploded from the curb. Murphy dropped the aerosol when he was thrown backward, but he recovered enough to dive headfirst into the back of the open cab door.

Smythe leveled the gun on the fleeing cab, but held his fire, as he was concerned about the pedestrians being hit either by a stray round or by the cab if he hit the gas tank. He would get Murphy later. He put the pistol back into his shoulder holster. Doc got up and quickly retrieved the brown bag. He took out the aerosol. It was undamaged. He held it up so Gabe's scanner could confirm it wasn't leaking. He stared at the helicopter in the distance hoping that he would not see a trail of fire from a rocket. He held that position for a good two minutes.

"What in hell are you trying to do, imitate the Statue of Liberty?" quipped Smythe as he approached.

"I'm trying not to get us toasted," responded Doc. He handed the container to Smythe, "You get to walk this up the hill to Gabe. Where have you been?"

"I've been eating a sweet roll and drinking coffee," answered Smythe grinning. "I got to see the transfer first hand."

"You were in the pastry shop?" asked Doc.

"Yes, but I couldn't leave until after Murphy did. I wanted to follow him. "Good thing I did. You almost gave him the aerosol back."

"Thanks," nodded Doc.

"You're welcome. Do I still have to walk back up to the hospital?" grinned Smythe.

"Yes, you need the exercise after those pastries." Doc handed Smythe the aerosol "Get this into a sealed unit. Have someone take it to Great Lakes for destruction. I've to clean up here."

Smythe turned on his heel and walked across the street, starting up to where the helicopter was still sitting on the helicopter pad at the hospital.

"A hundred," said the prostitute as she handed the communicator back to Doc.

"Yes." He opened his wallet and pulled out two fifty-dollar bills. "Thank you again." The girl took the money and scurried down the street, avoiding the Secret Service agent approaching Doc from the other direction.

"What do you want us to do with these men?" he asked.

"Have the local police hold them on something. Attempted murder would be good. But make them disappear for about two hours. I don't even want them talking to anyone for that length of time," ordered Doc.

"They have constitutional rights. We need to recognize their rights," stated the young Secret Service agent.

"Okay, lets play your game. These boys just tried to expose the central area of downtown to a bio-toxin capable of killing thousands of people. That makes it an act of terrorism. Such an act is under the jurisdiction of the Federal Bureau of Investigation. Call them and have the prisoners taken to Quantico. Upon arrival at a secure room in Quantico, notify their parents and get them lawyers," ordered Doc.

"Who the hell are you to give me orders," said the younger man in a fit of anger.

"You don't want to know," replied Doc calmly.

"Leave it alone," said the older agent to his partner. "Lets call in the FBI to do the collar and transport." He looked at Doc and Ruby. "Is it safe to have the meetings with the Second Lady, or do we call it off?"

"It should be safe. Relate what went on here to the FBI when they show up. I'll have someone call Quantico with the particulars of the charges," said Doc. He looked at Ruby, "Lets see if you've a parking ticket yet." Without further words, the two walked side by side down the sidewalk as though nothing had ever happened.

The younger agent looked at the older one. "What do we do with this truck?"

"Call the police and have it towed."

Doc held out his hand as they walked. Ruby took it. "Are you all right?" he asked.

"I was a little worried when Smythe started shooting. Jade could have ended it. She is an excellent shot. If Smythe had hit the aerosol it would really have been all over."

"He didn't hit the aerosol. He also is an excellent shot," responded Doc.

"What do we do now?" she asked.

"Punt."

Chapter 23

Jade swore when her shot didn't kill Murphy. It would have killed him had Smythe's shot not knocked him slightly backward with the impact of his own shot, which hit Murphy's Kevlar vest. She watched Smythe take the toxin-filled aerosol. When she realized that the danger was over, she disassembled the rifle and put it into the case. She packed the tripod and closed the window. She made it back to the helicopter in less than three minutes. Gabe was watching, and as she approached, he flipped a switch that automatically opened the back door so she could put the cases into the back section of the Nighthawk.

"Ready?" Gabe asked Jade.

"Damn, I missed." she responded in a dejected voice.

"Let's see if I can get you another shot," smiled Gabe.

"What do you mean?"

"I intend to follow that cab. You had better buckle up."

Gabe gave power to the rotors and the bird lifted off the hospital's helicopter pad. The cab headed into the tunnel. "We'll pick him up on the other side."

"What about Smythe?" asked Jade.

"He seems resourceful, I'm sure he'll get a ride with Doc and Ruby."

Meanwhile Doc and Ruby had made it to the car. Doc triggered the communicator. "Carrie, we recovered another aerosol. Any idea why the Second Lady or the Vice President were the targets?"

"I checked the voting records and there were no tie votes in the last two years having any bearing on Vaught's businesses. It must have been something that isn't in the public records. I've people working on it in Washington. Initial reports are that the V.P was influencing a bill, which would limit the profits of drug companies. Vaught Pharmaceuticals are almost ready to release a new anti-rejection drug for transplanted organs. It should be worth billions. Vaught was openly supporting an international organ bank system. There seems to be a big stink about the funding overseas to start the organ banks in third world countries. People are worried that the organ banks will be stocked with political dissidents. You know – 'Kill your enemy and sell the body for profit.'"

"Any idea of the target city?"

"Vaught's offices in Boston and Washington are normal, but the office in New York closed and put notices on the doors that they'll be closed tomorrow due to a computer failure. The note continues to say they will be down for only one day, as the parts for the machine are on overnight delivery and expected shortly. The phone service is relaying the same message."

Doc asked Carrie, "Have you been able to mobilize anyone to help stop the attack on the subway system?"

"We have FBI on every Vaught employee. We had a judge signing phone taps until he was really pissed at us. Since Vaught has a large number of employees, we are routing the conversations through a speech recognition computer. It's scanning each phone call for certain words that could mean the person is in on the spread of the virus. If the conversation includes any of the key words, it's routed to a live person to listen to both sides of the conversation. So far we have zilch."

Just then there was a knock on the window of the car. Smythe looked in the window and asked, "I appear to have been left without either wheels or wings. Can I bum a ride?"

Ruby pressed the electronic locking switch and the rear door clicked open. As Smythe swung into the seat he said, "Thanks. Where are we going?"

Ruby interjected, "He is right, we should be moving. Where do you want to go?"

"Hold on Carrie," Doc said. He then spoke to Ruby, "Let's head for the airport. We have to go to New York."

Ruby pulled out into traffic, just missing a local policeman who was writing tickets. Smythe couldn't help himself, "Where is a cop when you need one?"

Ruby started laughing, "Writing tickets, naturally." She gave the car gas and it took off, pressing Smythe into the back seat as he started laughing uncontrollably.

Doc spoke into the phone, "Carrie are you still there?

"Yes."

"By any chance did you send down anyone from the Center for Communicable Disease to pick up our parcel?"

"As a matter of fact, yes. People you know. One might say that you left them high and dry when you went for your swim."

"The commander and Brown?" asked Doc.

"They will transport your parcel back to Great Lakes for destruction."

"Are you still in Great Lakes?"

"Actually, I'm in a temporary office in a train car now headed to New York City," replied Carrie. The CDC has a special train complete with containment cars to handle outbreaks of disease in case of a biological attack. I'm in the command and control car."

"How many agents do you've?"

"Eight hundred are closing on New York. We do have one problem."

"What would that be?"

"Orders are to use rubber bullets. Can you imagine some dumb shit, sitting behind a desk being afraid of killing the bad guys before they kill thousands of people? Don't they realize that these people have declared war on us?" said Carrie, with more than a little frustration in her voice.

"Try to get Shelly to use her influence and get the order changed to use lethal force."

"I already tried; whoever is issuing the orders on behalf of the White House is the person who changed the CDC directive."

"Is this a secure line?" asked Doc.

"Yes, double secure."

"Tell CDC people with you that we need a second response team in Washington. Explain that another 20 aerosols are going to be used in an attack on the Capital building and other government building in the DC area."

"Christ, did we miss that many containers?" asked Carrie.

"No, but I'm willing to bet they change the orders to shoot to kill if it means protecting themselves. Vaught must still have some highly placed people he has bought off. Profit's one thing, but if it means that their own life is on the line, I think they will always vote to save their own ass."

"I'll do it."

"I've to go now, we're going into a tunnel and will lose signal," said Doc.

Doc turned in the seat to look at Smythe, "Why didn't you kill Murphy?"

"A couple of reasons. I knew that he only had one aerosol on him. He carried it in a brown paper sandwich bag. I also saw that he was wearing body armor. I wanted to be sure that there was only one aerosol for the building. I know Murphy. If there were a second aerosol he would have used it. Since there was only the one, he would retrieve it at all costs, and return it to Vaught like a dog returning a bone.

Ruby asked, "But why didn't you kill him with your shot or let Jade kill him?"

"I knew Gabe and Jade were watching with a sniper scope, I wanted to save Murphy so I could find Vaught," said Smythe as though the explanation were perfectly clear.

"So, indulge us," said Doc.

Smythe continued, "Murphy never met me, so I planted a bug in his pocket while he was in the pastry shop. I wanted him to snatch the aerosol. That would mean that this location would be safe. I had to stop him from taking it, and since he had the body armor, all I had to do was shoot him. The trick was to hit him just before Jade, or else she might kill him and then we would have a harder time tracking Vaught. Quite simple actually, just shoot him in the chest. Did you hear the clink when the slug hit the safety plate? I bet that really stung. Anyway 90% of the time when someone is shot in the chest, they drop whatever they are holding. The nice thing about hitting the body armor, there is no muss no fuss, and no blood or bodies to explain."

The fluorescent lights of the tunnel flashed by as the car sped through the tunnel and Smythe continued talking. "Does Carrie want us in New York?"

Suddenly Doc saw the light at the end of the tunnel in more than one way. "We have to split up, I'll have Gabe shadow Vaught with Ruby and Jade while we go to New York." As they came out of the tunnel the communicator rang. "Yes," said Doc.

Gabe was on the other end of the connection. "Pull off at the next exit. There is a mall parking lot to your right. Park at the far end so I can pick you up."

"Is there a problem?" asked Doc.

"I need to get you out of that car so that we can make some time. The cab dropped Murphy off at Vaught's private hangar. In this race you're falling behind. It's time to get wings."

Ruby pulled into a parking space near the far end of the parking lot and they all got out of the car. Ruby took two aluminum cases with her. Doc gave her a questioning look. She replied, "We don't want anyone to steal the car and find these play-toys."

They boarded the Nighthawk, stowing the two packages in the rear compartment. In a few minutes they were airborne and headed to the airport. They each put on headsets so that they could talk to one another. Smythe asked, "Do you still have the homer signal that I planted on Murphy?"

"The signal is still coming from Vaught's private hangar," responded Jade, as she studied the green screen in front of her.

When they got within two thousand feet of the hangar, Gabe asked, "Flip for a heat signature and see how many people are in the hangar."

"Which button?" She asked.

"Third on the left side of the screen," answered Gabe.

"Only two heat signatures in the building," replied Jade.

Smythe asked, "Do you think its Vaught and Murphy?"

Gabe responded, "Vaught left in the company's Lear jet four hours ago."

Doc asked, "Has the homer's signal moved?"

Jade stared at the screen, "Not that I can tell."

Doc shook his head; "He is gone. Homer or not, he is gone."

"He has to be there," stated Smythe.

"Let's find out," said Doc. He turned to Gabe. "Can you land this out of sight of the hangar?"

Gabe maneuvered the ship behind the National Guard barracks. After the rotor shut off, Smythe made a profound statement. "You know there is only one way to find out if Murphy is in the building."

"Yes?" said Doc skeptically.

"I'm going to order one of those pizzas that come in a half hour and then knock on the door and get in as a pizza delivery man," said Smythe with a degree of certainly.

Gabe interjected, "If you order a pizza, I want one with pepperoni."

Jade added, "I want mushrooms on mine."

"And onions," added Ruby.

Smythe got out the door and motioned, "Come on girls. We can order at the phone in the barracks headquarters." All three got out of the copter and went to the building, leaving just Gabe and Doc in the Nighthawk.

Doc asked Gabe, "Can we still monitor the signals from here?"

"Sure."

Doc used the device to confirm the three images were still inside of the building, then switched off the machine. He reached and picked up the emergency medical kit, choosing two sets of latex gloves and half a dozen individually packaged aspirins. "I'll be back."

"I'll be here, watching and listening," grinned Gabe.

Doc walked around the National Guard barracks and crossed the tarmac directly to the Vaught hangar's side door. He knocked three times. After a few minutes without a response, he knocked again. Finally a man came to the door. "What do you want?"

"I'm here to pick up Murphy's clothes," stated Doc.

"Don't know any Murphy," growled the man.

Doc reached into his pocket and slowly and deliberately put on the latex gloves. "I hope you didn't get too close to Murphy. Now cut the shit. We have to get Murphy's clothes for the incinerator. You do have some plastic bags; we should double bag them for safety. If you want to bag the clothes, you'd better put on a set of gloves."

"What's on those clothes?"

"Bad shit. You know what, we better take the antigen now to be safe. Do you've water?"

The guard motioned Doc in, locking the door after Doc was inside. He said, "Follow me, the lunch room is this way."

"Are you the only onc hcrc?" asked Doc.

I'm Bruno; Morley is cleaning up the locker room. We're the only ones here."

"Well Bruno, You had better get Morley so he can take the antigen or else he could get sick," instructed Doc.

Bruno hollered at the top of his lungs, "Yo Morley. I need you in the lunchroom. Now!"

Doc went over to the water cooler, filled three paper cups with water, and set them on the table. Just then Morley came into the room. "What's this all about?"

Doc asked, "Did you touch anything that Murphy might have touched?"

"Yea, probably. What happened?"

"Well, Murphy was in a sensitive part of the lab. A new security man told him to freeze. Murphy told him to do something physically impossible and kept moving toward the sensitive material. The guard ordered him to stop one more time. Murphy turned around and extended a finger to the guard. The guard shot him in the center of his chest. Murphy was testing the guard, but never expected to be actually shot. As a safety he was wearing body armor, with a steel insert to protect the heart area. The bullet ricocheted off the steel plate and broke a vial with some very bad bugs in it. We didn't notice it until after Murphy left the building."

Doc looked at the three paper cups of water he placed on the table. He took out the individually packaged aspirin continuing his lie. "We'd better take the antigen before we go back and get the clothes. The packages are marked aspirin, but we were in a hurry when we packaged the antigen and that label was in the pill machine." He tore open one package and gulped the aspirin.

The two men then followed his example taking the aspirin. "What does this bug do?" asked Morley.

"Well, did you ever have mumps?" asked Doc.

"Both men nodded yes. "Do you remember people saying that if you lifted anything heavy your testicles would swell up to the size of oranges?" continued Doc.

Both men were nodding. "This bug is like mumps, only it will make you sterile and your testicles will swell up to the size of cantaloupes."

"What do we do?" asked the men in unison. Their eyes were going wide.

"Two things; First you must not lift anything at all. It would probably be best if you would lie down with your legs spread apart. Second, you've to hold your testicles to support them while you stand," explained Doc as he could hardly hold a straight face.

"How long will we have to be like this?" asked Morley, as he reached down to hold his testicles with his left hand.

"Only about ten hours. By then the antigen will be giving you full protection and you'll be back to normal. Now we had better get those clothes so I can destroy them."

"Follow me," said Morley. He led the way to the locker room. He pointed to a locker at the end with a lock on it. "That's Murphy's with the lock."

"You do have bolt cutters here don't you?" asked Doc.

"I'll be right back," said Bruno. Doc could tell that Bruno was terrified. In two minutes Bruno returned and handed Doc the bolt cutters, "You better do it, cause I don't have any extra gloves."

Doc cut through the lock's hasp and opened the locker. Inside he found a complete set of clothes including the body armor. Holding up Murphy's shirt he said, "This is where the bullet hit."

"For God sake man. Put it in the bag. I've a wife and kids," screamed Bruno.

Doc dropped the clothes into the plastic bag cinching it at the top. He double bagged the first garbage bag. As he turned around he saw both men holding their private parts with one hand. He nodded to the men, "Smart move. It's always best to protect the family jewels."

As the men were ushering him toward the door, someone started knocking. "Let me get that," Doc said.

He opened the door to face Smythe holding a pizza. Smythe was uncharacteristically speechless. Doc turned to the men. "I ordered a pizza for you so that your time will not be totally unpleasant." He then took the pizza from Smythe and handed it to Bruno. "Now you both better go lie down and rest for the next ten hours. If your testicles haven't swollen up to the size of melons, you'll be alright." Bruno and Morley both nodded agreement. "But I need to ask one more question? Where did Murphy go, I've to get the antigen medicine to him as soon as possible, by now his testicles are probably starting to hurt."

"He caught the shuttle to New York," volunteered Morley.

"How long ago did the flight leave?" asked Doc.

Morley looked at his watch and said, "It will be leaving in about 2 minutes.

"Don't worry about Murphy, he'll be fine. Now lock the door behind us and get some rest. If I were you I would'nt even answer the door," ordered Doc as he closed the door. He and Smythe left the building.

When they were about twenty feet from the building Smythe recovered, "How in the hell did you know that he wasn't in there?"

While you were ordering pizza, I overlaid the heat signatures of the people in the building with the location of the homer. There was no person in the area where the homer signal was coming from, hence no Murphy. I needed to find out where he went. The best way was to scare the men in the building."

Smythe stared at Doc, "AND?"

Doc smiled, "And we are going to New York."

Chapter 24

Luck was with Doc and Smythe. As they returned from Vaught Pharmaceutical's hangar, they saw Brown packaging the aerosol, containing the toxin, in a hermetically sealed container for transport to Great Lakes for destruction. Doc nudged Smythe, "Do you know what that means?"

"Yes, she probably ate my share of the pizza. What are you talking about?" asked Smythe.

Doc smiled, "Where we find Brown, we find a fast plane. I think we can borrow a ride to New York and get there, possibly before Murphy." Both men started running toward the Nighthawk as Brown walked away, carrying the silver aluminum case.

"Hold on a second!" yelled Smythe.

Recognizing Doc, she stopped in mid-stride. As they came up to her she said, "I bet the commander that you would end up in the water. He would not take the bet. I see we were both wrong."

"Can we get a ride?" asked Smythe.

"We'll be going back to Great Lakes to destroy this bug," she said, motioning to the aluminum case she was holding.

"Could you take a detour?"

"Where?" said Brown, eyeing Smythe suspiciously.

Doc came directly to the point. "Could we please have a ride to New York City? We have to get there before a plane that just left this airport. But first we must divide to conquer." He motioned them back to the Nighthawk helicopter.

When Doc opened the side door he saw Ruby, Jade and Gabe each with their mouths full of pizza. Gabe was the first to speak, "We didn't want to waste anything."

Doc asked, "Do you've any information as to where Vaught went with the Lear jet?"

Gabe looked up, taking a drink of soda to clear his throat. "We have two fixes on his location. One is from the flight plan he filed. The second is from satellite monitoring and a Ground Positioning Satellite confirming the jet's movement. He's at his experimental ranch in Montana. It's a ranch owned by Vaught Pharmaceuticals for experimentation with drugs on animals."

"How far is the ranch from civilization? Is there any way to get out in that area and watch his movements without causing suspicion?" asked Doc.

Gabe responded, "To the north north-west of the ranch there are some mountains that are public land. Sometimes the military uses it for training. We could take this bird out there on the pretext of a training session. I don't think anyone would be suspicious."

"Okay. Gabe you take the Nighthawk with the women out to monitor What's going on at the ranch; Smythe and I are going to New York and see what havoc we can cause there. If things work out, we'll come out and meet you in Montana."

Gabe grinned at the women, "Are you with me?"

Both women nodded their consent.

Doc and Smythe followed Brown as she started back across the tarmac to where the commander was waiting with the jet. Brown strode straight to a blue-gray Sabreliner. The commander was doing a walk-around, checking the tires as part of the pre-flight inspection. He left nothing to chance. When they got closer he acknowledged them with a nod of his head. The commander spoke directly to Brown, "While you were gone I had it topped off. We now have a full 8,800 pounds of fuel, just in case we have to go somewhere else in a hurry." Looking at Doc, "Do we have to go somewhere else in a hurry?"

"If you would'nt mind, we have to get to New York as soon as possible," explained Doc.

"The city?" asked the commander.

"As close as you can to the commercial airport," responded Doc.

A portable stairway was attached to the plane. The commander took a small xenon flashlight out of his uniform and blinked it twice toward the hangar area. A young enlisted man came running over to the plane. The commander ordered, "As soon as we are in, pull this away."

"Yes sir," said the crewman as he saluted.

The commander turned and went up the stairs, taking his position in the cockpit. Brown, Smythe and Doc followed. Once Doc was inside, the crewman pulled the ladder away from the aircraft as Doc locked the hatch into position. Doc and Smythe took seats and fastened the seatbelts. Brown, holding a clipboard, worked with the commander to go through the pre-flight checklist. Upon completing the commander asked, "How fast do you need to get there?"

"As fast as possible, I want to beat a commercial flight that left 20 minutes ago. I know this version of the Sabreliner is listed for about 436 miles per hour," replied Doc.

The commander smiled as he taxied onto the runway, "You're referring to the civilian model, this is a military version that has been tuned by yours truly. Buckle down, we are preparing for takeoff. I'll register the flight plan as a medical emergency."

Doc and Smythe were pushed back into their seats by the 3,700 pounds of thrust at takeoff. The plane went into a relatively steep climb until it leveled off at 38,000 feet. Smythe looked out the window, "Nothing down there but clouds."

The commander came over the intercom, "We're lucking out. I've the plane positioned in a natural jet stream that is going from west to east. It will add to our speed."

Doc cupped his hands by his mouth to form a megaphone, "Is it alright to use the communicator?"

"No problem," replied the commander.

Doc keyed in the number for Carrie and pressed SEND.

Carrie answered, "Where in the heck have you been?"

"What's wrong?" asked Doc.

Carrie answered, "I leaked the information of a probable change of target from New York to DC. The powers that control things pulled everyone to Washington. The train I'm on with the CDC is scheduled to leave in 20 minutes. I thought you said they would use real ammo when they realized the danger? Well they are, but in Washington. What do you want me to do now?"

"Do you've a laptop?"

"Yes."

"Download street maps of New York and also maps of the subway system. Overlay those with locations of Vaught's properties, and finally with the tactical maps of the old military tests of the subway system from November 1968."

"I've it already on my machine."

"Then get off that train. Take a cab to Kennedy. Stand outside the luggage pickup area. We'll pick you up in about ninety minutes. "

"What will you be driving?"

"No idea, but it will be fast."

Smythe asked Doc to give him the phone. "Carrie, I want you to call the British consulate and ask Jim to pick you up in the Hong Kong Special." He handed the phone back to Doc, smiling.

"What's the Hong Kong Special?" asked Doc as he hung up the phone.

Smythe answered the question with a question. "Have you ever been in Hong Kong while the British controlled it?"

"Yes."

"What do you remember above everything else?"

"The city was extremely crowded."

"Exactly!"

"Exactly what?" asked Doc.

"With all the crowding there would be traffic accidents. The traffic would be similar to what we'll experience in New York City. When the British Government controlled the emergency systems we used a very special ambulance system."

"Ambulance system? Now I really don't understand."

"We used a panel truck ambulance. The back of the panel truck held emergency equipment and motorcycles to cut through traffic to get to the victims. Now do you understand?"

"Not really." Doc was puzzled.

"We could respond to an accident, but because of heavy traffic that builds up around an accident, it would be difficult to get a paramedic to the injured people. So, we would get close with the medical truck, then the paramedics would drive through traffic using the motorcycles. These motorcycles were equipped with communicators and nested tubing stretchers. They could cut through the heaviest traffic. When the Chinese took over Hong Kong we took our equipment out. We modified it to be an ambulance with excellent surveillance monitoring. We happen to have it in New York City. Jim is our primary driver."

Carrie came back to where Doc and Smythe were plotting strategy. "I've a ride arranged."

"What do you've?" asked Smythe.

"A taxi," said Carrie as she started laughing.

"You're kidding," stated Smythe.

"Not really, we have a specially modified taxi. It looks like a taxi, but it has a very large engine and a reinforced frame. The trunk is armored with a variety of weapons. I'm sure you'll get more that a bang out of it. Our Christians In Action - CIA friends are giving it to us on loan. They do ask that you return it in one piece." Brown smiled at the men and left to go back to the co-pilot's seat.

Smythe suddenly seemed to be in a somber mood. "Doc, What happens if we can't stop this?"

Doc answered directly, "First we have a plague. There will be no controlling it. With no controls it will probably develop a pestilence. People panicking will cause a lot of indiscriminate killing and vandalism. I don't know where it will end, but probably the stresses to the municipal authorities will cause a breakdown of authority, at least at local levels. If it spreads fast enough, New York City might as well be dead. If it spreads beyond the immediate infected area, and reaches to other cities, we'll have a disruption of the world economy. On the bright side, it only seems to be lethal for the first and possibly second exposures to the original toxin. The sickness will tie up a lot of hospitals and support people. I believe the old saying was 'Kill one enemy and you remove one man, wound an enemy and you remove ten support people from the front line.' About that time Vaught will announce and sell the anti-toxin. People with the money will buy and support him. I think he may then make a bid for political power. The world could have a serious problem with a maniac like that in a position of power."

Smythe grinned, "Don't tell me you're being optimistic?"

"I really am being optimistic. If we get all of the toxin, and none gets released in the process, we stand a good chance of surviving this."

Smythe then asked the critical question, "Where and how will the toxin be released?"

"If it were me, if I had knowledge of a previous plan for spreading gas in New York that worked, if I had the complete details of how the prior plan was carried out, I would not reinvent the wheel. I would copy the prior plan and maybe try to improve on it. Vaught has just that information from the 1968 test by the United States in preparation for a Soviet biological attack on New York. They synchronized the release of the gas and timed when it showed on the meters at the different platforms in order to see how fast the movement of the trains spread the virus. They also monitored the intensity of the virus at each train terminal. They monitored the hospitals for the number of persons admitted to track the spread of the virus. I saw the plans in the office in Toronto. I'm betting Vaught duplicates them."

Smythe pressed, "If you were going to improve on it what would you do?"

"In 1968 military personnel took knapsacks into the subway system and released a smoke and gas containing what later became known as Hong Kong Flu. They triggered the release of the gas from the service tunnels a short distance from the terminal. If I were to do the same tactic, I would use stealth to get into the tunnels, and a timer to release the gas to protect the person triggering release. Finally, I would not use 18 men as they did back then. I would use as few as possible. Fewer tongues to talk, means less chance of being caught. I remember marks on the maps in Canada; I think there will be only two insertion points. I'm betting my life on it."

"You're betting a lot of lives on it," agreed Smythe.

The rest of the flight was uneventful. The descent was steep. Normally a glide path is an easy descent. This landing wasn't a glide but a powered dive. The 16,000-pound Sabreliner, still carrying most of its fuel, leveled off just before it touched the runway with the gentleness of a lover's caress. The commander kept up the pretense of a medical emergency. As they taxied to a stop just off the main runway, an ambulance pulled up along side. The commander radioed the tower to alert the ambulance, "We just received notice that the patient died. We are standing down. Tower, may we proceed to the hangar?"

The tower gave permission, and the jet taxied to a military hangar. The hangar door closed until it was only open with a fifteen-foot gap. Everyone exited the plane and as they did an officer inside the hangar pulled a white cloth car cover that was hiding a yellow vehicle labeled as a New York City Cab.

Smythe looked admiringly at the vehicle. Turning to Doc he suggested, "Flip for dibs on driving?"

Brown stepped between the men. "It's my responsibility, so I'm driving."

"Fine with me," said Doc as he opened the back door and climbed into the passenger seat. "Drop me at the main terminal. I need to see Carrie. If I'm right, between her information and where our man, Murphy, goes after the plane lands, we should be able to wrap this up with minimal problems."

The commander stayed with the jet. Brown drove the armored cab with Doc and Smythe to the main terminal. "Wait for my directions," said Doc as he closed the cab door and walked toward the luggage pick-up area of the main terminal.

Across the airport the commander had left the Sabreliner and entered a hangar near the outer edge of the base. Inside was a black helicopter with a rack of four missiles underneath. The armed security guard saluted. "Sir, I've the explosive tip missiles with 80 pounds of napalm in each."

"Good. Now help me wheel it out of the hangar."

The helicopter was sitting on a wheeled skid. Together they pushed it onto the tarmac.

Chapter 25

The terminal door opened when the sensor recorded Doc's body heat. Doc found Carrie sitting in a molded plastic seat in the waiting area adjacent to the baggage pickup. Carrie stood up. She was carrying a small black nylon bag. Doc realized it was her laptop computer. Opening her arms in a welcoming gesture, she approached with a large smile.

"Later, maybe after this is over," Doc returned the smile. "Now we have an ambulance waiting. Doc turned around and Carrie followed him. Just as they exited the automatic doors, the ambulance pulled up across the parking lane. They continued across the lane to the ambulance.

The driver rolled down his window, "Someone need a ride?"

Doc answered, "Only if you're going to Hong Kong." By answering in this manor he signified that they were the party the driver was looking for.

The driver answered, "My name is Jim, I never know what that damn Smythe is up to, so I loaded this with a little of everything. Which country do you want to take over? We have enough intelligence-gathering equipment and armament here to do almost anything. What do you need to know or where do you need to go? Your wish is my command."

"We have a man named Murphy coming in on a flight from Pittsburgh. I need to know where he goes," explained Doc. "Smythe is in a taxi about three cars back on the left side"

Jim swiveled to the right in his seat and released a computer keyboard from the dash panel. In a matter of seconds the little display panel showed the flight arrival times. "I tapped into the display monitors of the airport terminal that shows arrival and departure times. It looks like your plane is about to land in about 5 minutes at Gate #8. Do you know what the fellow looks like that you're trying to tag?"

"I know him," answered Doc.

"Okay, now we try to tap the gate camera." It took several minutes and a few tries to cameras that were at different gates. Finally a flickering image appeared of Gate #8 just as two service people prepared for the passengers to disembark. All three of them were staring at the video screen when there was a tapping on the side window.

Carrie jumped, Jim swore, and Doc calmly opened the door, "What has been keeping you Smythe?"

Smythe smiled, "I've this little pocket radio from Brown's vehicle. It will let us talk over a digital channel so no one can listen to us. Brown and I are going around the front of the airport just in case he leaves from that direction. I trust you've the baggage area covered," he said, motioning to the computer display.

Carrie recovered, and opened her black nylon case. "Do you've a 12 volt plug I can use?"

Jim answered without looking up, "Feel under the seat for a little black plastic plug. Pull it out and you can plug in almost anything."

"Found it, " she said as she ran the wire to her laptop.

"There he is," said Doc pointing to a man carrying a suit coat over his arm.

"Now we watch," said Jim. "He pushed a few more keys and the screen divided into six separate views of the airport from six different cameras he had tapped. As Murphy walked away from the disembarking area, his image appeared on the hallway camera. Jim worked the keyboard and a camera showing the front gate replaced the older camera showing the disembarking area. They watched as Murphy continued to thread his way to the main entrance.

"Smythe, are you in position outside the main gate?" asked Doc.

"We have a good view. Is he coming out our way?" replied Smythe.

Carrie intruded, "I've my computer up."

Doc asked her, "Can you bring up the city maps so that we can try to figure where he intends to go?"

Two keystrokes later Carrie had the street maps on her screen with the airport area highlighted. “Good enough?”

Doc looked at the display, “Excellent.”

Smyth’s voice came over the little radio. “He’s crossing the main driveway. It looks like he’s expecting someone to be waiting.”

Silence kept the tension high until Smythe finally interrupted. “He’s getting into a blue Chevrolet Cavalier.”

“We are coming around,” said Jim.

“They’re heading into the city,” reported Smythe.

The site of a cab was common around the airport and didn’t arouse any suspicions. Still, the blue Cavalier pulled off to the side of the road after an hour. Smythe called in, “They pulled off, we’re maintaining speed. Hang back.”

“We understand.”

Two miles down the road there was a cross street. Brown wheeled the cab into the side street and did a U turn, hiding the cab behind a parked car. “Now we wait,” said Brown.

Jim pulled the panel van ambulance onto the western highway and went down the road about a mile. “That pull-off is about a mile ahead, so we’ll pull onto the berm here.” He asked Carrie, “Can you reach into the cabinet to the left? I need the scope clamped inside the door.”

Just as he had indicated there was a night vision scope inside the door panel. “Here,” she said handing it to him.

Jim looked into the scope and adjusted the eyepiece. “It looks like they are talking. We’ll just wait.”

I’ll radio Smythe,” said Doc.

Five minutes passed, then the turn signal of the Cavalier started blinking and the blue vehicle pulled out into traffic. Doc pressed SEND. “Smythe, they’re just pulling out into traffic. We’ll follow. You pull into line behind us.”

They followed the blue Chevrolet, taking turns so that one vehicle didn’t stay behind the target vehicle long enough for it to realize it was being followed. Doc kept looking at the track of the vehicle and finally said, "I got it. Smythe – stay with him. Jim pull off now!"

The ambulance screeched to a stop. Doc went to the back and worked the hydraulic holding locks that held the motorcycles upright. Jim realized what he needed and opened the back doors and positioned the ramp. Doc stripped off the magnetic medical emblems and took the helmet that Jim held out. "There is a lip microphone inside the face piece and earphones built inside the ear pads. Keep in touch," said Jim. "You've driven one of these before?"

"No." Doc grinned wickedly. Not this particular model anyway. Have Smythe meet you here. I'll be back shortly," said Doc, as he rolled the bike down the ramp. Straddling it, he gunned the starter pedal and revved the engine. He sped down the street exceeding the speed limit. The road he was on paralleled the road of the Chevrolet. He sped past a number of older buildings in poor condition. This was part of an old warehouse district. Watching the cross streets, he counted two more blocks until he would cut over. Slowing to 40 miles per hour, he had to lean the bike to make the sharp turn. Traveling only a block he waited at a stop sign. He could see the lights of the blue Chevrolet with Murphy approaching. As he waited at the stop sign he could see the vehicle slow. It pulled adjacent to an old warehouse. Doc pulled from the stop sign and turned onto the road, driving directly toward the parking Chevrolet. He timed his speed so that he passed Murphy and the driver just as they were entering the building. He could see several people inside the doorway. He continued down the roadway for another six blocks, just in case anyone noticed a lone bike rider.

"Everybody there?" asked Doc into the lip microphone.

"Everyone is here, be careful what you say, this isn't digital," said Jim.

Doc continued at a normal speed. He turned a left and then another left. Finally he pulled the bike directly behind the cab. He put down the kick stand and stepped off the bike. "Nice ride. I was thinking of getting one, but with my luck it would always rain when I would want to ride." He grinned at Smythe, waiting for a comeback.

Smythe responded, "I hope that our luck is better than that. Now how did you figure where they were going?"

"Simple, Carrie's maps. This was one of the locations. Vaught owns the warehouse. The warehouse is over the maintenance access for the subway."

"Carrie, do you've your laptop fired up yet?" asked Doc.

"Yes," she answered.

Doc continued, "This location was one site marked on the map, unfortunately there is a second." Looking at Brown and Smythe he said, "I need both of you to check out the other location, and do whatever is necessary."

Brown answered, "No problem, the commander is up there." She pointed up in the air. If we screw up he will drop a package and this area will cease to exit."

Smythe interjected, "Let's have him keep that package and we just kill anyone who needs killing. I intend to retire eventually and roast slowly in the sun in the Bahamas, not be toasted in an instant."

"What orders cause the commander to release the package?" asked Doc.

He has a monitor that is set for the toxin. If it triggers, he will release the missile."

Doc summarized, "This is simple. All we have to do is stop them from releasing any of the aerosols."

Jim interjected, "I've a toy that may help. He went into another cabinet and pulled out two devices that looked a lot like the radar guns used by police. "These are heat sensing imagers. They will effectively let you see through walls so you can determine where people are inside a building to give you an edge. I've two." He handed one to Brown.

"We better get going," said Smythe. "I don't want to be late for my own roast."

Brown and Smythe got into the cab and headed toward the second location. Brown wheeled the cab out of the parking area and did a U turn. As they disappeared down the roadway, Doc turned to Jim and Carrie. “If a package gets dropped here, everyone in a two block area will be incinerated. If you could reposition this vehicle several blocks away, I’ll take care of business.”

Jim didn’t answer, but instead lifted the padded seat in the back of the van. “What do you prefer?” He asked, motioning to the assortment of armament inside the gun safe.

Doc picked up a Colt Python. Jim reached into another compartment and pulled out some 357-caliber ammo. “These are Glassier. They are lead shot in a plastic casing. If you’ve to kill someone, it releases the full energy of the charge in him or her and the shot stays there. There isn’t a chance of ricochet. Another effect, there is no slug to trace rifling.”

Carrie picked up a shotgun. “I’m going in. This lady isn’t going to miss the party.”

Jim chose a Mac-10 and put in a clip. He pulled back the receiver sliding a shell into the chamber. He put two more clips into his pocket. Shrugging, he commented, “I’ve nothing better to do, and there are re-runs on television tonight.”

Doc and Carrie said, “Thanks,” in unison.

The trio locked the ambulance van to protect it and allow a stealthy approach. They walked the three blocks to the warehouse. Upon arriving, Jim used the imaging device to determine that there were five individuals inside the warehouse. Three were to the back area and one was to the far right of the door. The fifth person wasn’t showing.

All three went over to the old wooden door and tested it. A large bolt was thrown across to a hasp, securing the door. Looking at Jim's shoes, Doc asked, “Could you give me your shoelace.”

Jim looked puzzled, “Are you sure that this type of work isn’t getting to you?”

“Just loan me your shoelace,” Doc demanded. “And do you happen to have a long bladed knife?”

Carrie bent her leg at the knee and deftly reached down with her right hand to remove a Sikes Fairbaine knife from a leg sheath. She handed it to Doc, hilt first. "Will this do?"

Doc raised one eyebrow.

In answer to the unasked question, “A girl has to be prepared to protect her chastity.”

Doc used the knife to thread the shoelace into the crack of the door over the bolt. He used the point of the knife to bring the shoelace out through the crack underneath the bolt. He repeated this a second time making a cinching knot around the metal rod of the bolt. He applied pressure on the shoestring and by loosening one end as he pulled the other end, he rolled the metal rod of the bolt to release it from it’s metal catch. Using the blade of the knife he applied pressure to the metal bolt, working it from right to left. The bolt moved only a fraction of an inch each time and it took several tries, but finally the bolt was free of the hasp. Doc carefully rolled the handle of the bolt down so that it would not click when he released the pressure from the shoestring and pulled the string free. Handing it back to Jim, Doc whispered, “Thanks, do you want to put it back on?”

Jim looked at the imager again, “No time now. Originally there were five individuals showing, now there are only four.”

“One possibly went down into the tunnel. You’re probably right, we’d better move now.”

“Will you watch the back?” Doc asked Jim. “I’ll go in the front.”

“What about me?” asked Carrie.

“Stay out here, as our surprise. I’ll try to take out as many as I can before they can release the toxin. If you hear any shooting, come in and shoot to kill.”

“Silly boy, if someone is shooting at me I always shoot to kill.”

Doc cracked the door slightly and slid through the opening. He made it into the room and rounded a pile of packing crates when a guard coming around the same pile of crates spotted him.

Doc leaned against a steel beam with his left arm. His revolver was in the waistband of his pants. He spoke slowly and in a commanding voice to the guard, "Put down your rifle and walk away."

Doc watched the guard's tip of the rifle. It was rising. The guard started to say "Die you m…."

Doc pushed with his left arm against the steel beam as he tucked his legs close to his body. While the momentum of the guard's rifle kept the muzzle rising Doc fell to the floor out of the field of fire. The momentum of the arm push propelled his feet toward the guard's legs. Doc straightened his right leg, catching the ankle of the guard with the steel arch of his shoe. The ankle snapped. Doc used his legs to scissor lock around the guard's legs, and the momentum of his own body to flip the guard to the ground. Simulatiously, as the man's head hit the concrete floor, Doc flexed his torso upright, and slammed his right elbow down into the guard's throat as he fell backward. The combined force of the sudden thrust of the elbow and the weight of his upper body crushed the guard's larynx, preventing any further sound except a slight bubbling of blood as the guard died, drowned in his own blood. Doc looked at the blank eyes staring at him. "I told you to walk away. This was your choice."

Inside the warehouse, Murphy had gone into the cold room where medical supplies were refrigerated. He had already passed out the aerosols and timers to his men. He had gone back into the refrigerated unit to see if anything else was left that he might want to take. The refrigeration room's insulation and the cold of the room masked his body signature from the imaging system that Jim had used earlier. Murphy continued to work in the refrigerated room.

Outside, the three remaining men used duct tape to fasten a small explosive timer to groups of three aerosols. They strapped them together as units to disperse later in the tunnel. They put the units into four knapsacks. One of the men looked up. "I'm going to get something to remove this glue from my hands." He came into the main room just as Doc was getting to his feet. The dead guard was at his feet.

The man pulled a Glock from his own waistband and had it leveled at Doc. "You son of a b…"

At that instant Doc experienced time effectively slow. Some people explain times of stress as a time where the brain works at a higher than normal speed giving the illusions of things slowing down around you. He saw the Glock rising, ready to fire at his chest. He observed that the man was right handed and didn't hold the gun properly. Still, this wasn't the time to give a lesson. By the way the man had his finger on the trigger it would cause the gun to pull to the side. All of this information was gathered in a fraction of a second. Doc's brain told his muscles to twist sideways to avoid being shot in the chest. His muscles were stuck in real time, not the hyper speed of his brain. As his mind willed his body to move, he couldn't react fast enough to counter the muscles he saw tighten on the trigger. He expected the shot to hit his chest. The trajectory was right, still he tried to twist out of the way.

The concussion of the muzzle blast echoed in his ear. He felt no pain. Time was still so slow he didn't know if he were breathing, but he saw the gun separate and fall from the guard's hand. Time returned to normal speed and Doc's mind slowed to match his body's reactions. He twisted away from the shot the man never fired just as Carrie fired the shotgun a second time, catching the man in the chest, throwing him back against the boxes.

Murphy heard the shotgun blast and closed the door of the refrigerator room, leaving only a crack showing. The two remaining men reacted differently. One grabbed his weapon and came out into the room firing. Carrie emptied two shotgun blasts into him. The remaining man grabbed a pack of three aerosols with the timer attached and ran to the stairs leading down into the tunnels.

Doc looked at Carrie, "Get these containers into bags. You and Jim take them back to the van. I'll go after Murphy and the other man." He raced down the steps, following the echo of the footsteps ahead of him. He pulled the Colt from his belt and ran with it held at waist level. The building had a sub-basement. Doc continued the chase to where Vaught's men had dug into the subway maintenance tunnel. He stopped and listened. Doc didn't want to descend the ladder only to be shot in mid-rung. He put the Colt back into his belt and took off his shirt. He grabbed the tail of the shirt and ripped it in half. He wrapped the cloth around his hands. Somewhere below him was a very bad man with a gun who would like nothing better in the world than to kill him as he stepped down the ladder. All things considered that wasn't a good idea.

Doc straddled the hole. Looking down, he estimated it was twenty feet to the bottom of the ladder. Shit, he had to do it. He jumped onto the ladder. The arches of his feet slid along the sides of the ladder; his cloth-covered hands steadied his descent by sliding in a loose grip alongside the outer edges of the ladder. At the bottom he rolled left and came up with the Colt, ready to fire. Doc held still for a second. No one fired at him. He listened. Finally he heard it. Steps in the distance running along the passageway. Doc started to sprint after the man. He thought he heard a shot come from the building overhead.

Above Doc, Carrie set the shotgun on the table and organized the knapsacks with a total of 69 cans of the toxin. She yelled for Jim to come in. When he didn't come into the building she went to the back door with the intention of unlocking it. She opened the lock and looked out. Jim had started around the building to come in the same entrance Carrie and Doc had used. She caught his attention and motioned him to use the back door to join her. She walked back to where she had filled up the knapsacks. She had several sacks slung over her arms when Jim came in the back door.

Murphy watched everything that Carrie had done. He weighed all of his options. Essentially he realized that this operation was compromised beyond recovery. He could naturally just go in and start shooting the containers. That would release the gas. Unfortunately the effects would be that he receives a lethal dose and dies. That wasn't on his agenda. He could stay there, but it was also possible that someone would look in the refrigerator unit and find him. His best option was to escape out the back door. He watched Jim come in the back door when Carrie beckoned him. Jim walked directly to where Carrie was working. Murphy opened the door and slipped out after Jim had walked past. He was almost to the back door when he stepped on a creaky floorboard. Jim turned around. He had the Mac-10 to his side. He saw Murphy as he turned. Jim started to raise the muzzle of the weapon when Murphy's bullet tore at his shoulder twisting him around. The bullet had effectively disabled his right arm. Murphy was out the back door before Carrie could react.

Jim swore and got to his feet as Carrie approached. "That son-of-a-bitch was really fast."

"The hell with him, lets get these canisters out of here," said Carrie.

She tried to carry as much as she could, but Jim said." I may be shot in my right shoulder, but if you loop a couple of those over my head I can carry some on my neck and some with my left arm."

Together they left the building and hurried across the street to get the toxin containers into the ambulance.

In the tunnel below Doc continued to follow the man. He heard a rusty creek as a door was opened. He sprinted forward. The man was on the main tracks of the subway, walking backwards. "Leave me alone and I'll let you know where I planted the containers.

Doc yelled, "Stop!"

"Let me go. If you shoot me you'll never find it in time."

Doc yelled, "Please stop!"

The man continued to back up. Doc had seen the third rail the man was backing toward. If the man didn't know that the third rail held a powerful charge of electrical current, he was about to learn the hard way. The nails in his boots arced as his boot almost touched the rail. The man's body lurched as the current raced up one leg and out the other. It was only a second or so until his clothes and body burst into flames. He was dead.

Doc looked around; the door that creaked was a flood door to prevent back flooding into the service tunnel. Somewhere in that tunnel was a timer with three aerosols of toxin. He spotted the door and tried to close it. It was moving slowly. He was forcing it and still it wasn't closing properly.

"What are you trying to do?" said a voice to his right side.

Doc had not noticed the maintenance man who had just spoken.

Behind him was a set of acetylene welding equipment.

"Is that tank full?"

"Yes, but it wont help you open the door. All you need is this big lever extension." He held up a tool that slipped over the door lever and extended the leverage by an additional three feet. The maintenance man slipped the handle over the door and closed it.

"Wait a minute, open it up again," said Doc.

The man worked the lever and the door opened a foot. "Hold it there. Now help me with the tanks."

"What are you going to do with my tanks?" asked the maintenance man.

"Help me lift," said Doc as he muscled the tanks to the door.

Together they got the tanks into the tunnel and pulled them back into the passageway about thirty feet. Doc cut the hoses with his pocket knife to the horror of the maintenance man

"What are you doing? Those tools cost a lot of money."

Doc opened both valves and the gas started to flood the passageway.

Across the tracks on the platform a couple of elderly people sat waiting for the next train. The man had a wooden cane. Doc sprinted across the tracks and used his arms to propel himself up onto the concrete platform. Pointing to the wooden cane he asked, "May I borrow that for a minute or two?"

The old man answered, "Sure thing Sonny, but you've to tell me what movie you're filming. It looks like it's going to be a humdinger."

"I'll be right back,"

Doc pulled a smoking piece of clothing from the dead man by using the wooden cane to insulate himself from the electricity still surging through the corpse. As he picked it up and air got to the smoldering cloth, it burst into flame. He walked over to the flood door, holding the flaming material high to keep it from the dense gas of the acetylene just in case any of the gas started seeping out the door. "On the count of three get ready to close the door." He threw the cloth into the tunnel.

The maintenance man was pulling on the lever. Doc added his weight to the task and the steel flood door slid into place. An instant later the heard and felt the concussion as the acetylene and oxygen combined to form an explosive gas. The gas ignited The concussion of the initial explosion blew the gas upward and the entire warehouse building above the tunnel became ablaze.

Across town Smythe and Brown arrived at the other location. They used the imaging system and found the building empty of any trace of human heat form. Time was of the essence so Smythe just shot the lock. It took two shots to splinter the wood and lock enough to let him kick in the door. Inside the warehouse they found several vehicles. It didn't take a rocket scientist to realize that this was the escape point. The plan had Vaught's men enter the subway system from the first warehouse, travel underground, spreading the toxin containers, and exit through this building that held six vehicles pointed toward the door. Brown raced outside and then triggered the communicator in the cab. "Commander, this is Brown. This location is the escape point." Just then a plume of fire reached high into the sky.

The commander answered, "I think we just saw a signal. Shit. There is a trace toxin on the spectrometer." The unseen helicopter fired two heat-seeking missiles. The inferno redoubled as the missiles hit. The commander maneuvered to a different angle and fired his remaining two missiles. The inferno raged as the missiles struck.

I'll miss them. I was really starting to like that guy," said Smythe.

Inside the ambulance Carrie and Jim put down their sacks of toxin and Jim collapsed in the passenger seat. Carrie gave him a flask of water and told him to sip on it while she locked the motorcycle into its stand. She locked the wheels with the hydraulic pistons to hold it in place and was pushing the ramps into the back door when she saw the plume of flame and heard the explosion. She slammed the back doors shut and jumped into the driver's seat. Just as she locked the seatbelt, the first set of missiles hit. Carrie turned over the motor and drove away from the explosions. From her rearview mirror she saw the second set of missiles hit. She hit the sirens and lights as she sped down the highway. "I've to get you to a hospital."

Jim nodded," I know, I'm starting to go into shock. I think I lost too much blood."

"Hold in there buddy." Carrie grimaced.

Three minutes later she screeched to a halt in the semicircle of a local hospital. She jumped out of the seat and ran into the hospital. "I need help out here. This man has been shot in an attempted mugging. He is going into shock."

The nurse behind the check-in desk said, "Do you know what medical insurance he has? I need a number before we can admit him."

"He is a British diplomat. If you fuck up and he dies I guarantee that you'll lose every bit of funding from the government. Now get your ass off that seat and get him some help."

Two orderlies were bringing Jim in on a stretcher. He heard what Carrie had said. "I'll give them a phone number to get everything. You get out of here. Deliver those packages to a safe place. I think that doctor fellow died to make sure you got away."

Wiping a tear from her eye Carrie said, "I think you may be right." She turned and went back to the ambulance. Pulling out into traffic she didn't know where she would go. Still she drove. She caught a freeway that led to Delaware. When she came to a roadside rest, she used her radio to contact the CCD. "I've sixty-nine canisters of the poison here in the vehicle. I'm feeling exhausted. Come and help me."

The man who answered from the CCD confirmed that he would get people to her. “Are any of the containers leaking?”

“No, they are recovered, but my friend died.”

“We’re sorry about your friend. Stay on this line. Do not break this transmission.”

***

In the subway everyone felt the concussions of the missiles hitting above them. A few pieces of concrete fell from the ceiling. Doc shook the maintenance man's hand. "Thanks to you we made it. By the way, what’s your name?”

“My name is Bobby Johnson. I’m probably going to be fired for letting you destroy those welding tools.”

“Mr. Johnson, it’s a distinct pleasure to have you on my side for once,” said Doc. "I guarantee that you’ll have all of your equipment replaced and you’ll get a bonus for helping and saving so many lives.”

Doc crossed the tracks again and returned the cane to the older man. “Thank you.”

The older man said, “Damn good show. Now if you need any cameo appearances, Mildred and I’ll be glad to be a part of your movie. Here, I’ll put our names and address on this card. Now you give us a call if you need any extras.”

Doc looked at the card. The man's last name was Law.

Chapter 26

Location: Colorado Vaught Pharmaceutical testing ranch

The flight from Pittsburgh to the private airstrip at the Vaught's ranch was smooth. Vaught used the airtime to plan how he was going to exploit the sudden incidence of a plague. As his flight landed, he was confident of his plan for the deployment of the anti-toxin. He had used computer data to define the areas of highest income, and then cross-referenced it by the hospitals in those areas. He took these results and found out which of those cities had easy access to international airports. Last, he made sure that his pharmaceutical salesmen made calls on each of those hospitals doing a data survey to find out who actually purchased the drugs in each hospital. He was pleased with his scheme. Good detailed planning would make him richer.

The only thing that held up the undertaking now was waiting for the news services to declare an outbreak of plague. He had an open line monitoring CNN and MSNBC for any announcements dealing with the Second Lady. She should be sick by now, and be dead by tomorrow. That type of press release would make news, but so far nothing had come across the wire services.

Vaught listened to a portable radio as he rode the five minutes from the private airport to his ranch house. Still no reports were released on a plague. Once in the house he paced his private den in frustration. Finally, after his evening meal, a reporter on the 6:00 p.m. broadcast made an announcement that 70 people who had attended a political rally were being admitted to a local hospital in Pittsburgh. The reporter suggested that doctors were looking into some kind of flu, or possible food poisoning. He continued that this was probably not anything like the Legionnaire's disease that affected a convention in Philadelphia back in the late seventies.

Vaught finally relaxed. His plague had started. The money would start rolling in shortly. According to his plan, he should be the richest man in the world. He figured that he would be rich enough to call Bill Gates a pauper. He would control and own anything, or anyone he wanted.

He walked over to the desk, and dialed the extension for the housekeeper. He asked if the masseuse would meet him in the spa. Vaught kept a private health club with a Swedish steam room adjacent to his private bedroom. His plan was now implemented. All he had to do was wait until the other breakouts occurred. With the incubation period, he could do nothing for about 18 hours. He intended to get fully relaxed and get a good night's sleep. The key to that sleep would be relieving stress that had built up from waiting for news of the outbreak. He opened the door to the spa and was greeted by a rush of warm air, and a beautiful Japanese girl named Penny.

"Does the master want to take some steam?" asked Penny.

"It may help to open my sinus. They always get blocked when I fly," answered Vaught.

Penny was a small-framed woman standing about five-foot even and weighing possibly one hundred pounds. Although she was actually from the Philippines, Vaught treated her as though she were a Japanese Geisha. Her name was actually Marie. He called her Penny, a subtle reference to the incident where he bought her from her family. Her mother taught her about human physiology and psyche of sex. Sex and sexual release were complicated. Her mother instilled the difference between love and sex. She remembered her mother saying that sex is an experience of the mind that is only acerbated by the body response.

For a man, sex is a mental experience brought on by physical stimulation. If a man thinks the woman is enjoying the experience, he will reach a heightened level of stimulation. To control the act, a woman gives effective stimulation neuron ganglion in the legs about a finger width above the kneecap. The man will pop off before the woman would have to commit to actual intercourse.

Using these techniques Penny was able have the reputation of the most sensual and exotic female, giving the most sexual fulfilling experience that most men ever had. She did this for Vaught and occasionally for some of his better clients. In truth she hated Vaught. She played with his body and mind, letting him fool his own body into ejaculating before she would have to submit to intercourse. She approached, wrapped in a translucent rob with a cherry blossom pattern. “Sit,” she ordered Vaught.

He did. She knelt in front of him, untied his shoes and removed them. She rubbed her hands over his thighs, and down working around his ankles then outward onto his toes. She repeated this twice on each foot and in the process removed his socks. She slowly rose, standing directly in front of him and undid his shirt.

Vaught was anxious and stood up, removing his shirt himself and bent forward to remove his undershirt. “I appreciate your courtesy, but I need massage now.”

She stood back feigning embarrassment. “You don’t want my help?”

“I need to un-kink my muscles now.”

“Do you want a bath?”

“That would be nice.”

Penny walked bare foot into the tiled shower area and ran steaming water into a large ornate crock. The water in the crock was scented with camphor, oils, and spices. When the hot water mixed with the water in the container, the solution gave off a very pleasant scent. She took out a wooden bowl and sluiced water onto a naughehide-covered bench. She repeated this three times before Vaught entered behind her. He was now totally naked.

“Lie down,” she ordered.

He stretched out face down on the bench. There was a gel pack encased in plastic to be used as a pillow. He rested his forehead on the gel pack. Penny reached into the hot crock and pulled out a loofah sponge. She pulled his one arm out to the side and worked the sponge over the back of his arm, holding his hand under her arm in such a way that his arm brushed against her breast. She worked the loofah sponge under the arm scrubbing away a layer of skin. She went around the bench and repeated the procedure with his other arm. The sponge seemed to take all of the dead skin from his flesh. Something in the water, possibly the camphorated oil seeped into the pores, opening them to a spectacularly sensuous tingling sensation. Penny went to work on his legs. Since he was still on his stomach, she bent his leg up, forcing his foot out and worked the rough sponge over his soles to remove all odors and sweat from his feet, and between his toes. Vaught winced several times in response to Penny's scrubbing. Penny worked her powerful fingers between his toes. She grabbed his ankle and used a squeezing pinch as she worked the Achilles tendon area of each foot. She used the sponge over his legs from the back of the knee to the ankle. Vaught wondered if any hair would be remaining on his legs.

"Spread you legs," she ordered.

Vaught was still on his stomach. He extended his legs as far apart as they would go. Penny took off her robe and crawled on to the table with him and knelt between his legs. She bent forward, scrubbing his back. As she reached forward she made sure to brush her breasts against his back in a sensuous stroking manner. She kept the pressure on the sponge. He could feel the blood flowing to the surface of his skin. The sensation was almost as if he were getting a brush burn in slow motion. She finished with his back and his buttocks and upper thighs.

Finally she ordered him, "Turn over."

His anticipation of sexual release was extremely heightened, causing his manhood to be fully erect. Just then the intercom for the ranch paged him. "Mr. Vaught you've an urgent phone call."

He sat up and reached for the intercom button on the wall. Punching it with the side of his balled fist, he ordered, "I don't want disturbed for anything! If the President himself calls, I'm unavailable until tomorrow morning."

Martin Vaught had just made a critical mistake for the sake of sex. He never asked who was on the phone, not that it mattered. Vaught could care less that Murphy was calling from a pay phone in the New York warehouse district. Vaught was thinking with his sexual need, not his mind.

Location: New York City –Warehouse district

Murphy left the back of the warehouse after shooting one man on his way out. Realizing that his operation had been compromised, he wanted to see who was behind the failure of his mission. When he left the warehouse, he circled behind the loading dock of an adjacent warehouse, which came out in an alley where he could see the intruders as they left the building. Only two people left the front of the building. A man, bent over and obviously in pain, and a woman. They were carrying the knapsacks, probably with the toxin filled aerosols. They checked behind themselves only twice. Murphy stayed in the shadows of the buildings and followed them to a vehicle that looked like an ambulance. The man fell into the back of the ambulance, probably from blood loss. He watched the woman push a cycle up into the back area of the vehicle, lock the back, and get into the driver's seat. He had just written the license number when he heard explosions behind him. He watched in amazement as a plume of fire erupted from Vaught's warehouse. Continuing to stare as additional explosions drove the inferno to higher flames, he was so engrossed watching the destruction, he didn't see the ambulance pull away from the curb. He turned when the ambulance switched on its siren at the intersection and headed for the main highway.

As he worked his way around for a better view of the warehouse, Murphy saw two of the rockets just before they impacted into the center of the flaming wreckage. He was three hundred yards from the closest point of what used to be a warehouse. The inferno was heating his face. The fire had eerie phosphorescence. He had seen it before. Those rockets he had seen hitting the building had Napalm in them. He knew he'd better get away. He calmly walked down the street, away from the destruction. His mind whirled. Napalm could be made by anyone, but the government had napalm. It made sense that somehow the government knew. Just how much they knew was the question.

He saw a phone booth and called a cab. He called Vaught while he waited for the cab. The ranch operator refused to put him through to Vaught. When he reached the ranch, he would ream the ranch operator another ass hole. That was only if the operator were lucky. There was no sign of the cab, so he dialed another number to rent an executive jet. He put the charge on the company card. The cost was in excess of $10,000 for the rental of the jet, with company discount. He didn't care about the cost. Some of the parties for pharmaceutical distributors had entertainment costs of over $20,000.

The cab arrived and he headed for the airport. He had to make it to Colorado tonight.

Location: New York City –adjacent to the flaming warehouse.

Smythe and Brown approached the flaming building. Brown used the hand held detector to check for any trace of toxin. The toxin would not show on the device, but the VX gas component did register. They stopped the vehicle ten blocks from the inferno, but nothing registered on the machine. They worked their way closer, going only one block at a time, checking for any trace of toxin. The commander was overhead in the flat black helicopter. "No sign of any toxin from up here. Go in and check for witnesses."

"Yes sir," said Brown.

They pulled to within three blocks of the flames, and parked the vehicle. The steel girders of the building had fallen in. The roof had collapsed and the residual debris was actually glowing with a radiant intensity.

The commander came over the radio, "Is there any sign of other operatives?"

"Nothing yet," responded Brown. "Can you see any sign of the Hong Kong Express?"

"Nothing from up here. There are several real ambulances and fire trucks approaching. Are you sure there is no trace of toxin?"

Brown responded, "I confirm there is no trace of any toxin. We are going to circle north and recheck, but I think if any toxin were in the building it was destroyed by the heat." She slowly drove north concentrating on the scanner. Nothing registered on her instrument. "Commander, did you receive any transmission from Doc?"

The commander clicked open his microphone transmission circuit, but didn't speak for a few seconds. "I think he was the one who triggered the initial fire, I didn't. The building just suddenly exploded in a massive amount of flames. I fired the rockets as a measure of safety, but I'm sure any toxin was destroyed by the initial conflagration. I'm sorry to lose a man like that."

Brown and Smythe stopped the car and were concentrating on the fire. They never noticed Doc approaching the cab on foot. He rapped his knuckle on the glass and both Brown and Smythe jumped. "Care to scan me for safety. I don't think any gas escaped but I sincerely doubt you would give me a ride if I were exposed to the plague."

"You SOB," said Smythe. "We thought you were toast."

Doc explained what had happened in the tunnels. He then asked, "Have you talked to Carrie?"

"We haven't found her, or the Hong Kong Express," answered Smythe.

"Just as well, your man was hurt and she was leaving with him and a lot of canisters when the fireworks started." Looking directly at Smythe Doc said, "Your man took a bullet. She will get him medical attention. Smythe, would your Harrier fly from here to Colorado?"

"Sure, I can fly anywhere," answered Smythe with an air of self-satisfaction.

"Brown, mind if I drive? I think you need to start arranging a plausible explanation for the explosion and fire. If I'm not mistaken, you've the connections. I suggest a pocket of gas, like a dinosaur fart finally surfaced and caught fire. For goodness sake don't say natural gas like in a pipeline. We don't need any liability lawyers poking around with lawsuits. I also need a favor by making a maintance man named Johnson the hero of the subway."

"Can do," said Brown, as she got from behind the wheel and into the back seat. "Where are we going?"

"I'm going across town to get a jet ride to Colorado," said Doc, smiling at Smythe.

"I can arrange a ride to Colorado with the commander and myself," offered Brown.

"I think you're both going to have your hands full with this cover-up."

Brown started communicating with her offices as Doc drove at high speed across town. Forty-five minutes later Doc wheeled the cab in front of the door to the hangar where they left the Harrier. He left the motor running as he stepped out of the cab. Grinning at Brown, he said, "I hope you can find your way home."

He and Smythe entered the hangar to prepare for takeoff.

Location: New York City –Not far from the warehouse district.

Candy Dietz, a freshman at the local college, majoring in journalism, was doing her Astronomy 101 homework. She pointed her camera at Ursa Major and was framing the photo in her viewfinder when she saw a flash of light from the right of the camera. She unlocked the tripod handle and swung the camera around to where the light originated. She saw an orange light from a fire. She took a photo. Something flared to the left of the fire. Candy shot another picture. She saw streaks of fire from the left go toward the fire, and then the fire doubled in size. She grabbed her phone and dialed her girlfriend.

"Marsha, you won't believe it. There is a UFO firing at a building. I got the photos. We're under attack by aliens." She continued to shoot photos until she was out of film.

Marsha was her classmate at college, and a level headed co-ed. "Candy, are you serious? Do you really have pictures? I've a boyfriend who works for a scandal sheet downtown. Do you want me to call him?" Sirens in the background caused her to believe Candy and her mind was racing. "Candy, I'll call you right back"

Marsha dialed her boyfriend at the newspaper. "Brandon, you know Candy don't you? Well she has photos of a UFO shooting and causing the fire in the warehouse district. It's burning now. Can you see if someone will buy the pictures?"

Brandon answered, "Come on down to the paper. Come in the main door and have security call me. I'll take you up to see the editor. Be sure to bring the film. They'll need to see what they are buying."

"Okay. See you shortly," answered Marsha. As soon as she hung up she was dialing for Candy.

"I'll pick you up. We're going down to the paper to see the photos." She didn't even wait for Candy to answer. She needed to get her keys and get to her car. She didn't have time to waste small talking with Candy.

Marsha picked up Candy and the girls drove to the newspaper. They followed Brandon's directions and ended up in the assistant editor's office. They relinquished the film so that it could be developed. The editor listened. The story of a UFO attacking a warehouse didn't seem reasonable. He wondered, why a warehouse? Why not attack the White House, or an airport. He was thinking that he was going to have a very serious talk with Brandon about wasting his time.

The photo darkroom technician knocked on the door and came into the room. "Sir, you had better see these!"

Location: New Jersey Turnpike rest stop.

Carrie had listened to the Center for Disease Control people. She waited and talked to them on the radio. The corporal she had worked with in Great Lakes was on board the helicopter that was coming to pick up her cargo. She was finally relaxing.

Two hoodlums, noted for drug dealing, pulled into the rest stop and spotted the ambulance. In their minds ambulance meant medical supplies, which translated to drugs. They parked their vehicle and walked around the ambulance, one on each side, on the way to the men's room. They joined up in the rest room. "I only saw a lady, no one else."

"I say we go in the back door, I tested the handle. It's not locked. If that bitch in the front gives us any problem, we can have some fun with her."

"Good," said the one hoodlum and held out his hand in a fist. The second hood made a fist and hit his friend's fist in confirmation of the plan. They went back to their vehicle, took out two 45-caliber automatics from the trunk, and tucked them under their belts. They approached the ambulance from the rear. One grabbed the handle and fumbled with the locking lever as the back door opened.

Carrie heard the noise and raised the shotgun beside her to a point just below the level of the back of the seat to keep it hidden. As the hoods broke into the back of the van Carrie ordered, "Get out now!"

The one hood raised his weapon to threaten Carrie. Carrie raised the 10-gage shotgun and shot the first would be thief squarely in the chest. The impact threw him out the back of the open doors. She fired again as the second thief was raising his handgun. She hit him in the shoulder with the first shot. She fired again, catching him in the abdomen. The impact threw him out of the van and onto the ground beside his friend's corpse.

On the radio the corporal heard the shots. He was asking what was going on, but Carrie couldn't hear. Her ears were ringing from the concussion of the shotgun blasts in the enclosed area of the ambulance. The corporal ordered the pilot to speed things up.

As luck would have it, a police car pulled into the rest stop. The police saw two bodies at the rear of the ambulance. They pulled the patrol car adjacent to the ambulance at a distance of 30 feet and saw Carrie still holding the shotgun. The one officer got the bullhorn from the back seat and ordered, "Put down the gun and come out with your hands in the air."

The corporal heard the orders over the radio. Carrie was still not answering because she couldn't hear anything. She saw the police and rested the shotgun on the seat and waved.

"What do we do now?" one officer asked the other.

"I say we have to get her disarmed and out of the vehicle. We have to take her in. Those men look dead to me," he said pointing to the corpses at the rear of the ambulance. They had both taken up a position on the other side of the patrol car, using it as cover.

Just then the helicopter pilot spotted the ambulance. "There!"

The corporal flipped the switch for the outside bullhorn and, as he spoke, his voice boomed from the speaker mounted to the underside of the helicopter. "This is a matter for the CDC." Police – Please stand down. Again- this is a CDC matter."

The officers didn't know what the mnemonic CDC meant. They only knew that this was their area and that they had two dead bodies at the back of an ambulance and an armed female inside the ambulance. They responded to the helicopter with their bullhorn. "This is a police matter. Please clear the area. We have an armed female in the ambulance. We may have to use force to get her out."

The corporal was getting irritated. He told the pilot, " I'm going to extend the sterilizer. Watch your balance." He pressed the red button. Five-foot sections of telescoping tubing extended to a total length of seventeen feet, ending in a nozzle. The length left the nozzle just outside the main blade wash.

The corporal picked up the microphone again, "I told you to leave her alone. This is a CDC matter!"

The policeman responded, "I told you to leave the area."

The corporal looked at the pilot. "Ready?"

"Ready," the pilot responded.

An instant later the corporal shot a stream of flaming liquid onto the ground between the patrol car and the ambulance. The fire made a wall of flame between the two vehicles. "I told you to leave her alone. Now put down your weapons and stand down."

The policemen both holstered their guns. One spoke into the bullhorn, "I believe this is a matter for the CDC."

The corporal responded, "Thank you." They landed the helicopter on the far side of the ambulance.

The corporal loaded the toxin containers into a special fiberglass chest. The toxin containers were loaded into the helicopter for transport back to the CDC train. The two policemen helped put the corpses into body bags and loaded them into the back of the ambulance. Carrie got into the passenger seat and the corporal drove her to the hospital to see what damage she had done to her ears. It was coincidental that they were going to drop the bodies off at the morgue. The police were nice, or perhaps intimidated and gave a police escort so that no one bothered the ambulance.

Location: Colorado – Outside the Vaught Ranch

Gabe landed the Nighthawk, with Ruby and Jade, in a clearing on the public forestlands. It was shielded from the ranch by a ridge of land. Ruby volunteered to do the reconnoitering. Jade set up parameter security around the Nighthawk. Gabe worked the radio, setting up monitoring of communications from the ranch.

Ruby took a laser microphone device with her. She got to within 400 yards of the ranch house. On the ride to the ranch, Gabe had accessed computer files and satellite photos of the ranch. She knew which room was Vaught's office with the bedroom to the side. She first bounced the laser onto the glass of the office window. The laser bugging device worked by vibrations from sounds in the room making the glass vibrate. The laser could pick up the vibrations. A computer chip would convert the light variances back into sound. Essentially she was planting a bug on the window to listen in on what was being said in the room. Unfortunately nothing was transmitted back. She tried again, targeting the bedroom window. She heard sounds, but couldn't make out what was being said. From the weak signal they must be in an adjacent room. She tried another room. The signal was proper. She had her target. She relayed the signal back to the Nighthawk and worked setting up two more laser bugs on the bedroom and the office. She linked these to the repeater to send the signal from those back to the Nighthawk. She listened in on the first bug.

What she heard was surprising. Evidently two people were engaged in something very passionate. She could hear heavy breathing and panting. She took off the earphones and put then into her carrying bag and headed back to where she had left her sister and Gabe.

On the way there, a large hand clapped over her mouth, and a male voice suddenly surprised her. "I don't know where you're headed, but I know where I'm going to take you now."

She struggled and tried to bite the hand over her mouth. The big man held her firm. "Now if you just behave yourself, I'll take you back to the ranch house."

She nodded, assenting. He responded by letting go of her mouth. "How did you find me?"

"Simple, I listened to the animals. They quit talking to each other when you invaded their homes."

She turned to face the man. He was dressed in a fringed leather jacket and carried a large belt knife. For all the world he looked as though he were a Native American from a different age. "Who are you?' she asked.

"My name is Bertram Little Waters. My friends call me Bert. I work on the Vaught ranch making sure that the animals stay on the ranch and that wild animals don't enter the grounds."

"Well I don't belong on the ranch, so let me go so I can leave," explained Ruby.

"I must take you back. That is also part of my job. There are people who would steal information from the ranch. I've to protect the ranch from thieves."

I'm not a thief."

They will talk to you. If you're not a thief, you'll be let go tomorrow. For tonight you'll be a guest of the ranch. You'll get a hot meal and a soft bed for the night."

Ruby was praying that Bert didn't see her set the lasers, and had not found the repeater. "I'll be glad to accept the hospitality of the ranch. Thank you Bert."

Together they walked down an animal path to the edge of a field. Bert stopped and looked back at the edge of the field that was shrouded in ground fog. He pointed to a spot, but didn't speak. Ruby saw the hole in the fog with what looked like a buffalo just visible in the center of the fog. Then light reflected off some high flying plane, casting a golden flash at the buffalo.

Bert asked, "Did you see?"

Ruby answered, "I saw a light colored buffalo at the edge of the field."

"We have no living buffalo in this area, and no white buffalo. What you saw was a spirit. Do you understand the meaning?"

"No."

"Before the sun rises again you must jump through fire to save your life. If you don't, you'll die." Bert turned and walked toward the ranch house without explaining anything else. They crossed by the barn and went into the main ranch house.

Meanwhile at the Nighthawk, Vaught, going through the throws of passion, was entertaining Jade and Gabe. Gabe laughed out loud when he overheard Vaught tell the intercom that he didn't want to be disturbed. "That is really *coitus interruptius*."

Jade interjected, "I don't think he even got that far." She joined in the laughter.

Chapter 27

Doc and Smythe drove the Harrier onto the runway under it's own power. They took off and attained cruising altitude in short order. Doc asked, "Smythe, is this plane expendable?"

Smythe answered after a few seconds. "Well the armament is totally expendable. I guess the plane is really expendable, but they will dock my pay for the rest of my life if I lose it. In reality, my supervisors would prefer that I save the plane even if it costs me my life. Personally I consider the plane a weapon, and I'll use it as a weapon. If I destroy it in accomplishing my goal, well, at least I accomplished my goal. Now why did you ask a question that makes me think so hard my head hurts?"

Doc answered, "I was just wondering." He paused in thought "Were you serious when you said there is enough armament to annihilate a small nation?"

"Yes, I'm totally serious on the armament. Realize that I only have conventional weapons. No nukes."

"Smythe, if things go right, I'll give you a signal. It may be on the pen or something else. Give me two minutes, I do mean a full 120 seconds. The 121st second I want you to blow up wherever the signal comes from."

"Actually, I don't think 120 seconds will give you any edge to escape. When I release the weapons, there will be a hell on earth," explained Smythe.

Doc answered, "I may not get out, but I want to be sure the other guys don't get out either."

Smythe came over the headset, "Now damn it, I don't want you depressing me. Are you having a premonition of something?"

Doc laughed, "The only premonition I've is that we better end this with the death of Vaught. That man has too many political connections and too much money. He can and will buy his way out of anything. If all else fails, he will escape to a place where the law can't touch him."

"Can you raise Gabe on the radio?" asked Doc.

"Shortly. We are going to meet our gas station in about fifteen minutes. I'm going to have my hands full."

"I didn't think you'd have any problem reaching the ranch."

"I can reach the ranch, but I want fuel to get out in a hurry. We're getting the juice airborne so that the Harrier isn't seen on any base, It will also let us keep up pace. Scott Air Force Base thinks this is a Nato flight courtesy."

The tanker was on time in the expected flight path. After confirming the identity of the Harrier, the tanker dropped a fueling line with a funnel-like device on the end. Smythe extended the fueling tube from the Harrier and connected to the fueling line. Once the connection registered on the tanker's monitoring system, they downloaded the fuel to fill the Harrier's tanks.

"Thank you," said Smythe as he disconnected.

"Glad to be of service. When you get a chance to stop, we'll be glad to show you some high test fuel for pilots. It beats tea, hands down." With that the pilot of the fuel tanker pulled away from the jet.

"Next time I'll take you up on it," answered Smythe, as he gave fuel to the thrusters. He headed directly for Colorado. The indicator light on the radio blinked. He had an incoming secure transmission from the British Embassy. He motioned to Doc. "Incoming message, you may as well listen. I'm not keeping secrets from you."

"Smythe, are you there?" came the coquettish voice of the embassy receptionist.

"If I'm not here, I don't know who is flying the plane," answered Smythe.

"Don't be a smart ass! You don't have time to waste. We have word that Murphy rented a jet and is on his way to Colorado. He left almost an hour before you, although you should be catching up."

Smythe pushed the speed a little faster. "How are Jim and Carrie?"

She answered, "Jim is in the hospital. He lost a lot of blood, but he received three pints and is now stable. Carrie had an incident.

She's all right except for a temporary loss of hearing. She was checked out at the hospital brought back to the embassy. The doctors say her hearing will probably return after she wakes. They gave her a pretty heavy sedative."

Doc interjected, "Were the packages delivered safely?"

"The CDC took delivery of the merchandise. It arrived safely. The Hong Kong Express wasn't damaged too much either. We have a body repair man scheduled to do repairs and painting tomorrow."

"What happened to the ambulance?" asked Smythe.

"Some of the shot shell BB's hit the door and damaged the metal frame, she replied.

"Could you please explain, what happened?" said Smythe as the bits and pieces of information he was receiving were incensing him.

"Carrie had to shoot the two men who tried to rob the ambulance. They had just broken into the back of the van when she fired the shotgun. The concussion caused temporary damage to her ears," she explained in a bout of frustration.

"Take care of Carrie and Jim. I'll call back when we finish our business," said Smythe as he signed off.

They flew in silence for the next half hour, each contemplating what they may encounter when they arrived. As they got closer to the target Smythe raised Gabe on the radio. "Have you any suggestions on where I can land the Harrier? I don't want to start a forest fire with the hot exhaust."

There is a clearing that has a shale parking lot for vehicles about two hundred yards from where we landed. It's clear of trees and shrubbery so nothing should catch fire.

Smythe did a fly-over to verify the location. He made a second pass, slowing and maneuvering the thrusters of the Harrier to a vertical configuration. The Harrier is a jet that has the capability of vertical takeoff and landing. Most pilots wobble in trying to keep the balance of the plane when they either land or take off. Smythe knew his plane. He swooped down toward the landing area, and then slowed to hovering status as he eased back the engines and landed smoothly on the parking area.

Gabe came over the radio, "You did a damn smooth landing."

Smythe and Doc climbed down from the Harrier. Smythe went to the rear of the plane and pulled out a carryall canvas bag. "Give me a hand, Doc." Together they unrolled a spool of camouflage screen netting and strung it along side the plane. Smythe anchored the tie downs of the netting to the ground with small spikes. Smythe set up little rockets that clipped onto the spikes. Smythe looped the netting into a hook of the rocket. There were six rockets total. "Now for my next trick I'll make this plane disappear." They stepped back and Smythe triggered the rockets electronically. The six rockets fired simultaneously, lifting a curtain of camouflage up and over the plane.

" Nice trick," said Gabe as he and Jade watched the events.

Smythe wasn't done. He set an additional six spikes on the other side of the plane. He didn't fasten the netting to them but instead set the rockets onto the spikes as little launchers and hooked the netting onto the rockets. "What are you doing now?" asked Gabe.

"Just in case we have to take off in a hurry, these rockets will pull the camouflage netting back over the plane so that we can take off," explained Smythe.

Smythe and Doc walked over toward Gabe and Jade. Doc asked, "What's the status now?" He noticed that Ruby wasn't with them. "Where is Ruby?"

Jade answered, "Ruby went to set the laser microphones to listen in on the ranch. She did set the microphones, but she didn't come back. One of the microphones was listening to Vaught having sex. We, she motioned to Gabe, were having fun listening in on the frolicking. We thought that she was listening also. Vaught retired to his bedroom and Ruby didn't come back. I went out to look for her and saw a man escorting her to the main ranch house. In short, we think she's a prisoner."

Doc listened with concern, "What about Vaught?"

Jade answered, "He was pissed off at being interrupted by a phone call, and then again by going off prematurely. He told everyone not to interrupt him, then went to bed, alone."

"Then he doesn't know about Ruby?"

Gabe answered, "They're holding her in a guest room with bars on the window. From the conversations I've listened to with the bug, they're expecting Murphy to arrive shortly. They'll turn her over to him for questioning rather then test Vaught's anger."

"What assets do we have available?" asked Doc.

Gabe answered, "All phones and radio communications are monitored. We have three laser bugs on the house. We have major and minor firepower. We do have some liabilities. Ruby is inside, along with maintance personnel who are innocent."

"Now we need a plan," said Smythe.

"Well whatever you're thinking, you're not going in shooting up everything. I want my sister out. I could just pop Vaught when he walks outside," offered Jade.

"We can't just shoot Vaught," answered Doc. "I'll go down and try to get Ruby out. We need to get Vaught to panic and run. If he and Murphy leave the ranch, they will take the toxin with them. Then we can then capture the toxin. If they have an accident, it will be all the better for us. What small arms do you've in the helicopter?"

Gabe named most of the equipment by memory. Doc stopped him when he mentioned flash cord and C-4. Gabe got the two items, along with duct-tape, and magnetic screwdriver with multiple heads, from the toolkit. Doc pulled the foil from the C-4 and pulled the flash cord through the clay-like compound. Small bits of the plastique explosive stuck to the ribbing of the flash cord. Doc wrapped the cord around his waist, and pulled his shirt over it. The duct tape and screwdriver went into his pocket. He still carried the Colt python under his windbreaker. Doc looked to Smythe, "Explain the two minute delay to Gabe. If they run for the plane, let them. Follow within striking distance. I'll send a signal." He looked at Jade, "I'll get Ruby out."

Doc started walking down a path. Gabe asked Smythe, "How did he know where the ranch was located?"

Smythe answered, "When we flew over, we could see it."

Jade looked at the path where Doc had disappeared, "Where is he?"

Doc moved quickly. He circled and went to the Harrier. He lifted the camouflage to get under and left the Colt Python and a note on the pilot's seat. He approached the ranch house from the side facing the cattle corals. The barn gave him cover. He moved keeping in the security of the shadows. The back of the house had an open window secured only by a screen. He used his knife to release the spring clips on the screen and removed it from the window. He put it diagonally through the window, setting it inside the building. Pulling himself up, he entered through the window. Finally, he replaced the screen. As he did, he heard the turbines of a plane landing. Subconsciously his mind registered that it must be Murphy's plane.

Once inside the residence, he tried to locate Ruby. He had spotted the room with the barred windows from the outside. Now he knew that it was down the hall to the left. He promised Jade he would get Ruby out, so he went down the hall. He tested the lock to the room he thought Ruby was in. It was secure. He pulled a pick and lever from his inside pocket. Working the tumblers, he opened the lock. He saw Ruby lying on the bed. "Are you tired of lying around and want to get out?" Doc whispered.

"She opened her eyes. "We still have to find the toxin and then I want to talk to Vaught myself. I'm not about to leave," answered Ruby.

"Are you alright?"

"I'm fine, I understand that Murphy is going to question me. I'm going to convince him that I'm Pearl. I'm going to let him know that I'm really angry about the attempt on my life and that I want one million dollars to make a new life."

"You're going to play hardball?" asked Doc.

"I intend to scare the hell out of Murphy," explained Ruby. "Murphy knew Pearl, but he didn't know she had any sisters, let alone that she was one of identical triplets."

Doc thought for a minute, "How bad can you freak them?"

Ruby looked at him, "Why are you smiling?"

"If you can panic them enough to make them run, they'll take any toxin with them. We'll have the men and the toxin isolated in the air. We have both Gabe and Smythe here with air power to make sure that all the toxin burns before it hits the ground, I think we have a plan."

Ruby motioned to the door, "You'd better get out, I just heard a plane. If that's Murphy, he'll be here shortly."

Doc left the room, closing and locking it. He had an idea. It might just work. He needed to find Vaught's plane. He went down the hall, and back out the window. He carefully reset the screen. No one was outside. He slipped into the shadows and went into the barn. He liked barns. Large barns like this on a working ranch were filled with wonders. He found a pair of coveralls and a wheelbarrow. He put on the coveralls and pushed the wheelbarrow to a stall. He used a shovel and filled the wheelbarrow with fresh manure. He pushed the wheelbarrow across the compound to get close to the airplane hangar. He looked and acted like he knew what he was doing. No one questioned him. He used the shovel to dig a hole in the ground at the side of a door. One of the security guards did look in his direction, but dismissed him. He filled the hole with half of the manure, then leveled the dirt around the top of the freshly filled hole and patted it down with the back of the shovel. The entire time he had an eye on the hangar window. He wheeled the wheelbarrow to the opposite side of the hangar and repeated the process. From this vantage he was able to see that no one was around the plane. Finally he moved the wheelbarrow and shovel around the far side of the hangar where he wasn't readily visible to anyone.

Doc eased next to the hangar door and eased into the entrance. He moved to the side and stood perfectly still, listening. When he didn't hear anything, he slipped out of the coveralls and went to the plane. Vaught flew in style. The plane was a Beachcraft King Air 300. Doc went to the workroom and rummaged around. He found several sport parachutes. He took one with him as he went into the plane. The plane had a bedroom and office inside. There was a small kitchen in the rear. Doc found a closet built against the outside wall. With his knife he removed the plastic finish buttons that were fitted into the Phillips screw heads. He removed the outside bottom panel of the hull of the plane. He removed the insulation from inside the panel exposing a three by four feet section of thc outside metal of the hull. He unwrapped the flash cord from around his waist. The C-3 plastique explosive made the flash cord slightly sticky. It was an ideal consistency to adhere to bare metal. He used it to frame the perimeter of the exposed panel, then used duct tape to hold the flash cord in place. Finally he set a little button detonator into the cord and taped it securely. He finished by setting the insulation back into place. He didn't put the panel back; instead, he duct taped the panel into the inside of the closet so that it would not make any noise.

He placed the parachute inside the closet. Doc was planning alternatives. His old teacher always taught him to keep track of egress. He used to say, "Getting out and away when all hell breaks loose can make the difference between life and death, yours and mine." Doc knew the plane had limited entrances and exits. The doors were bevel fitted so they would not open into the vacuum of high altitude. If he needed an out, he would have to make his own door. He planned that the flash cord would heat the metal of the hull to an extreme temperature difference from the temperature on the outside of the metal. The difference would cause immediate metal fatigue. The C-4 imbedded in the flash cord taped to the inside of the hull would cause a focused and shaped explosion. If everything worked correctly, it would blow the panel off the plane, making an instant egress. It should work.

Meanwhile the executive jet had landed and Murphy got out. He jumped into a golf cart that was used as a shuttle between the airport and the ranch house. He drove directly to the ranch house. The jet took off shortly after he was clear. When Murphy reached the ranch house he went directly to Vaught's bedroom and knocked loudly on the door.

"Go away – I need my sleep," said Vaught from the inside.

"Boss, we have a problem. You better get up fast. I do mean now!" responded Murphy. The urgency in his voice set off every alarm in Vaught's head.

Doc put the coveralls into a trash container and went to a sink to wash his hands. He took a silk tie from his pocket and tied it into a full Windsor. As he finished his second loop, he positioned the micro detonator's remote trigger into the folds of the tie. He finished the knot and checked it in the mirror. He used his forefinger to make the traditional dimple at the bottom of the knot. Doc checked the communicator pen in his pocket. He was ready.

Chapter 28

Murphy was interested in the female who was found on the grounds early in the morning. He went to the far end of the ranch house to see for himself. He unlocked the door and knocked.

"Come in," replied Ruby from inside the room.

Murphy opened the door and was taken back as he recognized the woman sitting in a chair facing the door. Ruby invited, "Come in and have a seat. I want to discuss why you paid so little to kill me."

Murphy walked over to the woman. He backhand slapped her mouth, drawing blood to her lips. Looking at her bleeding mouth he said, "Dead people don't bleed."

"Genius, I'm not dead. Dead people don't need money. If you touch me again, I'll tell Mueller. He may have Otto break every bone in each of your hands." She smiled coquettishly. "Have you sent the demands for the blackmail?"

"No blackmail, we're going to use it and sell the antitoxin to make the money," replied Murphy.

"Shut up Murphy!" came the order from the door. Vaught stood there. "You," he said pointing at Murphy, "Come with me."

Murphy and Vaught left the room and Vaught locked the door. "I just saw the news. Two things bother me. That perky female newscaster on the morning show was interviewing the Vice President's wife about her views on proper desserts for luncheons. She should be on death's door. A second news segment showed my warehouse in flames. The reporter said some shit about a natural gas pocket from an old swamp that worked up into the basement of the building. Now I want the truth, did you succeed in the gassing the building in Pittsburgh?"

"I was shot trying to gas that building in Pittsburgh. I did escape, but somehow they found us again in New York. I shot one of them; they followed one of my men into the subway. I got out and there was a series of explosions. I don't think anyone made it out. I did try to call you but you would'nt take my calls." Murphy was stammering trying to explain the unexplainable.

"So someone found out about our plan?" asked Vaught.

"Yes, and they stopped our plans," replied Murphy.

Ruby slipped the lock to the room and walked up behind the two men. "More like stole your toxin. Maybe now you'll listen to some sense. I'm here to offer to sell your stuff back to you, and make a profit myself. I also need some of the anti-toxin."

Vaught stared in amazement at the woman. "Who in the hell are you?"

"My name is Pearl. That bastard beside you had me carry a bomb aboard the flight so you could steal the toxin recovered from the Gulf War."

"If that is true you should be dead," replied Vaught.

"I would be if I had stayed on the flight." She spread her hands to the side accentuating her figure. "But as you can see, I'm here in the flesh." She touched her cut lip. "No thanks to your Mr. Murphy and his little helpers."

Vaught looked her in the eye. "Since you were effectively killed in the plane crash, why shouldn't I just kill you here and finish the job that my Mr. Murphy botched?" he mocked.

Ruby, playing at being her sister, wiggled, giggled, and then pointed her finger at Vaught. "Because my lover is Mueller. He was really disturbed that you tried to kill me. He stole your pretty little toxin. He is a businessman. He will sell it back to you for a price." She then pointed to herself for emphasis. "I'm here to negotiate a price." She paused for drama, "Right after you've him apologize for trying to kill me" She pointed at Murphy.

Vaught looked at Murphy, "Tell her you apologize and let's find out where our canisters are located."

Murphy looked at the woman and offered, "Okay, I'm sorry that I tried to kill you. It was just business." He then swallowed to wet this throat. "How many of the canisters do you've?"

"Silly boys, I don't have any. I told you that Mueller has them. You made a mistake thinking he was only connected in Europe. He has all the ones from the boat. He also hijacked your little truck. Finally, he had a team steal all but one canister from your warehouse. The one leaked and he had to terminate your people and your building with a flaming vengeance." She spread her fingers in the air to emphasize the extreme destruction of the fire.

Vaught was getting irritated. He glared at Murphy, "Did you really let them steal all the toxin? Are all our plans for the deployment of the stuff literally up in smoke? Do I have to pay some blackmailer to get the toxin back?"

Ruby interjected, "I don't appreciate being called a blackmailer, besides it takes one to know one." She smiled coquettishly, "I prefer to consider myself a negotiator in setting up your new partnership."

They were standing in a hallway adjacent to the main lobby of the ranch house. Just then someone started a commotion in the lobby. They overheard the receptionist telling someone that they needed an appointment to see Mr. Vaught.

"I've to see him shortly. I'm from CNN and need an interview before the Feds arrive to arrest him."

Vaught heard what was said, and ordered Murphy, "Take her in the side room." He went to the lobby. Doc was playing the part of a reporter. "What can I help a member the press with today?" Vaught offered his hand for a handshake.

Doc took the hand and shook it. "Thank you for seeing me. I would like to interview you as quickly as I can to get your opinion on the charges being processed against you."

Vaught smiled a non-committal smile, "You mentioned that charges are being filed? What exactly am I being charged with?"

Doc answered, "My informant tells me they are going to hit you with everything from terrorism to atrocities. I know you've always helped people and I figure you're being framed. My brother-in-law was a volunteer at one of the hospitals you set up in Indonesia. He said you always sent plenty of medicines for the people. Anyway, I wanted to get your side of the story out before the assault teams arrive."

Vaught's eyes widened. "You said assault teams?" Vaught asked. "Wait here for a minute." Vaught went around the corner and commanded Murphy, "Take the girl and get the Beachcraft ready. We are leaving as soon as you get it out of the hangar. Get the briefcase in my office. The aluminum one beside my desk has the remaining canisters."

Both Murphy and Vaught were pilots and often flew the Beachcraft when they entertained for business. Murphy nodded his acknowledgement of the order and took Ruby with him in the golf cart as they headed out to the airplane.

Vaught came back into the lobby and was very polite. "I do have to go to a meeting. I'll let my lawyers handle the false accusations. In the meantime, I would like to give you an exclusive interview. Would you like to join me on my little trip?"

Doc replied, "I'm sure it will be the interview of my life."

"It may well be that," answered Vaught. "Follow me, we're going out to the private runway."

On the way out of the reception area, Vaught turned to the receptionist. "If people want to talk to me, be polite. Invite them in and phone my attorneys. Let them handle this bad publicity."

He and Doc left the building and boarded another golf. They arrived as a little tow motor was bringing the aircraft out of the hangar. Murphy was visible in the pilot's seat. When the plane stopped moving, one of the ranch hands held the steps as Vaught, followed by Doc, boarded the aircraft. Vaught closed and locked the hatch, then went to the front of the plane and took the pilot's seat that Murphy had just vacated when he moved into the copilot seat.

Meanwhile Jade, Gabe and Smythe were watching as the plane taxied down to the end of the runway and turned. Vaught held the brakes as he pushed forward on the throttle. He released the brake and the plane jumped forward, speeding down the runway.

Jade gasped, "He was to get her out!"

Smyth spoke the voice of reason, "If they are flying out, we better get back to our aircraft and follow."

Gabe asked, "Do you need help to remove the camouflage?"

Smythe answered, "I can get it off faster than Copperfield could make it disappear."

Smythe went back to the Harrier and triggered the rockets to lift the camouflage off the plane. He left the camouflage on the ground and climbed into the pilot's seat. He found the Colt and note under his helmet. Reading the note he muttered, "I hope you know what you're doing." He tucked the revolver into the map pouch and fired up the engines.

Gabe and Jade went back to the Nighthawk. Gabe used an expandable aluminum pole to remove the netting that covered the Nighthawk. Jade gathered the camouflage and stuffed it into the back of the helicopter. Gabe got in and fired up the rotors. He spoke into his headset. "Smythe, that Beachcraft can go pretty high. I'll follow on the ground, but it may turn out to be your call."

Smythe answered, "I can climb faster and higher than they can. They can outrun me, but I don't think it will come to that." He thought to himself, "Doc, you're a crazy bastard. How in the hell are you going to get the girl out?"

Onboard the plane Ruby and Doc were told to buckle down and enjoy the flight.

In the cockpit Murphy and Vaught were concentrating on the takeoff. Doc whispered to Ruby. "When I go to the back of the cabin, come with me. When I say 'Now' grab onto me and hold on."

She looked quizzically at him, "What do you mean?"

"I've a plan to escape by parachute. Unfortunately I brought only one chute, so we are going to share."

"I've never jumped from a plane," explained Ruby.

"Just hold onto me. Take a deep breath as we leave the plane. We'll be stepping into the cold. It will be very cold. It will suck the breath out of your lungs. Don't panic, as we drop you'll be able to breath again. Just remember to hold on."

How do we go out the door? I didn't even see a door back there," said Ruby in a nervous voice.

"Don't worry, the wind will pull us to safety when it's time," comforted Doc.

When they were at about 8,000 feet Vaught put the plane into a shallow climb and set the course for Mexico. Vaught set the automatic pilot and started to talk to Murphy. "We're in deep. Do you've any idea how much the Feds can link back to me?"

"I don't think they can trace much back directly to you," responded Murphy.

"Well you're partially right. You don't think. We are leaving the country until our lawyers can get a handle on things. Now I want you to go in the back and find out what that reporter knows. Use whatever means necessary. We can always dump the body in the desert."

Murphy went to the back of plane. He looked at Doc; suddenly there was recognition in his eyes. He remembered Doc from outside the hotel in Pittsburgh. Murphy drew out his pocket automatic. Pointing it at Doc he said, "I don't know who you're, but you're not a reporter."

Doc looked at him and said, "It isn't safe to shoot a gun in an airplane. You could puncture the hull and have a decompression."

"Yea, and smoking isn't good for you either. The bullet will not hit the hull if it lodges in your body," taunted Murphy.

He held the muzzle of the gun close to Doc. "Now I want you to stand up slowly and lie down in the aisle so I can cuff you. He pulled a nylon tie out of his pocket that he intended to use to secure Doc's wrists.

Doc complied, moving slowly. When he stood up, Murphy patted him down and found nothing, but then he was looking for a gun. Doc knelt in the aisle and Murphy started to bend over him. Ruby grasp both of her hands together in clutched fists and hit Murphy as hard as she could at the base of the neck. Murphy lurched and Doc reached over his shoulder, catching Murphy, and flipped him over his shoulder into the tiny aisle. They punched and chopped at each other to no avail. Neither man got the upper hand. Ruby followed as they fought their way to the back of the plane. Murphy had lost the gun and used both hands to lever Doc into a flip. As Doc impacted a seat he felt a rib break and tasted blood. Doc and Murphy were locked a wrestling hold.

Murphy grabbed at Doc's tie. Instead of fighting to counteract the hold, Doc reached into his pocket, triggered the communicator pen and threw it across the cabin. He grabbed Murphy's hand as Murphy tried to strangle Doc. Doc levered Murphy's thumb to the detention trigger in the Windsor knot of his tie. Suddenly there was an explosion, however the panel didn't immediately separate from the hull. Doc looped one strap of the parachute over his left hand as he fell to the floor and slid it up his arm. He grabbed Ruby's hand. Doc used his legs to throw his weight and that of Murphy against the weakened panel. It was still glowing in a rectangular flame. As Murphy's back hit it, the glowing panel gave way. The panel sheared off and Murphy made the mistake of letting go of Doc. Murphy's body was sucked out the hole. Doc and Ruby were sucked out of the plane immediately afterward.

Doc held Ruby's arm. The cold was numbing. What little breath he had in his lungs was sucked away by the low-pressure vacuum of the high altitude. The two bodies cartwheeled arm-in-arm through the air. Doc wrapped his legs around Ruby to hold onto her. She finally clutched him and locked her legs around him. They were falling. Doc was losing track of time. The lack of oxygen was getting to him. He tried to slip on the harness of the chute. He was able to get one leg into the harness and finally got both arms through the straps. He used a D ring to hook Ruby's belt just in case either one of them lost their hold. She was also suffering from lack of oxygen. Her grip was loosening. With Ruby secured by the D ring, he was finally able to get his other leg into the harness. He tried breathing. He could get a small amount of air now. He lost track of the plane.

Immediately after the decompression in Vaught's plane, the automatic pilot took the plane in a steep dive. Probably Vaught was on oxygen and regaining control of the plane. Just then Doc saw what he had been hoping for.

Behind Vaught's plane, Smythe was keeping in missile distance awaiting a signal, any signal. He watched as Vaught's plane climbed to 8,000 feet. One didn't have to be a mind reader to recognize the course was set for the direction of Mexico. He muttered to himself, "That SOB is going to South America by way of Mexico."

Smythe was low to the left of the Beachcraft when it decompressed. The communicator signal went off an instant before the decompression. Smythe had set a timer in the cockpit for 120 seconds. He tripped it when the communicator went off. He reached for the throttle and pushed it to full. He just started to close when Vaught's plane did its nosedive. Smythe closed on his target. At ninety seconds he started to talk to himself over an open microphone. Gabe was listening in. Referring to Doc, he said, "You dumb SOB, I hope you got him. I'm going to make that plane toast." At 20 seconds he had closed and locked on the plane with his missiles. Smythe counted down as he continued to close. At four seconds he stopped counting and uttered a prayer, "Doc, you rest in peace knowing the mission was completed." He fired two missiles, then two more five seconds later. Both of the first-launched missiles struck, causing the Beachcraft to burst into a ball of flaming wreckage. The second set of missiles struck the flaming debris, adding to the ball of flame. Smythe was depressed thinking he had just killed Doc. "I'll give you the best damn send off that any Viking would be happy with. Expendable, hell yes, all ordnance on this baby is expendable. He launched every remaining heat seeking ordnance he had on board.

Gabe came over the microphone, "Smythe, get hold of yourself. There isn't anything left to blow up. You used enough fire to kill any plague they had with them."

Gabe turned to Jade and expressed his sympathy, "I'm sorry, there was no way out or Doc would have found it."

Jade looked him straight in the eye. "I don't understand what you're talking about. I don't know about Doc, but Ruby didn't die."

"You saw the flame. Nothing survived."

"Sisters know, especially twins or triplets. I knew when Pearl died. I knew when Ruby had a tooth pulled. Trust me. She is alive, and I think very cold." Jade shivered involuntarily inside of her jacket.

Doc watched the flames as Smythe's missiles hit the Beachcraft. He had a sense of satisfaction knowing that the mission was complete in containing the plague. He looked down. The earth was coming up fast. He roused Ruby, "Now hold on very tightly, I'm going to pull the ripcord. It's going to slow us." They each interlocked their legs and Ruby wrapped her arms around Doc. He pulled the cord and the chute opened. It was a substantial shock, but they held onto each other. The rapid descent of the Beachcraft following the decompression had taken it about twenty miles away from where the parachute was going to land. Doc and Ruby were clear of any flaming debris.

As they got closer to the ground, they were coming down near the edge of a small lake. They were too heavy for a smooth landing. Doc ordered Ruby, "I'm going to release the harness above the water. I'll go into the water. You hold onto these cords and you should be able to float to a landing on shore. When you hit, let your legs and arms go slack and roll. You'll be fine. I'll be coming out of the water right behind you."

Ruby answered with only one word, "Why?"

"When I release my weight from the chute, it will slow its descent so that you can land safely."

"But?"

"Hold on here," he said guiding her hand. "Now hold on." Doc released the harness and dropped into the freezing water.

Ruby did stay with the chute as it glided onto the shoreline. She landed in scrub brush that cushioned her.

Doc knew he had to keep moving or he would suffer hypothermia from the cold. It was only eighty feet to shore. He forced himself the last fifteen feet. His arms worked in robotic movement, continuing to stroke water until he touched the mud bottom with one of his strokes. He crawled onto the bank. Ruby ran down to help him onto the shore. The wind was picking up, adding to his chill. Ruby was going into convulsive shivering, partly a result of the cold during the freefall, and partially from nervous release.

She and Doc stumbled to the base of a hemlock tree where Ruby had gathered the folds of the chute. Doc removed the wet jacket and pants leaving only his under shorts. He and Ruby wrapped themselves in the folds of the parachute and covered themselves with the dry pine as insulation. They hugged each other for shared body warmth. Within ten minutes they were both feeling the comfort of the shared body warmth and the insulation of the pine and nylon. They fell asleep in each other's arms and slept until the next morning.

Neither Gabe nor Smythe felt there were any survivors of the Beachcraft. They never mounted any type of search for either Doc or Ruby.

Morning came and wind had dried Doc's clothes overnight. He dressed. Ruby went down to the lake and splashed water on her face.

As she was coming back toward Doc he said, "I don't think we are going to be rescued. If we want to get out of here, we'll have to do it ourselves."

Ruby didn't complain, she simply asked, "Which way?"

Doc answered, "On the way down I saw a cabin due north of here. They walked for three hours and found the cabin. From there they were able to get a ride into town. Doc had three twenty-dollar bills sewn into a pocket in his belt. He used the money to get each of them a meal and to make a phone call.

Otto answered the phone. "Hello."

"Otto, Ruby and I are stuck and need a ride. Could you ask Mueller to arrange discreet transportation?"

Otto replied, "I saw the news. Congratulations, no survivors "Mueller is very well connected. Someone will pick you up in about five hours. Just stay in that small community by the lake."

"How will we know who it is?" asked Doc.

"You'll know when your ride arrives. You'll have access to whatever Mueller can provide. He does send his thanks."

Five hours later a Chevy Blazer pulled in town and parked at the town's only restaurant. Mueller himself drove it. Doc and Ruby walked over to the Chevy and climbed in.

"What can I do for you?" Mueller asked.

"Get us out of here," answered Doc.

"I want to go home," replied Ruby.

Doc asked, "How is it that you suddenly appear here to pick us up?"

Mueller smiled, "I came to the United States shortly after you left Germany. I needed a vacation and decided to do some big game hunting and got lost. I watched you at the ranch. I was very impressed. Thank you for doing what I couldn't do. I also thank you for returning Ruby. What can I do for you?"

"I would appreciate a ride to the train station in Chicago, and a little traveling money."

EPILOG

It's impossible to go through life and do anything without affecting the lives of many people.

1. The commander returned to his private office in Langley Virginia. He had been in charge of the antiterrorist team that found the original toxin after the Gulf war. He had just arrived at his office when an aid informed him that the director needed him immediately. He figured he very well might lose his position. He had violated a number of legal guidelines, including taking active action on United States soil.

When he knocked on the door, the director ordered him to have a seat. He threw two newspapers onto the desk in front of the commander. "Good work, I never would have thought of blaming a UFO for starting the fire. Normal people will readily accept the story of prehistoric gas. You did fine work."

When he returned to his private office he saw two boxes on his desk. Both were wrapped with a little bow. One card said, "Thanks. I told you I would return it. –D" the other said, "I figured you would need a new one. –D" He opened the boxes and found his original parachute knife in one and a brand new knife in the other box. Security had no knowledge of anyone entering his office, or any unauthorized entry in the building.

2. Elizabeth Rosemary Owens was the point person on the team usually used for covert operations. She didn't like the name Elizabeth and usually preferred Beth. The nameplate on her desk announced – **B**eth **R** **Ow**e**n**s. For fieldwork she shortened this to Brown. When she showed up for work there were a dozen long stemmed red roses in a vase sitting in the middle of her desk. The card said, - "Thanks for the rides. - D" Beth took the rose vase into the commander's office. "I thought he died," she said.

The commander held out the orange knives, "Evidently not."

3. The National Transportation Board, known as the NTSB did a cursory investigation of the crash. The conclusion was that Vaught was on a medical mission of mercy and possibly a canister of ether leaked, causing an explosion. All the wreckage was taken to a steel mill in a security guarded train car and melted to prohibit further investigation.

4. The maintenance man named Johnson was given an award by the Mayor of New York city for his quick thinking and saving many lives in a potentially disastrous freak accident. His four children were granted full scholarships. He was given a raise and title.

5. A gentleman greeted Mr. Law at the door. The man was from a fine men's store in New York. Three attendants followed him, carrying samples. He told Mr. Law that he was instructed to make sure that Mr. Law had a proper cane to replace the one that was damaged in the subway accident. He assured Mr. Law that price was no object.

6. Shortly after her husband had been fitted with five custom canes, another knock came at the door. Two men delivered a 38-inch High Definition Television set and a videotape system for the new television. After they set it up, thcy gave Mrs. Law a booklet featuring over 1000 video titles. They explained she could select 300 of the videos at no charge. Everything had been paid for in advance. As they left, one of them put a card on the table. Mrs. Law opened the card. Inside it said, "Thank you. Sorry you couldn't be in a film. Perhaps you can watch some. – D"

7. Shelly came back to her office from lunch. She had not eaten, but instead went to a church, lit a candle and prayed for the soul of her friend. On her desk was a dozen of red roses. The note said, "Don't count me out yet. You look sexy in black. – D"

8. Bert, the American Indian, didn't like the lawyers who came to the ranch. This one was very persistent. Bert left before sunrise and stayed out until long after sunset. Still the man waited. Bert decided to face whatever fate awaited him. The lawyer would probably fire everyone and sell the ranch. It was proper that he face this man.

Bert met him in the reception area of the main ranch house. The lawyer had forms to sign. The lawyer explained, "You now own the ranch. All taxes will be paid by a trust fund. Your job is to continue doing whatever is needed to help your lands and people. The ranch has a lot of potential. It's now yours. Bert was in shock.

9. The security guard at the Toronto plant was reunited with his wife and children. The necessity for his apparent death in the thwarting of a terrorist attempt on the sovereignty of Canada was rewarded with an appointment to a position as head of security for a large government building in Toronto.

10. About four weeks after the incident, Smythe took a vacation. He picked Germany. Coincidently he went to the bank where he and Doc had a safety deposit box. He signed in for the box and removed it in the private booth. He opened the box to find the gun, approximately 4,000 dollars of currency and a note. "I know that public officials are poorly paid. Leave this just in case you need it later. In the meantime $200,000 , your share of my fee, has been placed in a Swiss account for you. The instructions on the sheet told how to access the money. It ended with - - I hope you live to enjoy retirement. I intend to. –D"

11. Penny, Vaught's masseuse was awarded a tidy sum from Vaught's estate. She moved to California and opened a beauty shop. Her clients would be women only.

12. Otto went out to the front gate of the Mueller household. A Japanese man was there. He insisted that he see the lady of the

house. He said he had a present for her. Otto blocked the way until the man said, "This present is from Doc." Otto allowed him to enter and escorted him to the main residence. Mueller and his mistress greeted the man in the study. He opened the container. Inside was a black velvet-lined case with a beautiful necklace of large white pearls separated by small black fresh water pearls accentuated with gold beads. "It's lovely," said Ruby.

The Oriental man handed Mueller and Ruby a note. Mueller opened his, "Consider this necklace a wedding present. I'm sorry that Vaught killed Ruby when she borrowed Pearl's identity to go home to see her mother. Pearl had a lot of guts assuming her sister's identity to find the killer. Since her sister was killed under her name, I guess the only way to cure that is to make her an honest woman as Mrs. Muller."

Pearl in her guise as Ruby read her note. "I know that you may never reclaim your own name. I hope that this will be a nice remembrance. Look at Mueller – I think he has something to ask you. – D"

Mueller asked, "Will you?"

DOC will return in:

Body Parts for Profit -